Daughters

by

Kate Ennals

For Áine

June 2023

Prologue
December 2011

Grains of warm, white sand flowed beneath Clare's feet. As she walked, she could feel the pulse of the moon party fading with the curve of the beach behind her, a faint heartbeat.

For most of the night, Clare had danced in the flickering light of the fire, watching the shadows and silhouettes stretch and weave in the flames. Just before dawn, she had dragged Angie and Julie away to walk the beach with her to watch the new day dawn. When only tendrils of notes drifted over the sea, the three girls flopped at the foot of the pine trees, close to the end of the peninsula. Clare wanted to swim.

"It's too shallow," said Angie.

"I want to feel the sea on my feet one last time before I return to London; I'm going to watch the sun come up from the water."

Clare stood up and headed towards the shallows. Leaning back against the trunks of the trees, the two girls watched Clare meander down to the water's edge. She was wearing a silver threaded sarong over her black bikini. Her black hair was loose and damp. It hung down her back, rippling over her brown shoulders. She turned around and waved. They waved back.

"To be honest, I'm glad she's going home today," said Julie. "She is far is too intense and a demon for the sights."

Silently, Angie agreed, but didn't like to openly betray her best friend. Clare needed a man, Angie thought. That evening, Angie had been dancing with an Aussie lad, with long flickering limbs. Julie had fallen in with an American boy, fresh faced, with perfect teeth. The four were going to meet that evening after they took Clare to the airport. Angie closed her eyes. What would she wear? Maybe the orange flower sarong with green shorts. It would show off her tanned shoulders. She and Julie dozed beneath the trees, dreaming of the boys.

At the shore, the sky turned from grey to silver, to a pale blue. Standing in the shallows, Clare watched an arc of golden sun rise from under the ocean. An arrow of yellow light rippled across the sea towards her. Clare waded into the sparkling water until it was deep enough for her to lie on her back. She felt so tired. Soon, the golden arrow lost its shape, dissipating into a circle of glittering sea. Clare felt herself ebb away. Water flowed across her stomach. She could taste and feel the salt on her skin. Gentle waves tugged at her. She closed her eyes. She would become a sea horse. Her silver sarong unwrapped itself from her body and drifted through the water to the shore, glinting in the sun.

Chapter 1
October 2021

Gloria's bright red lipstick served only to emphasise her ill health. Miranda could see her low-slung breasts under her nightie, resting like seals on a rock. She averted her eyes. Seeing Gloria so frail, made Miranda feel uncomfortable.

Her mother started to cough and sat up to bring up the phlegm. She grabbed a paper tissue from under her pillow and spat into it.

"Yuck," said Gloria, looking into the hankie. She lay back on her pillows, breathing heavily. There were flakes of the red lippy on her teeth.

"Miranda, honey. What time is it? Where's Josie?"

"At Clive's."

Gloria grimaced, her face caving into powdered crevices. These days, Josie, Gloria's youngest, spent most weekends at her father's. Soon after her marriage to Clive which had happened late in life, Gloria had realised that she wasn't the marrying kind. Her girls were enough for her. She didn't mind that Josie stayed often with her father, though she would have preferred it if Josie wasn't so obvious about her preference for her father.

"So, you're back to being my baby girl, Miranda. I'll get up and make us dinner. Have you any plans for the weekend? Why don't you go out? Have fun like most people your age?"

"Don't start, mum. I'll make us an omelette."

"No, no. I want to," insisted Gloria.

"Mum, rest." It was an ordeal when Gloria decided to get up and 'do her bit' as she would say. Everything turned into a drama.

"I'm fine. Forget the cancer! You think you're being kind, Miranda, but you're not. You're killing me with kindness. I suppose that's what you want, isn't it, me to die so all this can be over. Well, it's what I want too."

"Gloria, stop being so dramatic."

Miranda tried to adopt her older sister, Rose's no nonsense tone of voice. Rose was best at dealing with her mother.

"Oh, so being on my deathbed is being dramatic, is it?"

"Mum, you're not on your death bed."

"Well, bring me a glass of wine, at least. Open that South African Sauvignon Blanc."

Later that evening, Rose rang while Miranda was filling the dish washer. Gloria was in the living room, with her bottle of wine, watching Ozark, an American thriller series.

"You don't have to look after her, Miranda. She's perfectly capable, you know. I knew Gloria would have you looking after her. You should really move out."

"Don't be ridiculous, Rose. I'm okay."

"I know, I'm wasting my breath. Alright, lets change the subject. How's Further Education College going for you? Is it very different to school? Have you made friends?"

Miranda hesitated. She had transferred to Kingsway Princeton FE College to do her sixth form exams. It had been her choice, but on the first day, she had decided that as nothing ever happened on the first day, she would go in the next day to pick up timetables. The next day, she convinced herself that proper classes would probably only start the following week. The following Monday, she felt that it would be odd if she turned up having missed the first week. No-one had come looking for her. Instead of going to college, for a month, Miranda had left the house, walked for an hour first thing in the morning, then returned home. She had spent her days scribbling the notebook that she had bought for Clare, her favourite older sister, ten years ago. She was writing about that year, 2011. She was writing about Simeon and Clive. She was writing about her family and in writing, she was discovering stories and angles she had never understood about the people closest to her. Everything was beginning to slot into place in a way it never had. Every day, at 4pm, she would close her notebook, lock it up and go upstairs to make Gloria tea, pretending she had just come home. She was lucky Gloria never came downstairs but Gloria had never ventured much downstairs, even when Miranda was a little girl.

"It's great," Miranda said, finally responding to Rose. "I get a little lost, moving between rooms."

"That's exactly what Clare used to say when she started at Camden School."

Both she and Rose were both silent for a minute.

"What about new friends?" Rose asked again.

"Yeah, there's a few girls I like. It's early days."

"Talking to you is like pulling teeth, Miranda! How is Josie?" asked Rose. "I hope Clive is taking some responsibility for her."

"Yes, of course. You know Clive. She's with him now. Rose, talking of responsibility," Miranda said, "Gloria is quite sick, you know. You should come and see her."

"I will," Rose answered, "soon."

There was another awkward silence which Rose broke again.

"Is something wrong, Miranda? You sound odd. I know it's a difficult time: Gloria sick, starting a new college, managing Josie, A Levels, and all that…" Rose tapered off.

Miranda felt a sob, rising. She took a breath to stop it.

She heard Rose's voice raise a pitch.

"Miranda?"

"I'm fine. I have to go now, Rose. I have an assignment to finish. It's a demon for homework, this college."

Chapter 2
January 2011

"Miranda, did you wash your hands before eating?" asked Clare. "That sofa is a nest of cat hair."

Miranda didn't answer, mesmerised by The Magic School Bus on TV. Clare watched her little sister lift the burger and bite into the Big Mac, not taking her eyes from the screen. Thick mayonnaise dribbled down her chin and splashed on to her nightie. Lettuce, mayo and gherkin splurged out the sides. Miranda wiped the mayo off her nightie with her finger and sucked it.

Clare got up and took the burger from her little sister.

"Here, I'll cut it up for you."

Miranda had short, black spikey hair, oval shaped brown eyes, and a little snub nose. Her sallow skin seemed to reflect a soft mellow light. She looked a picture of innocence, sat with her knees tucked up under her white cotton nightie. Absorbed in the TV, Miranda picked up the milk shake. Gurgling noises came from her straw as she sucked froth. Clare cut the Big Mac into quarters with a knife and tried to shove the lettuce and gherkin back into the bun. She glared at the large, bad-tempered white Persian cat, Sasha, which sprawled on the couch next to Miranda but didn't try to move it. No-one dared shift Sasha when she was in situ, except Gloria, their mother, who treated the cat with disdain.

Clare sucked the mayo from her own fingers and gave the bits of burger back to Miranda. In the corner of the room stood a bare, skeletal Christmas tree. Outside, dusk was nestling into the winter January trees. Clare liked the feeling of stillness at this hour. Not quite the time for the busy of evening. This afternoon's peace was interrupted by a shout from the bedroom next door.

"Have you two finished your McDonalds? If you have, make sure you put the burger cartons in the bin. Don't leave it for other people to clear up."

Miranda looked at Clare who raised her eyebrows.

"Fat chance of her clearing it up!" Clare said but then called back, "yes, Gloria."

Clare stood up and balanced her Big Mac box on the bare brittle branches of the dead Christmas tree. A scattering of dry brown needles fell to the floor in a shower.

"Pass me your milkshake carton, Miranda."

Clare steadied it between the branches, like a Christmas decoration. More needles fell.

"Art," Clare sighed.

"The Christmas tree looks horrible. When will we take it down?" asked Miranda.

"Maybe tomorrow. Now though, I've got to go. Miranda, I'll see you later. If I'm not back by nine, make sure you get yourself to bed."

Clare disappeared from the room. She returned wearing her new afghan coat. It was brown suede with curly white wool inside and red, green and blue embroidery down the front. Clare's long black ringlets toppled over it. Miranda thought of the Faun from Narnia. Clare bent down and gave Miranda a kiss. Miranda wrinkled her nose. The coat smelt like animal, but she hung on to Clare's pelt.

"Stay, we could read some more of Narnia."

"Sorry, Miranda. I'll be back later. Maybe a story then."

They heard slippers shuffling along the kitchen lino next door.

"She's up!" Clare whispered. "I'm going."

Clare slipped out of the room. Miranda heard the front door click open and then quietly shut.

"Clare! Are you still here? Will you make a cup of tea?

The shuffling came towards the front room. Miranda watched the door, waiting for her mother's entrance. She came in tying a grubby white cotton towelling dressing gown in a knot across her tummy. Her bleached blond hair, greying at the roots, was unbrushed. Gloria had dabbed make up on her face which made it look white and powdery. Her eyes darted sharply around the room.

"Oh, has Clare gone out? Damn girl. I wanted some tea. Miranda, what are you doing? Do you want mummy to read you a story?"

Miranda shook her head and turned back to the TV.

"Come on, angel. What are you watching? The Magic School Bus? Shall I watch it with you?"

Her mother hefted her herself down on to the couch. Sasha leapt to the armchair with a snarl. As Gloria sat, the programme credits came up on the TV. Gloria noticed the tree.

"Look what Clare's done to the tree! Honestly, she's a demon. Not like this lovely, little girl with me. Miranda, you love your mother, don't you, cherub? Okay, sweetie, let's watch the news."

Gloria reached out for the remote control lying on the coffee table among the clatter of dirty cups. She switched channels. Miranda slid off the couch.

"I'm going to play downstairs, Mum."

"Okay, sweetheart. Can you get me my cigarettes? They are by my bed. I think Uncle Clive is coming over shortly. Have you eaten enough? Oh, and do take those Macdonald's wrappers off the tree and put them in the dustbin. That tree needs to be taken down."

"Clare said we could do it tomorrow."

"I don't know how many times I've asked your sisters to do it. It's bad luck to keep it up after the 6th of January."

Miranda plucked the cartons from the tree as the news headlines were being read. She heard a woman say something about the consumption of alcohol being linked to breast cancer and her mother snorted. Miranda went into the kitchen to put the McDonalds cartons into the bin. The kitchen floor around the pedal bin was sticky. Miranda had to peel her foot from the lino. There was an unpleasant smell of stale food. She wrinkled up her nose and left the rubbish on the kitchen counter as the bin was over-flowing. She plodded down the stairs to her bedroom, holding on to each banister rail, as Clare had shown her, forgetting her mother's cigarettes. She wanted to play with her beanie babies.

Miranda's bedroom had once been her sisters' playroom. There was 15 years between Miranda and Rose, her eldest sister who was twenty. Clare was seventeen and Miranda was five. Everyone still referred to Miranda's bedroom as 'the playroom' and some of her sisters' old toys were still there: a jack in the box, a pogo stick, a painted wooden train set on the top shelves. The room led out into the garden through French windows. In the summer, Clare and Rose would trundle through with their friends, lingering over an old toy and reminiscing for a minute, exaggerating their maturity with a giggle of disdain at such childish things. Clare was Miranda's favourite sister. She was happy to watch TV with Miranda, read or even play with her dolls. Most of the books were Clare's.

Clare had introduced Miranda to Babar, the French elephant, Miranda's favourite. Now they were reading The Lion, the Witch and the Wardrobe together. Rose had been a pony fan. The top shelf was full of cutesy ponies with glossy manes and colourful reins. Her posters of sleek galloping horses were still on the wall. Miranda had added one of a ghostly white, bony sea horse with a long, curled tail and a regal head. She and Clare made up bedtime stories about it. It was gallant and brave and rescued children from the sea. The Beanie Babies on the bottom shelf were all Miranda's.

Miranda was pleased that she looked like Clare because she thought Clare was beautiful. Both she and Clare had thick black hair, brown eyes and dark olive coloured skin. Clare's hair was long. Rose had cut Miranda's hair, jagged. All the rage, Rose had said. Gloria said that one way or another, her girls took after her. Miranda found this hard to understand, except for Rose, who was her mother's spit. Both Rose and Gloria were pale with a mass of sharp triangles and features. Each part of Rose's face stood out. Her nose, her sharp cheek bones, her sharp blue eyes. And, Rose was skinny, not good for cuddling. Miranda liked to cuddle, most of all, Margaret, who minded Miranda sometimes. Miranda loved sitting on Margaret's lap. No one else could give a cuddle like Margaret. Not even Clare, even though Clare's skin felt like a beanie babies' when Miranda nuzzled her cheek.

Now, it was almost dark, and Miranda shivered. The overgrown, Virginia creeper outside scratched on the French windows. She went and looked out at the garden. The tree at the bottom of the garden tossed its bare branches back and forth silently in the wind. The rose bushes, cut back, looked like stunted ghouls. Broken sticks and twigs were scattered across the patch of muddy lawn. Miranda heard smashing glass from The TV news up-stairs. She didn't like the news. She got Bongo, her monkey, from her bed and sat on the rug. Upstairs the doorbell rang. The TV went silent and she heard her mother welcome in Uncle Clive. Miranda wasn't sure about Uncle Clive. He was always trying to tickle Miranda's chin. Miranda got up and shut her bedroom door and took down one of Rose's horses, one of Clare's dolls and introduced them to Bongo, her Beanie Baby. She began to play in the last of the light.

At ten o'clock, Clare climbed the eight wide front doorsteps, put her key into the porch door but before she turned it, she heard her mother's voice drift out from the slightly open bay window of the living room.

"I am worried about Miranda, Clive. The child is on her own such a lot. She needs company. The girls don't bother with her."

Clare bristled. That wasn't true. Clare spent more time with Miranda than her mother.

"Well, you're her mother, why don't you do something with her," Clive responded. Clare began to turn the key when she heard her mother say

"As the possible father, aren't you interested in her?"

Clare stiffened and stopped.

"I was clear at the time. I didn't want a child. I did it as a favour."

"A favour! You got to fuck me when you felt the urge!" said Gloria, laughing.

Clare grimaced.

"So did others, if I remember. That was the deal."

"There is DNA these days. We could find out."

Clive knew Gloria was teasing him.

"Fuck you, Gloria."

Her mother laughed. "I'm only joking, love."

Clare didn't want to hear any more but remained rooted to the spot. Gloria continued,

"You know, I'm not concerned about the paternity of Miranda. She's obviously not yours. But I am worried that she needs company. A little brother or sister, don't you think?"

"For fuck's sake, what are you saying, Gloria."

"Language, Clive."

"Another child! Good God, Gloria. Why add to an already dysfunctional family?"

Jesus, was her mother really thinking of having another baby? And, dysfunctional, Clare wondered. Is that what they were? Dysfunctional. She knew Gloria wasn't the best mother, but dysfunctional?

"They're teenage girls, for God's sake. Tell me what teenager is not dysfunctional? They're wired to do angst. Clive, it could be the same terms. No responsibilities. I do promise you, paternity will never be checked. No DNA tests. I will hold full responsibility."

"Have you discussed this with Rose or Clare?"

"No, why should I? Do you agree? It could be fun," she added slyly.

"Gloria, to be honest I'm not sure about your housekeeping skills. Jesus, look at the state of this place. If I wasn't a friend, I'd call social services."

Gloria looked around the room.

"It is a bit of a mess," she sighed. "Margaret hasn't been in to clean since before Christmas. She went home to Ireland for a month. And Rose is always off with Finn. Clare's usually hanging out with her friends, or studying, though I suppose I should be grateful for that."

Clare quietly withdrew the key from the lock and, barely breathing, peered through the small gap, where the curtain didn't meet the edge of the window. She could see her mother's legs lying on the couch with her feet in the lap of Clive. She was still in her dressing gown. Was Clive Miranda's dad?

Clare tip toed back down the front steps and down the side passage to the garden. The wind had died away. She knocked on the French windows of the playroom, peering in through the darkness towards the bed. She couldn't see Miranda. The bed seemed undisturbed. Finally, Clare saw Miranda lying at her feet, asleep on the other side of the glass. Clare squatted and knocked at the window.

"Miranda, let me in."

Her sister didn't stir. Clare knocked harder at the glass.

"Miranda. Let me in!"

Clare knocked again, more frantically. Miranda stirred and finally opened her eyes. When she saw Clare, Miranda smiled and stood up to open the French window, slowly. She stretched her arm and leg, stiff from sleeping on the floor. Clare pushed in and hugged her sister, lifting her on to the bed.

"Have you not been to bed?"

Miranda stared at her.

"I don't know," she stuttered.

"You can't sleep on the floor, Miranda."

"I didn't mean to. I fell asleep, playing. Uncle Clive was upstairs with mum. Clare, I'm hungry."

"We'll go food shopping tomorrow."

"I'm cold. Can I have hot milk?"

Clare looked at her little sister. She looked like a dishevelled angel. Upstairs, Clare heard Gloria saying goodbye to Clive and the front door close.

"Yes. I'll make you some hot milk. Brush your teeth and get into bed. I'll be right back."

Clare climbed the stairs. The musty smell of the coats flung over the banister was almost overwhelming. She added her Afghan to the pile.

"Mum?"

Clare went into the sitting room. On the coffee table, the ash tray overflowed. Two wine bottles and glasses stood empty. Two plates had rinds of cheese and apple peelings. The couch still had the imprint of her mother and Clive. Clare went into the kitchen. Gloria was at the sink with her back to Clare. She turned around. Gloria looked tired, Clare thought, though God knows how she can be, she doesn't do anything.

"You girls have got to help me more. It's a complete mess in here. The bin stinks.   Where have you been? Where is Miranda? She went downstairs to play but never came back up."

"Mum, you should check on her. I'm making her some milk. She fell asleep on the playroom floor."

Her mother flinched or was she just unsteady after the wine, Clare wondered. Clare turned to open the fridge door to get the milk. It was practically empty aside from two bottles of white wine, a carton of milk and half eaten bits of cheese, creviced and cracked. In the Perspex drawer at the bottom, limp green leeks dripped a pool of brown liquid. There were three carrots growing blonde hairs.

"I know, Clare, darling, let's do a shop tomorrow and cook a family dinner. Christmas is over. Time to start the New Year and look forward to its promise. We'll clean up, get rid of that tree. It's Sunday. And there's something I want to tell you."

"Ok." Clare said. Oh God, she thought, a family dinner but at least they would clean the house.

Chapter 3

The aroma of roast chicken and jasmine air freshener spray that Miranda had been spritzing about with great merriment, wafted up and downstairs.

"They should make incense sticks of roast chicken," said Clare.

Rose, Clare and Gloria deftly avoided banging into each other as they prepared the food and table for dinner. Miranda was now drawing and singing a nursery rhyme as she sat at the head of the table, out of the way. Gloria was wearing a long flowing dress. Her hair was washed and tied back. She was laying the table. Rose passed her the plates. In the soft afternoon winter light, the pine panelled kitchen looked cosy. The floor and surfaces were shining, and the table was laid for dinner. Gloria lifted the bird out of the oven triumphantly, her cheeks flushed with the heat of the kitchen.

"Perfect! Rose, will you carve?"

"I'll do it," said Clare, hastily. Rose was in a foul mood. She hadn't been pleased at being summoned to a family dinner. Clare knew Rose would simply hack at the bird. Rose was like that. If she didn't want to do something, she would do it so badly that no one would ask her again.

"I've got a nice bottle of wine," said Gloria. "I've been saving it for a special occasion."

"Not for me," said Rose. "I'm driving."

"Oh, one glass won't hurt. We're celebrating after all. Anyway, where are you going? I thought we were having a family evening."

"A family dinner," corrected Rose. "I'm staying at Finn's tonight. Anyway, what is this about? What are we celebrating?"

"Oh, let's wait until supper is served and then I'll tell you. Do you have to spend so much time at Finn's? You'll have to start paying rent soon!"

Gloria's words hung in the air.

"You're not paying Finn rent, are you?" asked her mother, sharply.

"I pay my way. I buy food, pay some of the bills."

"I do not give you an allowance to pay your boyfriend's bills. You have a perfectly good home here, Rose, and its free."

"Good home! You've got to be joking. Jesus, Finn's place is cleaner than this dump and it is lived in by four lads."

"Rose! Please don't start," said Gloria.

Miranda looked up from her drawing. Rose was standing perfectly still, the carving knife in her hand. Usually swishing, her ponytail was static. She held her head high, chin jutting out. She glared at her mother, her rose bud lips parted and Miranda could almost hear her snarling, like Sasha sometimes did when Miranda tried to stroke her. Miranda held her breath. Then Clare moved in and calmly took the knife from Rose.

"I said I'd carve," Clare said. She stood at the head of the table and started to carve the chicken. Clare continued talking.

"Mum, can you strain the veg? Miranda, clear away your crayons. Let's eat. Are you hungry, Miranda?"

"I could eat an elephant," said Miranda, while clearing away her drawings.

"I bet you could," said Rose, bitterly. "When I emptied that kitchen bin, it told me a story."

"The bin told you a story?" Miranda imagined the plastic flap of the bin top opening and shutting as it spoke to Rose.

"What story?"

"It was about a little girl who lived in a house built out of pizza boxes, McDonalds cartons, and Kentucky Fried chicken boxes."

"Rose, stop talking nonsense," said her mother.

Clare put the dish of carved chicken on the table and sat down next to Miranda. Gloria added the potatoes, green beans and broccoli. Rose sat opposite Miranda and Gloria sat at the head of the oblong pine table.

"Well, this is nice," Gloria said brightly. "I'm glad we got rid of the tree. It was horrible."

Gloria poured herself a glass of wine and passed the bottle to Clare who poured herself half a glass. She proffered the bottle to Rose who shook her head vehemently. Clare poured Miranda some water.

"Will someone teach me to ride my new bike tomorrow?" asked Miranda.

"I have school, Miranda", said Clare, "and it's dark by the time I'm home; I will next weekend. Is your chicken nice? You can pick up the drumstick with your fingers but wrap your serviette around it so you don't burn your fingers, like this."

Clare showed Miranda how to do this.

"Ok, Gloria, here we are having a 'nice' dinner, do tell us your news," said Rose. "Maybe you have made more millions from your South African investments?"

Clare winced. She wished Rose would sometimes just try and not continually provoke her mother.

"Well, girls, the good news is… I am going to have a baby!"

"A real baby?" asked Miranda excitedly.

"Of course, a real one, sweetie,"

Rose laid down her knife and fork. She stared at her mother.

"You are forty-five years old. You already have three daughters, one of whom is only five, none of whom you've reared."

"What do you mean? I have reared you all. On my own, more to the point."

"On your own! Don't give me that. I was passed down a line of minders. I looked after Clare and Clare is now looking after Miranda."

"That's rubbish. Oh Rose, you always see things from your own jaundiced point of view. You're completely blinkered. What have you ever wanted for? Just name one thing. You've had everything, home, a good education, clothes, money whenever you needed it, even a car. But you've done nothing since leaving 6th form college. You come and go as you please. Tell me one thing you've ever wanted and not got?"

"A father would have been nice."

"You've all got fathers. I'm not some immaculate Mary."

"You most certainly are not! Immaculate is not how I would describe you at all."

"Rose!"

"Am I going to have another sister?" asked Miranda. Gloria turned to her.

"Or a little brother, darling. Isn't it exciting? We could call it Jo, then it doesn't matter if it's a girl or a boy." She turned back to Rose.

"A little brother or sister will be company for Miranda. You two are out so often. She is on her own so much."

"I like Jo! A little brother or sister!" repeated Miranda, bouncing up and down on her chair.

Rose stood up.

"Gloria, you can't seriously blame Miranda's loneliness on me and Clare? You're her mother! It's fucking neglect! I bet you want this baby to convince yourself you are not getting old. Well, you are. Have you looked at yourself recently in the mirror? It's pathetic. I bet you have to pay men to sleep with you."

Rose pushed back her chair and stormed out of the kitchen.

"Oh, for God's sake, she is such a drama queen," Gloria tried to laugh. "Really, Clare, you have no idea how hard it is rearing three girls alone..."

Miranda slipped off her chair and got on to Gloria's lap.

"I think baby Jo will be lovely."

"Thank you, Miranda. Don't mind Rose."

"I'll help you look after it, I promise."

"You're a choti goty, Miranda, a beautiful girl. I know you will."

Clare looked at her mother. It made her uncomfortable when Gloria lapsed into Afrikans. Gloria couldn't be pregnant. Not overnight. What was she up to?

"Mum?"

"Yes, Clare."

"Are you actually pregnant?"

Gloria reached out across Miranda and poured herself another glass of wine, saying nothing.

"Oh God, Mother. You can't be and you shouldn't be drinking if you are. Miranda, go and sit down and eat your dinner. There will be no brother or sister for some time yet."

Miranda looked across at Clare and slipped off her mother's lap and went back to her seat and picked up her chicken leg.

"Gloria how can you have another baby? Surely, we should discuss this. It impacts on everybody."

"I want to have another baby, while I still can, Clare. I want a brother or sister for Miranda. You had Rose. A boy would be nice, wouldn't it? And since when have parents discussed having babies with their children?"

Rose stormed back into the kitchen with a bag packed.

"I'm leaving. Clare, come with me. We can stay at Finn's until we get our own place."

Her mother laughed.

"For God's sake, don't be absurd, Rose! How are you going to afford a place? You might belittle my inheritance, but you still live by it."

Clare looked at Rose.

"Rose, I'm about to do exams."

"Clare, you heard her. She wants another baby. She doesn't want 'to be alone'." Rose spoke in a Greta Garbo accent.

Gloria stood up, she towered above them. "How dare you behave like this," she yelled. I am sick and tired of justifying myself to you, Rose Van Standen. You go around like some sanctified martyr. So what, you have no father...millions of children have no father and are in far worse circumstances than you..."

Rose interrupted, "I have a father. I just don't know who he is."

"Nor do you want to."

"No, I probably don't, he probably paid you, and I was the resulting awful mistake."

"Ok Rose. You want to know about your father. Well, I'll tell you. He was a disgusting white South African rapist. Is that good enough for you? He raped me. Twenty years ago. In a police cell in Cape Town. He rammed me on the cell floor and raped me, over and over again. He slapped me when I screamed. Your beloved father was an Africaans police officer. Are you proud of that? I was a female prisoner and he raped me. Nine months later, there was you, with the rosebud lips. There, does knowing that that make you happy?"

Gloria took a deep breath and sat down. She was trembling. She took a sip of wine and avoided looking at them.

The three girls stared at her. Rose's face looked like a geometry set, sharp with lines. Miranda started crying. Clare stood up.

"Miranda, come with me," said Clare, "We'll eat in the sitting room." Obediently, Miranda pushed back her chair.

Gloria spoke, imperiously.

"No, Clare, sit down. I haven't finished. I've told Rose about her father. I'll tell you about yours."

Clare sat back down. She could feel her heart racing.

"You and Miranda have the same father."

Clare took Miranda into her lap.

Rose took a step forward, speaking slowly. Her voice was low and threatening.

"Gloria, you are full of shit. How dare you tell us in this way. Where is my father now?"

Miranda felt Clare grip her tight

"It's okay, Miranda," Clare murmured

Gloria looked at Rose

"Your father is dead, Rose."

Gloria spoke almost nonchalantly. She began to pretend to eat but everybody could see she was acting. Beads of sweat had broken out on her forehead. She picked up her fork and speared a piece of chicken. Rose spoke in a low voice.

"Why would you say that? I don't believe you."

Gloria slammed down the utensil on her plate. Food flew across the table.

"Rose, you think you know everything. You have no idea what it was like to live in South Africa during apartheid. The violence and fear. I hated everything, especially my parents. I rebelled. Just like you think you're doing now. Hah! Absurd. You have nothing to rebel about. But, let's get back to your father, shall we? I was on an anti-apartheid demo in Jo'burg. I got arrested by him. He threw me, alone in a cell and that's where he raped me. Hah, he thought he had power. Funnily enough, we had been at school together and he signed up for the police at the age of 18. I was always taunting him about his racist views. In the police station he was re-asserting his weak, pathetic sense of authority. My parents told me I deserved it. Happy now, Rose?"

There was a silence.

"Oh God, mum" murmured Clare.

"I left and came to England where my mother's sister, Aunt May had emigrated. I never went back. And, then, like Rose says, I had a whole pile of children to make me feel good and powerful."

"Mum, I'm sorry," Clare whispered, reaching out an arm to her.

"What is raped?" Asked Miranda

"This isn't a discussion for Miranda, Mum, she's too young,"

31

"Who is my daddy?" asked Miranda. "Is it Uncle Clive?"

Gloria suddenly laughed. "No, sweetheart,"

"I don't believe you," said Rose. "I don't believe any of this."

"How do you know Miranda and I have the same father?" asked Clare, "does he know about us?"

"No, he doesn't. Look at you, two peas in a pod. Same gentle nature, just like your father." Gloria looked at Rose. "Not like me and Rose."

"But you say we take after you," said Miranda.

"Rose takes after me, darling, except for her sweetheart lips. She got those from her father. Yes, Rose, you are a chip off the old block. When I was young, I looked and acted just like you but I expect you don't want to hear that. To be just like your mother must be a shock."

Rose grabbed her bag, her ponytail back in action, "I don't have to listen to any of this bullshit."

She stormed out of the kitchen. A few seconds later, the front door slammed.

"She'll be back when she runs out of money," said Gloria, calmly laying together her knife and fork and picking up pieces of scattered food from the table.

"Gloria, how can you be so calm? This is crazy stuff." Clare clutched Miranda around her waist.

"Who is my daddy?" asked Miranda.

"His name is Simeon, my love, and he is a lovely man."

"Simeon?" repeated Clare.

"He was half Indian, half English and involved in the London ANC with me back in the 80s. He was one of the tenants in the flat upstairs for a short while. He went to India not long after you were born. He had no idea you were his. He was a bit of a free spirit. You both look just like him."

"An Indian!" repeated Miranda.

Gloria pushed her chair back.

"Why haven't you told us this before."

"The time never seemed right. Shit, it's all Rose's fault. She would goad a sloth. I'm sorry, Clare. I'm going to lie down."

Gloria stood up from the table, lifted the bottle from the table and went into her bedroom adjacent to the kitchen, saying as she went.

"Clare, we'll talk more tomorrow, I promise. Put Miranda to bed, will you?"

Clare was trying to remember a Simeon. There had always been lots of people in the house, when she was young, usually men. Her mother had lots of meetings. She and Rose had spent much of the time downstairs with the different au pairs.

"Clare, are you going to leave? Like Rose?" Miranda suddenly asked.

"No, of course not, sweetie."

Miranda stared at her plate for a minute and then looked up at Clare. "Can we watch The Magic School Bus?"

"Yes, you go ahead, I'll come in a minute."

Miranda ran out of the kitchen.

Clare looked around at the debris and started to clear away. Simeon. Clare loaded the dishwasher and wiped the table. When she entered the sitting room, The Magic School Bus was ending.

"Come on, Miranda, bath and bedtime."

Rose might remember a Simeon. Clare got Miranda into the bath and started to play with her.

"So, maybe we are Indian princesses," said Clare, swishing the flannel up and down through the bath water.

"Are there arrows? And cowboys?" asked Miranda.

"Not American Indians. Indian Indians, from the continent of India"

"Quite the domestic scene." Rose stood in the bathroom door.

Clare dropped the flannel.

"Oh my God, you scared the life out of me, Rose."

"Rose, come play with us! We are Injun princesses" Miranda cried. Rose put her fingers to her lips.

"Not now, Miranda. Clare, we need to talk. Come on, Miranda. Time for bed, and a very quick story."

After they got Miranda to bed, Rose and Clare went to Clare's bedroom.

"Do you think she's telling the truth?" asked Clare

"Why would she lie?"

"After you left, she told me the name of our father was Simeon. Do you remember a Simeon? Or know his last name?"

Rose screwed up her nose.

"Hum. There was someone. He was quiet. He had long black hair." Rose stared her sister, "Do you think she was telling the truth about being raped?"

"As you say, why would she lie?"

Rose looked pale.

"God, I hate her. Clare, I know you're only seventeen and I know you have exams, but if you stay here, Gloria will have you skivvying, not just after Miranda, but her too, and another baby!"

"I can't leave, Rose. I don't want to. Anyway, she's not pregnant."

"How do you know she's not pregnant?"

"I heard her talking with Clive last night, suggesting they have a baby. She can't be pregnant already. She's just testing out the idea. Anyway, what are you going to do now? Really move in with Finn?"

Rose stood up, her eyes shining, her nose now straight and longer than ever.

"A baby with Clive? That's disgusting."

"Rose, if you want to know more about your father, you'll have to calm down."

"She's an old whore claiming she was raped! I bet she asked for it. I'm certainly not taking her word for it."

"Rose, stop. What else is there?"

Rose stood up

"God, I hate families. I hope I never have one. Don't come crying to me when Gloria gets the better of you. I'm going to Finn's. I'll call you later."

Rose stalked out of the room. Clare heard the playroom door click shut as Rose went out the French windows. I do want a family, Clare thought to herself. A big family with lots of children, a husband, a lovely home which would be clean and tidy and smell of roast chicken. A happy functional family.

Chapter 4

Rose was sitting up in Finn's bed, talking to an empty room and a closed white door. On the other side was Finn. She could hear him peeing, his flow splashing against the toilet bowl.

"She said she was raped, that my father was a rapist. A white South African rapist! Can you believe that? Why would a mother say that to her daughter? Gloria and the word 'mother' don't belong in the same sentence together. She doesn't know the meaning of 'mother'."

Rose was silent for a moment, waiting for a response and then plunged on ahead.

"Anyway, will it be okay if I move in, just for a while? I practically live here anyway."

Rose closed her eyes and took a deep breath. When she opened them, she noticed that the room was tidy. He'd even taken down the WWF wrestling poster she hated.

The bathroom door opened, and Finn came through, rubbing his head with a towel. He was tall with a mop of brown curly hair on his head, and big black eyes that Rose fell into when she looked at him. It made her wary, she was uncomfortable with the feeling. He was her weak spot. Finn was wearing a green shirt, unbuttoned and stripy pants. Rose felt her stomach undulate.

"Sounds harsh." Finn got into bed beside her. "But if it's true, well, isn't it better you know? I mean, I agree, it wasn't cool how she told you, but she's never been exactly, well…" he tried to pick his word carefully, "diplomatic". His slight American accent was soft and musical.

Finn liked Rose's mother. She was easy going, cool about dope and sex but she had always been an issue for Rose. Finn sighed. What was an issue for Rose became an issue for him. He had never known a girl obsess so much about her mother.

"I feel like I've been knocked over by a bus," said Rose. "Now, I know exactly what people mean when they say that. Feel how tense, I am."

Rose took Finn's hand and laid it on her stomach. It felt soft to him. It lay, smooth and flat beside the rise of her sharp hip bones. Rose wanted him to caress her.

"I'm going to do relaxation exercises. Have I shown you how to do these? You tense and relax each part of your body. One by one. Toes first."

Rose tensed her toes, then released, scrunching her eyes shut as she did so.

"Then knees."

She scrunched her knees, then released.

"Now bum."

She squeezed her buttocks, then released.

"Now stomach."

Finn felt the muscles beneath his hand harden and, after a moment, relax.

"Now fists"

Lifting her hands to show him, she clenched her fist, held it, then let go, and shook it out, as her mother had shown her. Rose's rigor mortis, her mother had called it. She had always been tense as a little girl. One of Rose's earliest memories was of Gloria lying down beside her and doing relaxation exercises. Together, they had tensed, clenched, squeezed and let go, lying down with her daughter, doing the same exercises with her own toes, knees, bottom, fingers, tummy, chest, neck, eyes, Gloria had relaxed herself.

Finn watched Rose scrunch herself up. She was like a matchstick person, all straight lines. Her breasts were small and even her nipples were pointed. He watched her muscles tensing up and relaxing. It was as if her body was a separate machine. She lay there, eyes closed, parts of her body performing. He felt his penis stir into action.

"Who did you think your father was? You must have asked before?"

Rose opened her eyes. He was on his side, looking at her. She avoided his eyes.

"Remember, I told you when we first met. The story was that he went travelling to Thailand and over-dosed at some hippy moon beach festival or something. He hadn't known she was pregnant when he left. It was a 'terrible tragedy'." Rose did air quotations. "She said she didn't know his family and didn't want to get them involved. Her folks were back home in South Africa, and she hated them. You know my mum, she's so crazy, that's it's all perfectly plausible."

Rose was silent for a moment.

"And, you know what, somehow it was never important. I didn't feel I had an abnormal life. I didn't realise it was unusual to only have a mum until school when I saw that most of my friends had a father knocking around. The men were hardly ever there. So, the fact I didn't have a father didn't matter. And there were so many divorces happening. Sometimes I was pleased I didn't have a father, particularly when I was a teenager. Fathers caused trouble."

"Did she never talk of her life in South Africa?

"Only occasionally, though she spouts Africaans in a very irritating way, as you know. She lived on a large farm in the Veld and despised it. Hated apartheid. That is why she left. In one way, I hated South Africa. It took up all her time. She was always holding ANC meetings in the house." Rose laughed.

"God, when I was in my teens, I used to think 'meetings' were this very important thing that would lead to freedom and change. It was only a couple of years ago that I realised they were not much more than an excuse for egotistical, mainly male, 'would be' politicians to make themselves feel important. Gloria always said we had to try and change the world. At first, I thought she was making a difference. But, really, all they are is a sad bunch of disillusioned lefties."

Finn was circling Rose's belly button with his fore finger.

"That's a bit harsh," he said. "Politicians are important. I mean apartheid ended. Nelson Mandela was freed," said Finn

"I don't think my mother had much to do with it," Rose sneered. "The worst bit is her hypocrisy. She gets her money from South Africa. Her parents, whom she hated, left her the land, the estate and she sold it for millions. You know she says I'm a chip off the old block. Jesus, there's not much hope for me if I'm like her and I have a racist rapist for a father!"

"Is he still alive?"

"She says not. I don't know. But I must have family or something. Grandparents. Shit. I'm going to have to deal with this." Rose took a deep breath and closed her eyes. Finn watched her. She was aware of him staring. Something was not right. She snapped open her eyes.

"By the way, where are all your posters? Why is the place so tidy?"

He looked away.

"Rose, I was going to tell you, but you got in first. I've got a job in the States, with Dad. A reporter on the local paper. I know it's sudden and obviously now, bad timing. But it's a great opportunity."

Rose's face lit up. It was one of the things Finn loved about Rose. She was like an electricity switch. If she was turned on, she glowed and shone. He was surprised. He thought she would be furious.

"Bad timing? Its great timing. I've always wanted to go to the States."

"Oh, no. I mean, you can't, well you can but, well...Not straight away. Maybe we can plan for you to come in the summer when I know what's happening."

He felt her body tense up under his hand. Rose turned on her side, her back towards him. Don't be like Gloria, she told herself. Don't react. Don't say anything. But she couldn't help it. She sat up, cheeks bones blaring.

"Fuck. How can you just go to America? Jesus. Finn. You obviously didn't give me a second thought. Is it that easy to leave me?"

"I'm not leaving you, Rose. Dad only told me about the job yesterday. I'm sorry. It's an opportunity. Would you want me not to take it?"

He sat up beside her and took her hand in his. Her fingers were long. He interlocked fingers.

"Rose, you've had quite a day. I'm sorry. Rose, I love you. You know that."

Tears started rolling down her face. "Oh, I know, I'm sorry, I hate girls who cry. It's just all a bit much. Of course, you must take the job. When do you have to go?"

"I leave in a month."

"Where's the job?"

"Montana. Dad's editor of a local newspaper. I'm going to help him. A local reporter"

"There's nothing for me?"

"Well, I never really thought you would want to come…I mean, I haven't asked."

Rose breathed in deeply. She turned around to face him.

"Finn, I'm delighted for you and I will come visit but I have decided something. I'm going to apply to do a diploma in journalism."

Rose laughed, taken aback by her own announcement. She had noticed the course advertised in the local paper this week, and wondered. Suddenly, now she had decided.

"And you and your dad can give me a job in two years."

"You daft thing."

Finn crept on top of her. Rose felt herself falling. She loved him. She wasn't going to lose him. She'd get herself a job in journalism. In America. She'd get away from her mother. She could write. She liked to write. Finn felt her sharp hip bones arch into him.

Chapter 5

At 7am the next morning, Rose let herself in the front door, lugged her bag down the stairs to her room which was under the front steps of the house. Rose had painted the underside of the steps black and stuck luminous ever-glo stars and moons on them. She liked the cave effect. The rest of the room was white with a thick fluffy cream carpet. She loved the feel of it between her toes. Rose threw her jacket over the chair and sat down at the table, staring out at the bricks in the side passage wall. She unzipped her bag and pulled out her laptop. She was going to apply to college. She would have to live in her mother's house a while longer. But first, a cup of tea. She went back up to the kitchen.

"So, you're back?" Gloria said to Rose, when she came out from her own room next door to the kitchen. She was surprised but relieved to find Rose making tea.

"I didn't expect you quite so soon." As soon as she heard herself, Gloria regretted her words. "Sorry, Rose, I'm glad you're back, if you are, that is. Anyway, can we talk? I'm sorry about last night. I shouldn't have let you goad me."

Rose looked pale. She was wearing a red dress and it clashed with her hair. Gloria almost commented on it but managed to hold her tongue.

"Do you mean you shouldn't have said things about you having another baby," Rose answered tersely. "Or me having a rapist for a father? I'm not sure which is more devastating. Is he dead, by the way, my father? Or is that another lie?"

Gloria pursed her lips, pulled her dressing gown around her. She looked out the window, taking a deep breath. The sky was still dark with cloud and rain outside. Gloria could see herself reflected in the pane, her face old and wrinkled. She'd be lucky if Clive would have her, she thought. She turned around to face Rose.

"Can we start again? It's a difficult conversation to be having as it is. Maybe we should agree to both try to be nice."

Rose looked up. Their eyes met. Quickly, Rose dropped her gaze.

"God loves a tryer," she said sardonically.

Gloria pulled up a chair beside her daughter and turned it around to face her. Rose ignored her.

"What I said last night was true about your father. And yes, he is dead. He was assaulted and found dead in one of the poorer parts of Jo-burg. It happened fifteen years ago. I only found out seven years ago when I was researching prison assaults in Jo-burg. I didn't know what I felt when I first saw it, relief or distress."

Rose looked up at her mother. She didn't know what she felt.

"Don't look at me like that, Rose. We both lived on the veld. We went to the same school, but I hated him, he was a racist. Then, of course, after what happened in the Police Station, well, I detested him. But still, no-one deserves to be beaten to death. I was upset and then angry that I was upset. I don't know, I am not putting it clearly.

"Did you not talk to his parents? Do they even know about me? Did he know about me?

"No, Rose. I discovered they left South Africa in 1994, after Mandela's release. I don't know where they are, if they are alive. He never knew about you. No-one knew about you, except Aunt May and my parents. As you know Aunt May died when you were a baby. Breast cancer."

"So why didn't you tell me all this before?"

"I don't know. I made up that other story about the moon party in Thailand. It seemed less harsh. I'm sorry. Maybe, I didn't want to face the vulnerability of being raped. I'm sorry I told you in a fit of temper. You provoked me."

The whistle of the kettle blew. Gloria put her hand on Rose's shoulder. Rose shrugged it off.

"I provoked you? You're the one who started it with your baby talk. A baby! You are being absurd, short sighted, and selfish. Who is going to father it?"

"Clive. We might get together."

"Yuck, the way he salivates after Miranda. You have no idea. Don't you see him staring at her? He makes me feel dirty."

Rose shivered and continued "I bet if he is screwing you, he's thinking of us."

Gloria stared at her, stepped forward and slapped her face.

"You little bitch."

Rose barely flinched. She walked out of the kitchen.

"I'm going downstairs."

"Oh, so you're home to stay, are you?" Gloria called after her. "Finn thrown you out, has he? Crawling back to the flea pit I raised you in. I'll send Clive down when he comes."

Gloria slumped down on the kitchen chair, exhausted. Rose slammed her bedroom door behind her.

Chapter 6

"Mummy has one of her headaches," said Miranda later as she snuggled into Margaret's square lap and comfortable bosom. "Will you read me a story?"

Margaret was reading the note left on the kitchen table by Gloria. Gloria's bedroom door was closed.

Welcome back, Margaret. And belated New Year greetings. We did a tidy up at the weekend, but it needs your touch. Could you concentrate on the kitchen and bathrooms after giving an overall hoover? I have the most god-awful migraine. Hopefully I'll be over it by the time you leave, otherwise see you Wednesday.

Gloria

Margaret hmphed. It's lucky I don't have migraines, she thought.

"Maybe after I've done my work, sweetheart. Is Clare at school?"

Miranda nodded.

"Rose. Where is she? With Finn?"

"In her room, I think, though last night she said she was going to live with Finn. But she was here this morning. She helped me get dressed when Mum said she had a headache but then she had to do a few things and said it was ok for me to watch TV. Can I show you what I got for Christmas?"

"I'd love to see."

Miranda slipped off her lap and scampered down the stairs. Margaret began clearing up the breakfast dishes, putting them in the sink. She grimaced at the grime of the sink.

"Look." Miranda was carrying a huge, floppy, cardboard book. She put it on the table.

"Hey," said Margaret, bustling over with her cloth, "I'll wipe that table. We don't want to ruin your book, do we? She wiped the table in big circular movements. " Now let me see."

"It's a paper family," said Miranda proudly. "You see, I cut out the dolls. And then I dress them with all these different clothes on this page. Look, they have little tabs that you bend over so they fit. See, this is a school uniform. Will I have one like that at my new school?"

"You will, indeed. Is this all you got for Christmas?"

"No, Clare gave me this. I got a bike from Mum, but I haven't learned how to ride it yet. And Clare got me Beanie Babies too."

"Well, isn't that lovely? Now for the moment, you sit here and get a few paper dolls dressed and then we can get you dressed."

"What are you going to do?"

"I'm going to clean this kitchen. We can play the shipwreck game when I wash the floor."

"Yes!" Miranda clapped her hands with glee.

"You get those paper dollies dressed now while I tackle this cooker."

Rose appeared in kitchen doorway.

"Margaret, hello. Happy New Year."

"It's a bit late for that. How are you, Rose, love?"

"Fine. Did you have a good Christmas? The baby well?"

"Great, thanks. It's lovely to show him off at home. All good here?"

Rose didn't answer.

"Margaret, I have to go out later. Are you ok keeping an eye on Miranda? Gloria has a migraine." Rose rolled her eyes to the ceiling.

"So I understand," Margaret almost smiled but continued, "don't worry about us. Miranda is going to give me a hand today, aren't you, sweetheart?" Margaret smiled at Miranda dressing her paper dolls at the table.

"Thanks, Margaret. It's great to have you back."

Margaret hmphed again and turned back to the sink.

Chapter 7

Royal College St. Had there once been a royal college here? Rose wondered. The railway bridge crossed over Camden Road with a vast yellow and red Michelin tyre advert spread across it. Underneath pigeons roosted, cooed and shat from black smoky bricks. Sitting in the back of a car, coming home from a long car journey, Rose always sighed in relief when she saw the bridge. These were her streets. For years Rose had walked home from the train station after school, past the four storey, ugly sixties flats, the eel pie and mash shop, now long closed. Wriggly eels had swum in a small silver containers in its windows. She had refused to eat them when they went in, she, just had mashed potato with the green liquor sauce splashed over. Now they came to The Favourite Café instead. Opposite was the Heavenly Corner Sweet Shop with its jars and trays of sweets, sherbet fountains, cola cubes, black jacks and pink chewy fruit salads.

Rose stared out the café window at the familiar shops on the other side of the street. There was Lennie's Electrical, Sari World and Super Save Sarah's with its messy displays of plastic bowls, mops, buckets, tiny stools disgorging onto the pavement. Rose loved the disarray of the Asian fruit and veg shop spilling across the road: the boxes of carrots, coriander, parsley, tomatoes, courgettes, yams, aubergines, chilis, oranges, apples and lemons, though she wouldn't know what to do with it all. Clare was the cook.

Rose watched a group of Jewish Free School boys, weighed down with school bags, grey shirts pulled out, making their way home, obviously slagging each other. A group of Camden school girls walked arm in arm, head to head, whispering, school skirts rolled up at the waist to make them shorter. She had been one of them not so long ago, a school girl, not at Camden School though. She and Clare had been sent to Haverstock, the comprehensive as Gloria didn't believe in grammar schools. She smiled to herself, momentarily happy, remembering her school days, in the familiarity of the wheezing coffee machine behind her, the condensation on the window, the white formica topped tables with the red plastic bottles of Heinz tomato ketchup. She could hear Nancy, big and busty behind her counter, shouting orders to the cook in the kitchen behind.

Outside, the sky suddenly darkened. It began to rain, heavy, thick drops. A train rumbled across the bridge, its lit windows flashing between the hoardings. She felt the table vibrate. Soon people began to emerge from the station. They hesitated at the exit, put up umbrellas, or lifted bags over their heads and hurried off. She saw Clare come out and cross the road. She wiped the steamed-up window with her hand and waved. Clare spotted her and waved back. She came in dripping, shrugged off her school bag and collapsed into the opposite seat.

"It's horrible out there."

"I got tea." Rose nodded at the small, stainless steel, tea pot.

"I fancy toast."

Clare caught Nancy's eye behind the counter.

"Hi Nancy, can I have some toast, please."

"Coming right up."

Clare turned back to Rose and gave a rueful smile.

"How are you? Have you seen mum? Did you tell Finn? What did he say?"

"I have seen mum. I have told Finn. And I'm fine. How was school?" asked Rose.

"Fine. Got an essay to write…about Shakespeare's Fool. So, tell me Rose, what's going on?"

Clare leaned into her, across the table to better hear her sister. "What happened to moving in with Finn."

"Finn neglected to tell me he was moving to America to be with his Dad. He's got a job."

"Oh my God. When? Are you upset?"

"Yes, I am but we haven't split up. Clare, it could be an opportunity for me, down the road. Anyway, so I have to stay at home in the short term. But, I don't want to be there any longer than I need to, particularly if Gloria's going to shack up with Clive? More than that, have a baby with Clive?"

"What? Shack up with Clive? How do you know?"

"She told me this morning. God, she is unbelievable, one rocket launch after another. I told her Clive is always ogling Miranda. It's gross."

"You didn't say that, did you?"

"I did. How can she think she can just set up house with Clive? It's our home too."

"Rose, you are so contradictory. You've just announced you're leaving home. Keep Clive out of this. I think he half thought Miranda was his. Did she say anything more about your dad or this Simeon?"

"Not really, just that she'd discovered my dad was dead and that there's no-one left in Jo'burg. She said nothing about Simeon, but I didn't ask. We got into arguing." Rose gave a rueful smile. Nancy bustled over with the toast.

"Here you are, girlies. More tea?"

She lifted the pot and poured out two cups.

"Is that too strong. Will I get you another?"

"No, Nancy, thank you. That's fine. I like it strong."

Clare buttered a triangle of toast and offered it to Rose who shook her head. Clare took a bite, chewed, looking at Rose.

"So, what are you going to do now? Are you going to try and find out more about your dad?"

Rose took a sip of her tea.

"Well, today I've applied to do journalism at Metropolitan University, starting next September."

"That's brilliant, Rose. You've always been good at writing. Are you going to stay at home?"

"Yes, and I need to find a job!" She turned around to Nancy.

"Hey, Nancy, any jobs going?" Rose laughed and turned back without waiting for an answer.

"Yeah, I do need a waitress, didn't you see the sign on the door?"

Rose nearly choked on her tea. "You serious?"

"Yep?"

"Oh my God, Rose, a job without even looking. Everything falls into your lap," said Clare.

"She ain't got it yet," said Nancy, winking. "I know she's reliable as a customer. But that doesn't make a good employee!"

"I'll be reliable, Nancy. I wouldn't want to let you down."

"Okay. A week's trial? Start tomorrow?"

"That is so cool, Nancy. You're a star! Thank you."

"Thank me when your feet are killing you, girl. This aint no easy work."

"You've saved my life, Nancy."

"Just be here at 7am in the morning."

"God, Rose, you're lucky," said Clare. She lowered her voice. "Rose, listen, I need you to think. Can you remember any more about Simeon? I know he's Indian! I guess that makes me half African and half Indian. That's exotic, isn't it?"

"I suppose. I guess having an African father makes me a full blooded South African. Maybe, I better start learning Africaans." Rose snorted. "I don't know anything, Clare, about Simeon. You'll have to ask Gloria."

"Hum. I'll get her in a good mood tonight. You keep away from her, Rose. You know what, I was thinking, maybe I could go to India for my gap year."

"Don't be silly. You can't traipse around India looking for Simeon. It would be like... looking for a needle in a haystack."

"Ha ha. I realise that, but, I'm going to find out as much as I can, and then we will see."

Chapter 8

Later that night, after Clare had read Miranda a bedtime story, and got her to sleep, she went back up to the kitchen to make tea. Rose had gone out to meet Finn. Gloria came into the kitchen. Clare handed her a cup.

"You're a pet, Clare, thank you. I'm going to put up a rota of responsibilities, so we all share the work."

"Good idea. Listen, Mum, I need to talk to you…about what you said. About Simeon, like who is he? Does he know about me and Miranda?

"I told you, he knows absolutely nothing, and its better if it remains like that. He is not interested, Clare. I don't even know where he is. India, I think. I haven't seen him since Miranda was conceived and I barely saw him for years before that."

"What's his full name? Don't tell me you don't know that."

Gloria hesitated. She couldn't see how she could avoid an answer.

"Simeon Ganapesh. He's not Indian, well he is. But he was born here. But I'm pretty sure he went to live in Mumbai."

"What does he do?"

"He was a student. Of politics. Clare, I don't know anything else."

"Mum, I want to find him. He's my dad. He's Miranda's dad. He has a right to know he has daughters."

"Vloeck, Clare. Please, don't interfere in my life, nor Miranda's."

"It's my life too. Rose said you and Clive are thinking of getting together. Is that true?"

"Maybe."

"Does Clive want to have a baby?"

"I think so."

"Will he take on Miranda?"

"What do you mean take on? He won't be her father."

"No, Simeon is. And he has a right to know that he has two daughters."

"Clare, it is not up to you to decide who Miranda's father is. If Clive moves in, then I guess, he will help raise Miranda."

"So, you'll become the regular little family."

"Don't be silly. You and Rose will always have a home here but, as you keep saying, you are independent young women. You can't have it both ways, Clare. I have a life, too."

"Mum, it is always all about you! We always have to fit in with you. I think Rose was right in one sense. All this baby business is about you not wanting to be alone."

"Clare, if I want another child, I'll have another child. I don't have to refer to you." Gloria got up. "I need to read some documents. Tell Miranda to come and kiss me goodnight."

"She's already in bed. You go down."

Chapter 9

On Friday night, Gloria scraped out the last of the rice from the pot and then curry from the casserole onto the plate and passed it down the table to Rose at the other end.

"Ok, smarklike eke, enjoy," Gloria said. Rose groaned. They all picked up their knives and forks except Miranda who used a spoon.

"Margaret and me planted wall flowers today," Miranda said.

"Margaret and I," corrected Gloria.

"I got a letter saying I've been accepted to the do the journalism course I applied for. I start in September." said Rose.

"Like me," piped up Miranda. "I start school in September. We can go together."

"Rose will be going to college, Miranda," said Clare.

"That's wonderful, Rose. Congratulations. I'm delighted. Will you live here or do you plan to move?" asked Gloria.

"Stay here until I can save more money and get my own place, if that's ok."

"This is your home, Rose. You know that."

"And Clive's home too?" Rose asked.

"That's still to be decided and none of your business."

"And, Clare's got some exciting news too, haven't you, Clare."

Clare looked at Rose, confused.

"Your news, Clare, tell us. Where are you going for your gap year after your exams this summer?"

Clare stared at Rose.

"I haven't fully decided yet."

"You have, come on, spill the beans."

"Well, I was thinking of going to India," announced Clare, her eyes flashing daggers at Rose. "With Angie… But nothing is decided." Clare turned to Gloria. "I wanted to have checked it out more before I told you."

Gloria looked at her in surprise.

"Can I go to Indja too?" asked Miranda

Clare laughed lightly. She wanted to smack Rose.

"You're starting school, Miranda. That is much more exciting."

"You kept that quiet, Clare," said Gloria. "It would have been nice to discuss it with you. When, how, and where exactly are you going?" asked Gloria. She leaned across for the pepper which she ground liberally on to her dish.

"Mum, obviously, nothing is decided. I hope to get a summer job after the exams, and then I'll work over there, if necessary. And you said I could have an allowance like Rose, when I finished school, to help with my gap year."

"Well, I can't give both you and Rose two hundred a month each."

Gloria put a forkful of curry into her mouth, looking from one daughter to the other.

"This is very nice. What do you think? It's not too spicy for you, is it?"

There was silence. Rose and Clare looked at each other.

"I don't need the money anymore. Give it to Clare," said Rose.

"That's very kind of you, Rose, and how do you plan to live while you're in College?" asked Gloria. "Gosh, you two do have great plans. Clare's off to India. Rose is off to college. Miranda will tell me next that she's moving out. Anyone would think you have money to throw away. Who do you think I am? Some fat wallah, here to hand out money as and when you need it? I find it amazing that while you sit here spending my money, my ill gotten gains according to Rose, and organising your lives, you still have the audacity to pass judgement on my hopes and plans. Why do you think that you have the right to say exactly what I can and cannot do!"

"Mum, that's not fair. You said I would have an allowance. It's my gap year," cried Clare.

"Sweetheart, that was before the roof started leaking and the council tax went up. Miranda starts school and will need uniform and books and, a childminder. You girls have no idea of the pressures I face. And the lodgers have given in their notice in the flat upstairs, so no rent for a while."

Gloria reached for the bottle of wine and poured herself a glass. How dare they assume that she would fork out for all their hare-brained plans without any discussion? Jesus, she tried to talk things through with them. Even Clive moving in. What other mother asked permission from their daughters?

"Why does Miranda even need a child minder? You don't work." said Rose.

"Just because I am not paid for the work I do, Rose, does not mean I do not work. I am the Vice Chair of the Equality and Equity Commission, not that your generation appear to have any interest in human rights."

"Don't be ridiculous. That's not full time. You're just being mean. How dare you try to stop Clare from doing what she wants. You, the paragon of human rights, and after all she's done to look after Miranda!"

"Enough!" Taking a deep breath, Gloria turned to Miranda and smiled, "well, Miranda, sweetie. When will we go and get your new school uniform? Shall we do that tomorrow?"

Miranda looked around the table and nodded.

"Is Indja far away, Clare? Will we be able to read stories at bedtime still? Who will take me to school?"

"We're not discussing it anymore." Gloria stood up and swept round to Miranda.

"Come on, Miranda, let's go and eat in the sitting room in front of The Magic School Bus and let your sisters plan their exciting lives."

She lifted Miranda out of her chair and held her in her arms. Miranda struggled.

"But I want to eat at the table, with Clare and Rose."

Gloria clasped her tighter and picked up her plate.

"They don't want to talk to us, Miranda. They need to discuss their travel plans. Come on."

Miranda started to squeal. "Mummy, you're hurting me."

"Mum, stop it. Don't be, what do you say in Afrikkans, belaglik?" said Claire, trying to make up to her mother. "Please sit down. Let's finish supper, as a family" said Clare.

"Belaglik means nasty, Clare. I was not being nasty."

"Stop trying to appease her, Clare," said Rose. "This is a perfect example of what will happen to you if you stay. She will manipulate you and make your life hell. She always has," said Rose.

Gloria left the room, calling back

"Take up Rose's offer to pass you her allowance, Clare. I can only afford two hundred a month. If Rose doesn't need it, you take it. Go and do your travelling. Miranda and I will be here when you return, won't we, sweetie?"

"You bloody better not return, Clare," Rose muttered. Clare turned on her.

"Rose…why did you do that? Create another scene. What is wrong with you? You turn this house into a …a Shakespearean tragedy. Don't you ever think before you speak? Jesus, I wish I hadn't mentioned it to you."

They heard Miranda crying next door, then their mother shout

"Miranda. If you don't stop, I will put you in your room and you will have no supper. You can't get what you want all the time. I've learned that from your sisters. Now settle down."

Rose and Clare looked at each other

"What the fuck has got into her? She's like a cat on a hot in rood?"

"Maybe I shouldn't go to India. I don't know if I really want to," said Clare.

"Of course you should go. You can't let her dictate."

*

Later, Rose was downstairs bathing Miranda. Clare could hear the whelps of delight. Bath time with Rose was always more fun, more water on the floor than in the bath. Clare took tea into the sitting room with Gloria.

"I'm so sorry, Mum. I should have spoken to you about India before I did to Rose. I just wanted to find out more about it before I did."

"Yes, you should have done, but actually, it's Rose. She really does get my goat. She sets out to deliberately hurt me. And she bloody well succeeds. I don't know where I went wrong with her. I don't know how you two are so different. But, India? For God's sake, don't do this to find Simeon. It will be a waste of time. Do you have any idea how large India is? I don't even know if he lives in India. He could be back here. He could be in Timbuctoo. Also, Simeon doesn't know about you, or Miranda. Suppose you do find Simeon and he is married with his own family. Suppose he is not interested. How will that make you feel?"

"It's not just about finding Simeon. India is an exciting continent. And it gives us a reason, other than just travelling. It'll be fun. and if we do find him, well…we can just be friends. I don't expect him to turn into my father over-night."

"Friends! God, Clare, you are naive. If he has another family, I'm not sure 'friends' will cut it."

"Mum, he is my Dad. I have rights too. And he has a right to know he has two daughters. I'm sorry, I am going to try and track him down. There's nothing you can do about it, except, maybe help me."

"Oh Clare. Stop being so childish. Okay, I'll put some feelers out first. I do have a number he used to be at. Or we could advertise. He always used to read *The Ham and High*, and *The Guardian*. Easier than gallivanting around India."

Oh God, Clare thought, I don't want Gloria getting involved.

"Mum, Angie wants to go to India, regardless. And, please, don't do anything. Just don't. Let me think over what you have said. Maybe you are right. I should leave sleeping dogs lie. I'm going to read Miranda a story."

Rose was drying Miranda in the bathroom when they heard Clare go into her bedroom and shut the door.

"Will Clare read me a story?"

"I will tonight."

Rose lowered her face to Miranda's and gave her a kiss on the cheek. For some reason, Miranda always remembered that moment. It felt strange, like a bird pecking her, Miranda thought.

Chapter 10

Angie had wanted to go to Thailand, but Clare had persuaded her that India was much more interesting. Everybody went to Thailand. And, in India, they would have a mission. But when Gloria suggested that he might have moved back to England, Clare wasn't sure. Maybe he was in London. After all, he was born here, according to Gloria, although she didn't know whereabouts (we had better things to do than discuss our backgrounds, Gloria had said to Clare who squirmed at the thought). He was younger than she was, Gloria had said, my 'toy boy', and looked fondly into the distant past (Clare squirmed again). He was interested in politics and poetry (weren't we all, Gloria had said, though actually, on reflection she added that poetry had never really been her thing). Apart from this, Gloria really didn't seem to know much about him at all.

"He was an occasional lover, Clare. Primarily, he was the lodger. A quiet boy, gentle. For God's sake it was the 1980s. We just fell into bed with each other, occasionally, after meetings. No-one really thought about it. Of course, we used contraception. Well, maybe not with Miranda. But I never was very good with the Pill, that's how you came along."

Gloria had added hurriedly,

"Anyway, I always wanted babies. I wanted, want, a big family."

Clare decided to advertise in the Ham and High.

"Just be direct," suggested Rose as they set in Rose's room composing an ad. "How about '*did you sleep with Gloria Van Standen in 1980s?*' No, maybe not, we could be inundated with calls. What about '*Indian birth father of two lovely girls sought?*' No, that won't work. We'll get a bunch of weirdos!"

"*Seeking Simeon Ganapesh who lived in Wilmott Place London NW1 in 1987. Very Important. Contact Clare on* cvs2@gmail.com.

"That does the trick. Short and sweet, I guess. What are you going to do if he does contact you?"

"I don't know. I guess I'll see. All I know is that I have to try."

"Ok, let's do this. It's quite exciting, isn't it? I'll have to live vicariously since mine is dead. Go on, Clare. send it off."

Chapter 11

Miranda was dressed up in a nurse's outfit, standing at a chair at the kitchen table, mixing peanut butter and marmalade medicine for an array of her teddies. Clare was just in from school, making tea. Gloria had come into the kitchen from her bedroom. She rubbed Miranda's head and tickled her chin.

"Clare, Gloya says Marget's going to look after me after school, every day."

"Sweetheart, call me mummy."

"Rose calls you Gloya,"

"Gloria. That's because she and Clare are grown up girls."

"I'm going to be grow'd up when I go to school."

"It's only March. You start in September. And you'll still have more growing up to do then."

"Miranda, will your patients want fish fingers and peas?" asked Clare.

"No, they are having medicine. Isn't she, mummy? Marget's going to look after me every day."

"Most days. Not at weekends. Talking of weekends, Clare, Clive and I are going out on Sunday night. Can you babysit?"

"Out! That's a first. Okay. Yes. We'll watch a film, will we Miranda? What about Winnie the Pooh?"

"I love Pooh. It'll make my teddies better too. They like Pooh."

"It will. Now, let them sleep while you eat your tea."

Clare put a plate of fish fingers, peas and potatoes in front of Miranda with a fork and a spoon and poured her some water.

"Put the kettle on, Clare. I'd love a coffee. Would you prefer orange juice, Miranda?"

"Too much orange juice is bad for her teeth."

"For God Sake, Clare, orange juice is good for you! You and Rose turned out ok, well, bossy, but okay."

"I wonder where we got 'bossy' from."

*

Clive had persuaded Gloria to go out to dinner. She didn't want to go anywhere fancy so they went to their local Chinese restaurant from where they usually got take away.

Gloria looked around. They were sitting at the only table in the window. There was a false wood partition behind them where there were more tables, but they were all empty.

"Why did we come here? It's like a ghost town. Maybe we should have gone to the Italian on Parkway. At least there's life there."

"It was you who suggested here, Gloria. You said you wanted Chinese."

"I did assume the restaurant would have people eating in it."

Gloria was facing the window. She could see her blurred reflection in the rainy black night. She looked grainy and misshapen. Her face faded in the headlights of the occasional car that drove past, tyres swishing along the wet road. She wished summer would hurry up and come.

"There's more atmosphere at home, and we could have smoked."

Gloria didn't like going out much. Shopping, and going to meetings was fine but social occasions...she felt awkward. And Clive, well she had never thought of him as boyfriend material. At home, it didn't matter. She wondered if she'd become a little isolated. Gloria looked at her reflection in the window again. She should get her hair cut, but at least long hair helped her hide her face which these days looked as if it was caving in. Back in the day, she had moved with panache. Like Rose did now. One day, Rose would find out, she thought with a slight sense of bitterness. Her time would come.

"I had a terrible row with Rose," Gloria said. "God, I'm sick to death with that young woman's hubris. It's unbelievable that a twenty-year old could be so arrogant."

"I think that is their prerogative. What happened?"

"God knows. She provoked me. I told her that her father raped me, and she was the product."

"Gloria! Are you mad? You have kept it from her all these years. Why now?"

"She just kept on at me, saying I was an awful mother."

"You must learn not to listen to her. She's young. She's rebelling. She doesn't mean it. Rose has had everything she needs."

"That's what I said. But then she said '*a father might have been nice*'. For God's sake. It's not as though all her friends are like happy families. Anyway, I just lost it."

"What about Clare and Miranda?"

"I told them the truth too, that they had the same father, Simeon, and that he had returned to India."

Clive looked up at her and asked her, sharply,

"How do you know?"

Gloria looked at him, surprised

"Well, they're clearly sisters. Can't you see that? And they look like Simeon."

"But Simeon is Indian."

"Yes, so what?"

"Well, they don't look Indian."

"Oh, for God's sake, Clive, what does Indian look like? They have lovely sallow skin. They don't look like me either, but I gave birth to them. Why are you so surprised? Did you think Miranda was yours? How could you truly think that?"

"Well, you kept hinting at it, always talking about DNA tests and stuff."

"Clive, I've never thought Miranda was yours. It's so obvious that she was Simeon's. I don't know how you can't see it."

"I only met the guy once or twice. I don't know. I just always thought…"

"But you've always said you don't want any responsibility."

"I know and I don't, didn't. But, I don't know, maybe it's different now. When you started talking about another baby the other night, well, I was just thinking, why mess around. If you want another. Well, maybe we could, I don't know, well do it together, official like, become proper parents.

Gloria stared at him. So, he was thinking the same way as her. Hardly romantic, but they were too old for romance. Clive was bulking out a little, but Gloria quite liked his size. And he gave a good cuddle. His eye-brows were growing ridiculously scraggy, but he was intelligent. He also had a steady teaching job in the local secondary school. He'd always been there for her, if she wanted.

"Is this a proposal?" she asked.

"Not a proposal as such. But maybe we could up it a notch. If I'm to father a child, I want to be part of the family.

"Well. I'm honoured. Clive, I think, in your oblique way, you are suggesting we become partners. Is that right?"

Clive stared at Gloria. He had hoped that Miranda was his. Yes, alright, she looked like Clare, but that could have been her mother in her, though Gloria looked nothing like Clare. Gloria was manipulative. Had she set him up? Gloria suddenly changed the subject

"In the meantime, what am I going to do about Rose?" Gloria asked.

He looked at her. About Rose? Oh God, Rose. If he got involved with Gloria, would that make him Rose's dad? Dear God. If they got married, what would he be taking on? If he wasn't Miranda's dad, maybe he should cut loose now.

"Clive, are you listening? Are you okay? Have another drink, sweetie, the blood has completely drained from your face."

"Gloria, can we talk about us and not Rose for once?" Clive's voice was a little shaky.

Gloria looked from her reflection to his face. So much had happened lately. How had all this happened?

"Clive, we are good friends, Clive. If we change the status of our relationship, will that change?"

"Gloria, and I feel stupid saying this, but I like us together. Here we are, in our late forties. We've been friends for ages. We've slept together. I even thought I might be the father of Miranda.

"Rose thinks your interest in Miranda is gross."

"What do you mean?"

"She accused you of having other interests, but I think she was trying to wind me up."

"What! For God's sake, Gloria. I hope you put her right, told her I thought Miranda might be mine. Rose, she's nothing but trouble. What did you say?"

"That she was talking nonsense. Anyway, sorry, I interrupted you. Do go on.

"Gloria, when you raised the possibility of another baby, something shifted in me. I realised, I might want a child and if I did, I would want it to be a secure relationship."

"Oh God, Clive, are you saying you want to get married? Don't we need to be in love?"

"Oh." He looked around, and half whispered. "Well, Gloria, I think I love you." He hesitated. "it sounds stupid."

Gloria played with his fingers. Jesus, this was weird. There was a silence while they both contemplated this idea.

"Living together? Could you cope with living with the four of us? Could you manage Rose? We are not an easy family. I think you would need your own separate space. I would need you to have your own space because I need mine."

"I can take the tree house!"

Gloria smiled.

"Seriously. But maybe we could get a man shed or something. And the girls. They are wholly mine. The decisions to be made are mine. I would look for your support, not your input.

"I'm happy to leave you the girls, particularly if you are serious about another baby! Also, Gloria, soon, they will leave home. Listen, we're in no rush. Let's take it bit by bit and see how we go. I'll keep renting my place for a while. But, let's try. You and me."

"Well, I'm a ticking time bomb. It needs to be sooner rather than later if we want a baby."

Gloria didn't feel sure. A baby was fine. But a baby and a man? Maybe it was practical. Maybe. Gloria glanced at her reflection again. She had nothing to lose. It wasn't all about Rose and Clare or Miranda. It would be good to share responsibilities. She might find it hard to relinquish control. But she could try. The girls seemed to be wresting it away from her anyway. She smiled.

"Okay. Let's try. And let's leave this dump and get a bottle of champagne and go out somewhere else to celebrate properly. We haven't ordered. Come on. I need a cigarette."

Chapter 12

At home, Miranda was curled up on the couch with her beanie babies. She had fallen asleep. On the tv, Winnie the Pooh was floating at the end of a balloon. Clare had turned down the sound and was reading Sylvia Plath poetry, wondering if Simeon liked Sylvia Plath. She heard the key in the latch. The door was flung open. It banged against the wall and she heard Rose throw her bag down and fling off her coat. Clare put her fingers to her mouth for when Rose burst into the room which she did, still wearing her Favourite Café apron and carrying a bottle of wine. Clare nodded towards Miranda. Rose beckoned her out, whispering

"Come to the kitchen. I need to talk to you."

Clare got up, covered up Miranda with a blanket and followed Rose into the kitchen. She was pouring wine into two glasses.

"There's shepherd's pie on the stove, if you want some."

"No thanks. I ate at The Fav."

Rose sat down with a sigh, sprawled back on the chair for a minute and then leaned forward to pick up her wine. She looked tired. Her hair was tied back in her usual ponytail, but it hung, listless, down her back. Her skin seemed tugged tight over her sharp angled face.

"What's wrong? Everything okay at the café?"

Rose nodded.

"Have you heard from Finn?"

"Yes. It's going great for him. He loves Montana. Says he misses me."

"So, what's wrong?"

"I don't know what to do."

"What do you mean? What about?"

"I think I'm pregnant. It's so stupid."

"Oh Rose, are you sure? Couldn't you be late? You're often irregular."

"It's more than two months. We last had sex in February before he went and its now April. I've got the pregnancy test. Will you do it with me in the morning?"

Clare nodded. She drank a sip of wine.

"Gloria will love this," Rose laughed a gritty laugh.

"Don't be ridiculous."

"Me making her same mistakes. Oh, I'm sure she'll crow."

"Hardly, Rose, Mum was raped. That is very different. And then being on her own over here. It must have been very hard for her. Anyway, I'm sure she won't crow."

"She'll probably want the baby."

"Rose, you're not sure you're pregnant yet."

"I think I am. My head feels funny. And I am so tired."

"It is Finn's?"

Rose looked up at Clare, surprised. What did her sister think of her? She knew she had a temper, and said things she probably shouldn't, but she was surprised Clare had to ask.

"Of course. There is no one else? There hasn't been anyone else. But, maybe I'm not. Maybe the shift work at the café is tiring me out. Maybe all this family drama is getting to me. Anyway, we'll find out in the morning. You'll help me?"

At 7am the next morning, Rose crept into Clare's room. She wanted to do the test. She watched Clare sleeping peacefully. It constantly surprised her how different they were. Both Gloria's children. It must be the genes of the different dads. Rose felt guilty waking her. Rose had barely slept, tossing and turning over different scenarios in her head, trying to feel her way through the possibilities. If she wasn't pregnant, she could go to college, get a qualification, get her own place, travel. If she was pregnant, she would have to stay here, if she could bear to live with Gloria. That was her least favoured option. She could have an abortion. But what about Finn? Should she tell him? He might not want an abortion or insist on one. She had no idea. Why should she tell him? He was the one that had gone off. Anyway, she'd never really missed having a father. Not really. She played that card sometimes, but Gloria had done quite well, and most of her friends' parents were divorced. There was something else worrying her. It had struck her suddenly in the middle of the night. Her father, now that she might be pregnant, that seemed important. It was absurd. She had never worried about the father thing before, when she thought her father was some young twenty year old who had a terrible accident. Somehow, he had never existed. Now she knew her father was a rapist. A racist rapist. She had the genes of a South African racist rapist and a neurotic controlling bitch. Genes couldn't get much worse than that. Would she turn out to be a mother like Gloria? People always said she was like her. Clare opened her eyes and stared straight at Rose.

"Good morning, Rose. Is everything all right?"

"Do you do that every morning?"

Clare sat up.

"Do what?"

"Open your eyes and address the world. No fluttering, snuggling, pulling the duvet over your head."

"Do you want to do the test? You look pale."

Rose always looked pale but this morning she looked pasty, Clare thought.

"Yes."

"Ok. Have you been worrying all night?"

Rose pulled a blue and white box out of her pocket. She felt strangely excited.

"I read the instructions. I have to pee on it and wait a minute. If it's two clear red bars, I'm pregnant. Oh God, Clare. I don't know."

"There's nothing to know until we know. Come on." The girls went into the bathroom and shut the door. Rose held Clare's arm, holding her back from walking across to the toilet.

"Clare, what if I'm pregnant and I have the baby? It'll have the genes of a South African, white racist rapist!"

"Christ, Rose. What are you talking about? You're way ahead of yourself. Racism isn't genetic and it'll have Finn's lovely American genes."

"But look at you and me. We are so different. That must be our genes."

"Yes, but social up-bringing is everything too; our belief system, love, family."

"Family! Well, I'm fucked then, with Gloria for a mother." Rose laughed "You're right. Sorry. I haven't slept much. Let's just get on with it."

Rose pulled the test out of the box and unwrapped it from the foil.

"Ok, it has to be mid flow."

She pulled up her nightie, sat on the toilet, started to pee then stuck the test between her legs. Then she laid it gingerly on the sink, dripping yellow drops of urine, wiped herself and washed her hands.

"I don't know how I feel. I love the thought of being pregnant, having a baby inside, being a woman, bearing life and rationally, I think and know that will be a fucking disaster. A true fucking disaster."

The three girls were having breakfast in the kitchen when Margaret arrived at 9.30. Miranda ran to her for a hug.

"Sit down, petal, and finish your breakfast." Margaret went straight to the kettle, filled it at the kitchen sink. "Anyone for more tea? Is Gloria in? Does she want tea or coffee?"

Rose nodded towards Gloria's bedroom off the kitchen.

"She's in there. I think Clive is with her."

Margaret raised her eyebrows.

"You late for school, Clare?"

"I have first two periods free on a Tuesday." She looked at Rose. Margaret made her tea and stood by the table. Something was wrong. She could feel it. She knew these girls well enough.

"Everything alright?"

Both Rose and Clare glanced at Miranda.

"Miranda," answered Margaret. "Have you finished your cereal? Why don't you go downstairs and choose some clothes?"

Miranda got down from the table, wrapped her arms around Margaret's legs.

"I'm glad I have lots of mummies…mummy, Clare," she beamed at Clare, then looked at Rose and said with less enthusiasm, "Rose, and Margaret." She gave Margaret's legs an extra squeeze and went downstairs.

"What's going on here?" asked Margaret.

Clare and Rose looked at each other and then looked pointedly at the closed door to Gloria's room.

"I'm going to get dressed," Rose got up and walked out.

Beckoning Margaret with her head, Clare followed Rose downstairs. Margaret followed them out of the room. What on earth had happened, she wondered. Just then, the doorbell rang. Margaret could see a dark tall, hatted, shadow through the glass of the front door. It was a bit early for visitors. Maybe Gloria had a meeting.

"Gloria," she called through the firmly shut bedroom door. Margaret always felt ill at ease in the kitchen when Gloria was in her bedroom with a man. One time she had heard Gloria squealing like a pig.

"There's someone at the door."

"I'm just dressing, Margaret. Show whoever it is into the front room. Thanks."

Margaret opened the door to a figure in a broad-rimmed black felt hat, and dark wool overcoat. He looked at her. She looked back at him. He was tall, dark faced with a deep voice.

"I'm looking for Gloria Van Standen."

"Is she expecting you?"

"No."

"Oh, well come in."

Margaret stood back to let him in.

"Go into the room on the left, the front room. I don't have time to be making tea or coffee now. Gloria will be out in a minute."

She hustled him through the door, shut it and made her way downstairs. A new drama every week in this house, she grumbled to herself. She opened Rose's bedroom door without knocking, smiling as she remembered how she'd come in on her and Finn one time.

Rose was tapping at her laptop, furiously. Clare was sitting on the couch with her knees pulled up.

"What's going on?" asked Margaret

"Who was at the door?" asked Clare.

"I don't know. I put him in the front room. A friend of your mother's."

Rose started to speak without looking at her.

"Margaret, I have discovered that I am the daughter of a South African rapist, a dead South African policeman, a racist and the daughter of a psychotic control freak who keeps having babies to ensure her continual youth and that I am pregnant myself and I don't know what to do."

Margaret stared at Rose who hadn't lifted her head from her laptop during this speech. Had she heard Rose correctly? She was pregnant? Gloria had been raped? By a policeman? Was she going mad?

"Well, you certainly know how to make an announcement, Rose."

Rose finally turned to look at her.

"See, a drama queen, just like my mother and Clare would say."

"Oh Rose," both Margaret and Clare said together.

"Are you pregnant?"

Rose nodded, defiantly.

"I'll put the kettle on," said Margaret.

"Said like the Irish mammy you are, Margaret. You do that while I google abortions in London."

"Rose, stop it," Margaret said sharply.

"I'm sorry. I don't know what to feel. If I'm pregnant, it will be a disaster, but I sort of feel excited."

Behind Margaret the door opened, and Miranda was standing next to her in half dressed, looking rather askew.

"What's wrong with Rose?" asked Miranda.

"Oh my God. Is there no privacy in this house?" cried Rose.

"Rose, you look terrible. I suggest you go back to bed and sleep, you'll be able to think better. I'll bring you tea shortly," said Margaret. "Miranda, Rose is tired that is all. Now, look at you. I love that elephant top, but I think it is on back to front. Will I help you change?"

Margaret bustled Miranda down the passage

"Clare, you should get off to school," she called back.

For sure, this house was nothing but a theatre full of divas. Pregnant indeed!

Clare closed the bedroom door after Margaret.

"Don't you have to be at school?" asked Rose

"I won't go in."

"Please don't stay on my account. There's nothing to be done here unless you're any good with knitting needles. Margaret is the sort of woman to have knitting needles, wouldn't you say?"

"Rose, stop this. What is wrong with you? What are you going to do?"

"Only one thing to be done. We can't have any more little rapists, white supremacists running around the world."

"Rose! Please be serious."

"Clare, I am being serious. I don't know anything about my father. He could be mad. Until I know more, I cannot bring a baby into this world.

"Rose, stop being so dramatic. Gloria brought you into the world, knowing him."

"Yes, and look at me. Nothing but trouble. Do I want to bring me into the world?"

"I don't think you are ready for a baby," said Clare.

"Same age as mum. And," Rose mimicked her mother's voice, "don't we have everything a young girl could ask for?"

"Yes, but as you said, Rose, no dad."

"Yeah, well, in this case there is a dad, isn't there?

They both jumped when they heard the door open. Margaret walked in with a cup of tea.

"Clare, what are you doing here? Go to school. Rose, take a few days. Mull it over. If you want to talk, I am here. But you must tell your mother."

Rose laughed.

"I'm not telling her. She'll gloat, then panic. She'll start calling me all sorts of horrible names in Africaans. She's the last person I need. She'll do my head in."

"She needs to know, Rose. And you might find she reacts differently to how you expect. After all, she had the same experience when she was your age, and she was alone. You need to tell her. She's the person who can help you most. And she will be dreadfully hurt and upset if you don't.

"So, as usual it comes back to Gloria. Poor Gloria. It's always about her."

"Rose. You twist things. I am saying these things to you to help. Believe me."

"Margaret, this is not help. I need to talk to someone who can be rational. I need good advice. You tell me. What should I do?"

"Rose. No one can tell you that. My advice is to tell your mum. Take a few days, absorb it. But before too long, you must tell your mum. She'll find out, one way or another. May be not today. She's too caught up in something else…that visitor…"

"Who was that, by the way?" asked Clare.

"Never seen him before. Anyway, I've got to go. Clive is reading to Miranda. Rose, believe me, this is not the end of the world, whatever happens. But try not to overreact, and you'll make your life easier."

"I wouldn't leave Clive with Miranda!"

"Rose, Clive is fine with Miranda! You are so exasperating," said Clare.

"Why wouldn't she be fine?" asked Margaret.

"Just one of Rose's mad notions. You know, the way he is affectionate with Miranda? Rose doesn't like it. I think he thinks he's her dad. We should tell him she's not. Or maybe Gloria has now."

"Anyway, I'm not over reacting," said Rose. "Genes make a difference. Look at the difference between Clare and me. Why are we so different when we come from the same place? She's kind, thoughtful, clever. I'm abrasive, bitchy and excitable."

"You have energy, enthusiasm, determination, Rose. I wish I did," Clare responded, but she sounded lame and actually Clare was glad she wasn't like Rose. Rose flashed her a look of pure resentment. Clare bristled in response. God, she was tired of her sister, always hogging the limelight. Even now, when it should be about Clare, Clare and her father, who at least was alive, Rose had to be fucking pregnant. Forget Gloria, it was all about Rose! Clare stood up.

"Ok, I'm going to school.

"Rose, things will look better after you sleep," said Margaret. "And stop being so bitchy. I never met anyone with a tongue like you."

"You know my mother, don't you?"

Chapter 13

Upstairs, Gloria threw on old slacks and a long tee-shirt.

"Who is it?" asked Clive.

"No idea. I hope to God it's not Len, you know the guy we helped get out of the Stamford Hostel. He's forever popping round with chocolates. He's harmless but a bit creepy."

"That'll teach you to do 'good works.'"

"Come and rescue me if I haven't got rid of him in ten minutes."

"I'm your knight in shining armour now, am I?"

Gloria gave him a grin, went out through the kitchen and opened the door into the sitting room. A tall figure was standing at the window, staring out into the street, holding a broad-rimmed hat at his side. He turned around at the noise of the door opening. Gloria couldn't make out his face against the bright light of the window, but she recognised him immediately.

"My God, Simeon! What are you doing here?"

"Hello Gloria. How are you? God, how long has it been six years? I'm here because there was an ad in *The Ham and High*, looking for a Simeon Ganapesh who lived in Wilmott

Place in 1987. I thought it must be you but wasn't sure. Look. This is the email address given."

Gloria looked at the folded paper he passed across to her. She sank down into the armchair, looking at it.

"It's Clare's email address. Oh my God. Simeon, I'm sorry."

"Who is Clare and why is she looking for me?"

"She's my daughter. You remember?"

"I remember Rose, and your baby. You had her just before I first left for India. Yes, you called her Clare. I'd forgotten."

"And I had another baby too, five years ago."

"That's nice. Congratulations."

"Thank you."

Simeon looked around the room.

"I haven't been back here since I moved out. Last time we met, you booked us into a hotel. You said you needed a break from the two girls. Where was it? Off Shaftsbury Avenue? A bit of a dive. Well, this place hasn't changed at all. It still reeks of cat. God, is that the same Sasha?"

He went to stroke the cat curled up on the sofa who hissed, jumped up and strolled to the other armchair. Simeon withdrew his hand, quickly.

"Yes, well, she hasn't changed. She must be ancient. Anyway, Gloria, you look well. Is everything alright? What's this ad about?"

"Actually, it's a different Sasha. I just keep the same names. How am I? Well, reeling a bit from this visit. But it is lovely to see you."

Gloria remembered the hotel. He hadn't really wanted to have sex. She had to be very persuasive.

"Simeon, I'm sorry, we can't talk now. Can we meet tonight? And I'll tell you why I think Clare is looking for you. Are you living in London?"

"Yes, for the moment."

"I'll explain everything tonight. Meet me at the Half Moon pub in Camden Town at 7.30pm. Do you remember it? And, Simeon, please don't contact Clare first."

"I wasn't sure whether to or not. Then I thought I'd come by and see what was going on. Gloria, stupidly, I'd forgotten you called your baby Clare. God, is she old enough to be putting ads in the Ham and High? What does she want?"

"I think I know. Now, I'm sorry to hustle you, but I'm really busy. You have to go. Let's meet later and I'll tell you what I think she is up to."

They heard footsteps approaching the living room door and both turned to watch it open. Damn, Gloria thought. She moved just a little in front of Simeon, trying to block the view from the door.

"Gloria, is everything alright?" Clive stuck his head around the door. "Remember, we have that meeting."

"Oh God, Clive, come in and shut the door. Quickly."

Clive entered the room and advanced towards Simeon and Gloria holding out his hand.

"I'm Clive…Gloria's intended." He looked at Gloria and grinned. She frowned in return.

Simeon stepped away from Gloria, held out his hand and smiled. His smile was broad.

"Clive! I think we've met. I'm Simeon, I used to live upstairs, was involved in the ANC movement, many moons ago. Congratulations. Good news. Congratulations Gloria!"

"Simeon! Hello"

Clive stared at him in surprise. Simeon had aged well. He had thin lips, a longish nose, pale brown skin and brown eyes. He had the stubble of a black beard on his face. Clive remembered him as a bit of a beanpole. He had bulked out a bit. Still slightly cross eyed though, but it gave him a wicked charm. Clive looked across at Gloria. A thought struck him.

"Er, does Clare know you're here?"

The front room door opened again. Both Clive and Gloria whirled around in front of Simeon.

"Mummy, can I get my crayons and my Babar book? I left them in here last night."

Miranda padded in. Her spiky black hair swung around her neck as she ran across the carpet to the coffee table which lay between the couch and two armchairs. She held out the book to her Gloria.

"Will you read to me, mummy."

"Mummy's busy now, darling. Ask Rose."

"Rose is asleep, and Margaret says she has to hoover, and Clare's going to school in a minute."

"Why is Rose asleep?"

"Margaret says she's tired."

"Go down to Margaret, say I said could she read to you for just ten minutes. I'll be with you then."

"Do you want me to read to you, Miranda?"

Miranda looked up at Uncle Clive. He never made the right animal sounds and made her read out difficult words. He didn't like to discuss the pictures either.

"No, it's alright, Uncle Clive."

Miranda became aware of a third person in the room, behind Gloria and Uncle Clive.

"Go on, Miranda, I am busy. Go and find Margaret now."

Her mother sounded cross. Miranda began to leave, carrying her books and crayons, peering at the stranger who stepped out from behind Gloria and spoke.

"Hello, Miranda. Good choice. I love Babar. He is the French elephant, isn't he?"

Miranda nodded. She looked at the tall man, and then at her mother. He crouched down and held out his hand.

"Show me."

Miranda looked up at her mother, unsure. Gloria shook her head.

"Not now, Miranda. You can show him another time. Mummy is very busy. Downstairs now. Go and find Margaret. Run along."

Miranda turned around and ran out, not looking back.

"Simeon, please. I'm busy now. Let's meet this evening. We can talk then."

"Okay. You'll definitely be there, Gloria?"

"yes, of course."

"Mum!," Clare called up the stairs, "I'm going to school."

Gloria caught Clive's eye, crossed the room and slipped out of the door, closing it behind her. Clive and Simeon heard them talking in the hall.

"Okay. What time are you home, Clare? We need to talk."

"Usual time, 4ish. Who is the visitor?"

"Oh, just Len, you know, bringing chocolates."

"It's a bit early."

"I'll get some cake in and we can chat at four. Off you go, got your coat and bag? Good. See you later." Gloria held open the front door.

"Jesus mum, the train isn't for half an hour yet."

"Bye darling."

Pulling on her coat, Clare left. She peered in the bay window on her way out. She could see Clive and a someone else and then her mother going back in the room. She drew away and headed towards the station.

"Well, Simeon," said Gloria. "I must go and find Miranda."

"Yes, well, she seems a lovely girl. So, I'll see you at 7.30pm

"Yes, yes. We need to talk."

"Yes, I think we do."

Chapter 14

Walking home that afternoon, Clare was thinking about Simeon. Were fathers so important, she wondered? Gloria was right, they had never wanted for anything. She had been envious, sometimes, when her friends talked about their fathers, and they turned up at matches, but she and Rose had agreed, fathers also brought problems with them. Now Rose was worrying about genes. Clare sighed. If fathers didn't matter, why did she want to find Simeon? No one had answered her advert in the Ham and High. It was disappointing. Should she try the Indian press in London? Which one though? She'd have to google. Maybe there were different papers for different regions, or religions? Was he religious? What were the religions? Jesus, did he wear a turban? And which religion wore the turban? She would ask Gloria. What would she do with a father in a turban? Was she doing the right thing, looking for him?

"I don't know much about the Indian religions," said Gloria when Clare brought Gloria a cup of tea in bed after her afternoon nap and asked if Simeon was religious. "but Simeon is not religious. Well, he wasn't. I think he came from a Hindu family not a Sikh. I remember asking about the turban. I wanted to try one on." said Gloria. "Actually, it was Simeon who I wanted to talk to you about. By the way, do you know where Rose is? I haven't seen her all day."

"Isn't she working?" Clare said. "I think she was doing a shift at The Favourite this afternoon."

"Oh, right. Clare, I'm out tonight again. Can you look after Miranda? But now, darling, we need to talk about Simeon."

"Why?" Said Clare suspiciously.

Gloria had tried to think all afternoon about what she wanted to say to Clare. She wanted to tell Clare how she had been truly in love with Simeon. Gloria wanted to tell Clare she hadn't been a mistake, nor had Miranda. Both were the product of love. Her love, but sadly, not Simeon's. Simeon had never felt the same. He had broken her heart. Gloria had told Simeon how she felt, at that hotel in Shaftsbury Avenue, but straight away he had said he didn't want a relationship. He liked her, but they could only be friends. Gloria wanted Clare to know that she was born out of love. Did she love Rose less because of her birth circumstances? Gloria had pondered this so often over the years. No, she didn't. The irony was that it was Rose who was Gloria's echo. She loved Rose's fire, antagonism, her determination. Clare had Simeon's reserve. And Miranda? Miranda was still a baby.

As Clare sat down on the bed, sipping tea, Gloria still hadn't decided what to say.

"What about Simeon?" Clare repeated.

"He was here today."

"Here! What do you mean?"

Clare remembered the visitor.

"That was who was here this morning. Why didn't you call me up? Had he seen my ad? Why didn't he email me? Why come to you?"

"Clare, he didn't know you and he was my friend. He wanted to ask me about it. It was, is, our life you are intruding into."

"Intruding? You should have thought about that before you had me…and Miranda."

"I didn't mean it like that. Anyway, I'm meeting him this evening, and I'm going to tell him about you both. I think it's better that way. I want to prepare the ground for you."

"Prepare the ground? What are you going to say?"

"Just that you two are his, that I didn't want to burden him."

"Burden him? Is that what we are to you?"

"No, stop it, Clare, darling. You're sounding like Rose. You know all three of you mean the world to me."

Clare stood up. She had wanted to tell Simeon that she was his daughter. She wanted to see the reaction on his face.

She wanted it to be a moment. Now Gloria was going to steal her moment. She didn't trust her. She would dress it up in her own frills and frippery. And, it would be all about Gloria.

"Clare, it's more sensible this way."

Clare looked at her mother. Clearly, the decision had already been made, but she could see Gloria wanted her approval. She didn't see how she could get around it.

"Okay, but please don't send him away."

"Of course not. I will be so proud to tell him he has such a beautiful, amazing, intelligent young daughter."

Gloria reached out for Clare's hand, her eyes shining. Clare could see she was excited.   "After that, I meet him alone," Clare continued. "I don't want you there."

Clare wanted to hurt Gloria and was satisfied to see Gloria grimace.

"Let's not fight, Clare, please."

Gloria wanted to be there. She wanted to be able to present her daughters to Simeon. Offer them as a gift, hand wrapped and prepared with pride. With love.

Clare felt her heart pumping. She put down the cup on her mother's bedside table. She should be leaping with excitement and joy but instead she felt her skin was swarming with electric eels

"I've got homework to do."

"Everything will be fine, Clare," said Gloria, getting up and going to her wardrobe. "Isn't this what you wanted? You've found your father. I'll leave money for you to order in pizza. Maybe Rose could collect it on her way back from work. Will you text her? You're okay to put Miranda to bed, aren't you? She's at the park with Margaret. Clare…what do you think I should wear?"

But Clare had left the room. Coming out of the kitchen, Clare saw Clive's bulk through the pane of the front door. She wheeled around,

"Clive is here. Is he moving in? Does he know about Simeon? What does he make of all this?"

"Well, maybe we're upping our stakes a little. We'll see, Clare. What do you think I should wear?" Gloria repeated, pulling out dresses and shirts.

They heard the front door open and shut. Clive stopped when he saw Clare in the bedroom door.

"Hi Clare,"

"Hi Clive. Excuse me, I have homework."

Clare slipped passed him. He positioned himself in her spot, leaning against the door jamb. Gloria held a knee length green dress against her and looked in the mirror. This dress used to pick up the red of her hair. Should she dye her hair. She had let herself go. It was time to change. New beginnings and all that. No, she would wear something demure. She smiled. She had never been demure.

"Gloria, we need to talk. I'm going to come with you to meet to Simeon. I don't think you should do this alone."

"Don't be ridiculous. You barely know him. Anyway, this has nothing to do with you, Clive."

"Maybe the pub is not the best place."

"I'm hoping we'll go out to dinner."

"Gloria, this is going to blow Simeon's mind. Have you considered what you are going to say…will you serve up Clare at the first course, and Miranda for dessert?"

"I don't know yet how I'm going to tell him. But it's not as if I am asking him to do anything. Anyway, this isn't my fault. Clare started all this."

"But you're behaving as if you are enjoying it."

Gloria put the green dress back and pulled out a black skirt. She turned to face Clive.

"Clive, our conversation the other night does not give you the right to interfere or tell me what to do. Let's make that clear from the beginning. This is between Simeon and myself. I make decisions about my children. Of course, I understand that Simeon knowing about Clare and Miranda could change everything. Everything."

"Gloria, does this change anything between us?"

"God, I don't know, Clive. How do I know what Simeon is going to say?"

"I want to come with you."

"No. I'll phone you later. Don't worry, everything will be fine."

Chapter 15

Gloria decided to wear the blue beaded peacock chiffon scarf she'd bought in Camden market over a plain white v neck jumper and blue jeans. She fixed her hair on top of her head with two chopsticks and put on blue dangly earrings. Her earrings had always amused Simeon but looking in the mirror, she saw mutton. Ah well, nothing she could do about that. She would have to wow him with her personality.

At 7pm Gloria got out of the black cab and entered the Half Moon pub. She found a small round table in the corner away from hustle and bustle of the clientele. She ordered a bottle of Sauvignon Blanc and two glasses. By 7.30pm the bottle was three quarters empty. She wondered if she should get some crisps. Gloria looked at her watch. Simeon used to be rarely late but now it was 7.40. Gloria looked around the pub again. There had been a bar billiards table in the old days. Now it was all stripped pine, low couches, and bookshelves. They had occasionally come here after meandering around Camden Market together on a Sunday morning. Again, she wondered how Simeon was going to react. Maybe he had guessed when he saw Miranda. The resemblance was striking.

Gloria saw the pub door push open and Simeon's hat silhouetted against the glass. She took another sip, trying to stop her hand from shaking. She was more nervous than she let on, even to herself. She watched him look around and waved to attract his attention. Taking a deep breath, she called.

"Simeon! Over here."

He saw her, smiled. Gloria was encouraged by his smile. It seemed genuine. She watched him edge between the tables coming towards her until he was standing over her. Her stomach turned. Simeon took in the nearly empty bottle of wine.

"I'm not that late, am I?"

"No, no, I was a little early. I wanted to get a quiet table."

Simeon looked around.

"A few changes," he remarked. He took off his coat, folded it in half and put it on the bench seat beside Gloria and perched his hat on top of it.

"I think I'll get a beer. You're ok?"

"Maybe a packet of crisps. I haven't eaten. I thought we might later."

She watched him go to the bar and chat with the bar man while his beer was being poured. They laughed. Well, he didn't seem too jumpy. Gloria wondered what they were laughing about.

"What were you laughing at?"

"The name of the beer. There's a beer called Duck's Fart."

"Weird."

Simeon set down and passed a packet of cheese and onion crisps. He looked directly at her.

"You look well, Gloria."

"I don't. I know I don't. I never shifted the weight after Miranda."

There was a moment's awkwardness. Gloria plunged ahead.

"Simeon, before we talk, tell me about yourself. What have you been up to in the last five years? Last time we met," she looked at him slyly, "in the dive, as you called it, you had just handed in your PHD. How did it go? What was it on again, I can't remember?

"'The Impact of Immigrants on the British Radical Left.' We discussed it."

"Of course, we did. I remember now."

"It was well received. I got a distinction. For the past three years I've been lecturing in Mumbai University from time to time on International Relations. I also guest lecture at LSE occasionally, when I'm in London."

"Wow, that's amazing. Congratulations. So, do you live in Mumbai? Have you family? Presumably, that's why I haven't heard from you."

"I haven't heard from you either, Gloria."

"Well, why would you? You were clear about not being together. And, then Miranda came along, and well, I've been busy, with three girls to rear."

"On your own? I rang and left a couple of messages, but you never responded."

"Did I not? I don't remember."

So many times, Gloria had nearly dialled the number Simeon had left. She did after the birth of Miranda, but the person who answered said he was in India. In a sense, she had been relieved. Gloria took a sip of wine. She let it swirl around her mouth, behind her teeth before she swallowed it. It was sharp on her gills.

"So, maybe we should get to the point," said Simeon, gently. "I think I know. Miranda, she's mine, isn't she? She looks just like my little sister. I've thought about the timing, and it fits."

"Really? She looks like your sister?" Gloria felt a sob rise at the back of her throat. "Oh, I'm sorry. I'm fine. Give me a minute."

She breathed deeply for a few minutes, trying to stop the tears rising. Simeon watched her, making no move to comfort her. Gloria took a deep breath, wiped her eyes and face with her chiffon scarf, looked at it, and laughed.

"Oh look, I've got mascara all over the peacock. Typical me." She looked up at Simeon. He was looking at her, but keeping perfectly still, and not saying anything.

"Say something, Simeon."

"I'm still coming to terms with it. I had no idea until this morning. And then I wasn't sure. Why didn't you tell me?"

"You said you weren't interested and I wasn't sure the baby was yours. I wasn't averse to having another baby. Clare was thirteen, and starting to go out, make her own friends. Rose was impossible…" Gloria chuckled, "mind you, Rose was always impossible. I began to feel a void. So, when I found myself pregnant, I thought, why not. I had good friends, daughters to help. It would never have been like before when it was just me and Rose. I have Clive. He is a good man. In fact, I thought the baby might be his. It was more likely."

Gloria's chatter petered out.

"I'm gabbling. I'm sorry. Anyway, that's the end of it. Yes, she yours. Obviously, now. As you say."

She looked up at him again. His face had contorted slightly. He might have guessed, she thought, but clearly it still hadn't sunk in. Simeon took a sip of his beer.

"So why was Clare trying to contact me?"

How to tell him about Clare.

"Clare? Maybe she thought Miranda should have a father. Well, now she could have two …what with me and Clive getting hitched, so it's all unnecessary."

Gloria gave a light laugh. This wasn't going to plan, she thought. Why was she talking about Clive? She should have thought this through. Gloria took another sip and said brightly,

"So, you never answered my question. Do you have your own family?"

"I'm getting married in four months, in August, in India. Gloria, what does Miranda know? Does she think Clive is her father? And how did Clare find out? Did you tell her? Jesus, Gloria, I wish you had told me. I had a right to know. I have a little girl! I can't believe it. What is she like?"

"I'm sorry, Simeon. Let's go for dinner and I can answer all your questions. And I have questions of my own…for instance, who are you marrying?"

"Dinner? No, I don't think so. Does Miranda know who I am?"

"To be honest, I am not sure how much she understands."

"Does Clive know?"

"Clive does know, now. He thought she might be his too. So, who is the lucky woman?"

"Her name is Minoo. So, will I be good news for Miranda? Jesus, I can't believe I have a daughter!"

"What will Minoo say?"

"I don't know. We will have to talk."

"Well, it won't have much impact on her, really. You know, you needn't tell her."

"Of course I'll tell her. I can't keep the fact I have a daughter from her."

"Why upset her? She's a million miles away."

Simeon stared at Gloria. Her face, although always strong, seemed hard. Gloria had never been a softie. He had liked her directness. She had always been honest, and principled. Things were right or wrong, black or white. Her sense of justice had always been acute.

"You don't think it's wrong not to tell her? You think it is okay for me to hide that I have a daughter from my wife? What sort of marriage would that be?"

"I suppose not but I don't want you to ruin your marriage for no reason. It may be difficult for her to accept you now that you have a family. I have learned somethings are best left unsaid."

"If I had hidden the fact that I had a daughter, not a family, that maybe true but I haven't known until now. I think she will understand," Simeon said coldly.

"You have two daughters, Simeon. Clare is also your daughter. I would call that a family."

*

Gloria fell, half laughing and half crying, into Clive's shoulder when he opened his front door.

"You should have seen his face. It almost turned white. He stood up, and I could see he wanted to punch me. And all I could do was laugh. I sounded like a witch cackling. I sounded like a mad woman. I have never seen him so angry. He left me there, laughing hysterically."

Chapter 16

Clare was chopping chilis, ginger and garlic in the kitchen with the big knife, standing at the thick wooden chopping board. She sliced the pink brown flesh of the chicken into fingers. When the oil was sizzling, she threw in the chopped chili garlic ginger mix. The aroma filled her nostrils. She stirred and added the chicken, turning each piece over until it sizzled white. She added the red chili, then the carrots, red and yellow peppers, stirring. The rice bubbled white and opaque, and a green salad was on the table. It suddenly occurred to her that spice might not work for Rose. Ah well, she thought, it's not too spicy. She'd been thinking of Miranda.

"That smells gorgeous, Clare."

Rose came in, her head raised and nose sniffing. She was shining.

"How are you feeling?"

"Much better. Listen, I'm sorry about…everything, about my erratic behaviour over the last few days. I'm tired, I guess, hormones and all that."

"Hum."

"Where's Gloria?"

"Out. Meeting a friend."

"Has she got friends, other than dear Clive?"

Clare hadn't yet told Rose about Simeon. When Rose had come back from work, she had made her go and have a bath. Miranda was watching children's TV.

"You look loads better."

Rose's pale skin glowed. Her elbows, knees, her nose, all her angles seem to be at rest. She had her hair up in a top knot. She looked...Clare searched for the word, regal.

"Yes. I feel almost excited," said Rose. "You know, I think I'm going to have this baby."

"Remember what Margaret said. Take your time. See how you feel with all the options. There's no rush. When are you going to tell mum?"

Rose shrugged.

"Well, take your time with that too. She seems to be in a bit of state." Clare turned back to her pan. "Will you pour me a glass of white wine?". She had picked up Gloria's habit of enjoying a glass of wine while cooking. The chef's glass.

"Why is Gloria in a state?

Clare couldn't contain herself.

"Rose, Simeon has been in touch!"

"Oh, my God. Why didn't you tell me? What happened? Did he contact you? Have you seen him?"

Rose leapt up and hugged Clare from behind. Clare was laughing when she turned around to hug Rose back.

"No, I didn't see him, well not really, through the window. He was the one who came around this morning. He wanted to ask Gloria about the advert. I didn't think of him doing that. Anyway, she insisted on seeing him first. They are meeting now. She's telling him about me and Miranda. I suppose, it probably is better coming from her. Oh my God, Rose. I don't know what I feel, excited, scared, sick."

Rose stepped back to look at her. Usually calm and serene, Clare looked drawn. She had tied back her dark ringlets. Her sallow skin had a tint of yellow and she had darkish rings around her blue eyes.

"Wow, Clare, this is worthy of celebration. I'll have one glass with you. One glass won't hurt. Anyway, maybe I won't have the baby. Maybe I'm too young."

Clare could see, there was going to be a lot of this twisting and turning about this baby. She smiled at Rose, raised her glass, and wondered how Gloria and Simeon were getting on.

After dinner, Rose stretched out on the long grey divan in the living room, the cat beside her and Clare was in her usual armchair, legs curled under her. Both were in their PJs. Clare's were stripy flannelette and Rose's green silk. Margaret had cleaned earlier and the square bamboo coffee table as clear of coffee stained cups, and dirty ashtrays. Gloria's magazines were neatly piled under the rows of bookcases which were full of manila files and thrillers. The mirror over the mantlepiece gleamed. Clare got up and pulled the floor length, grey velvet curtains together. Rose sipped at a second glass of wine.

"It's nice here, on our own. Funny, really, when you think about it: there we were going about our usual business, me dossing, you hard at study, Gloria being Gloria and doing what we've done for years, squabbling, living regular old life and suddenly wham bam, the next moment I discover my father is a mad rapist and dead, you discover your father is alive and kicking, Gloria plans to get hitched to Clive, I'm having a baby. How did all this happen?"

Clare sat back down and leaned forward to light the candles on the coffee table.

"It all comes back to you pushing Gloria too far. That was the trigger. If she hadn't had that outburst, telling you about your dad, none of this would have happened. Except you getting pregnant. Presumably, that would have happened."

Rose recalled her and Finn making love when she had got back from 'that' Sunday dinner.

"Maybe not," she murmured. "I think I conceived that night when I was so upset. It is strange how things happen."

Rose remembered how drained she had felt after the row with Gloria and the shock she had felt when Finn told her he was going to the States. It was the first time that she felt that

119

nothing was secure; and that what happened in her life was not pre-destined but also her responsibility.

"Do you think being conceived in stress will affect the baby?"

"Don't be ridiculous, Rose. You have some very strange notions about what makes a baby."

"So, what do you think Simeon said?" wondered Clare out loud. "Presumably, Gloria has told him by now. It's half nine, she should be home soon."

"I have no idea."

"Maybe he doesn't want to know. I've probably ruined his life."

"Clare, now who is being ridiculous?"

They sat silent for a few minutes.

"What would you like to happen?" asked Rose.

"I don't know. Have a dad but I'm not sure what dads do. I want him to have a relationship with Miranda."

"I wonder if you have half brothers and sisters. That would be strange. Not sure I wouldn't feel a bit jealous. You won't be all mine."

"I'll always be all yours…I'm not going to be able to escape you that easily."

They looked at each other and laughed but the feeling of discomfort lingered.

"Families, ay?" Rose sighed. "Do you think I could have a baby and go to college? It will be born in November."

"Maybe delay college a year. You know mum and I will help, don't you?"

"Gloria? You must be mad. We both know her child rearing skills. She doesn't know an arse from an elbow."

"Don't be silly. Anyway, it'll probably be different, being a grandmother not a mother."

"I wonder. She'll not like that either, being made a grandmother, I mean."

"Having a baby will change everything, Rose. You need to think about it...all the knock-on effects. College, work, income. Are you going to tell Finn?"

"I guess, but, I am beginning to see a little why she wouldn't have told Simeon. I feel it's my decision. If I tell him and he says no, that he's not interested, then I'll be angry, upset, and resentful. I'll probably have it to spite him." Rose laughed and continued, "And if he says let's have it, then I'll feel cornered and guilty because I don't want it. It's a no-win situation for him. If I make the decision to have it myself, it's all my fault. I'd have to live with the consequences. Like Gloria has to."

Clare considered this for moment.

"It's not all bad having a baby. Maybe Finn could help you think it through."

"But he's not here, is he?"

"You could skype or face time."

"No, I want to talk to him face to face."

"So, tell me, why might you keep it?"

Rose thought about it a minute.

"I love Finn. It might be sooner than I thought, but when is a good time to have a baby? I bet there's always a good reason to put it off."

"It will be interesting to see what Simeon's reaction will be then, won't it?"

"Jesus, I'll tell Finn when I have made a decision, not seventeen years later. Ssshhh, I think I hear Clive's car."

Rose got up, moved across to the window and peered out between the closed curtains.

"Yes, that's Clive and, it's Gloria too. Did he go with her? God, that was sensible but there's no Simeon."

Chapter 17

Clare put back her head, closed her eyes, and steeled herself.
She heard the key turn in the latch. Gloria took off her jacket
and threw it over the bannister.

"Girls?"

"In here," she heard Rose call back.

Gloria looked back at Clive and raised her eyebrows.
He shrugged. If she'd had a choice, it would have been Simeon.
Always, she thought, but, she didn't have a choice. Gloria
sighed.

"I'm off," Clive said.

"But we only just got here."

Clive indicated towards the sitting room.

"I think the girls are waiting."

He mouthed silently Good Luck. Gloria grimaced. He
leaned across, gave her a kiss, and whispered

"Just tell the truth and don't let Rose provoke you,
whatever."

Out loud, a little too loud, he said

"I'll see you in the morning. become round about ten."

Rose looked at Clare and rolled her eyes upwards. They
both looked towards the door to watch for Gloria's entrance.

"Hello girls!"

Gloria bustled in, pretending to be all bright and breezy. Clare looked at her directly. Her eyes were glistening. Had she been crying?

"Oh good, a bottle of wine. I'll get a glass."

Gloria hurried out again. They heard her go into the kitchen, walking purposefully, but she must have pulled the cupboard door too wildly for they heard it bang against the wall.

"Whoops," they heard her say.

"She's drunk," Clare whispered.

"She's fine. She's nearly always got a glass of wine on the go," said Rose.

Gloria came back in and poured herself a large glass.

"Can I fill anyone up?"

Both Rose and Clare put their hands over their glass tops.

"Why will you never drink with me?"

"We don't like to encourage alcoholics," said Rose. "So, Clare tells me you met Simeon tonight. How did that go? Did Clive go with you?"

"No, Clive didn't come with me. I went to his place after."

"Mum, did it go ok?"

"If wanting to slap me is alright, then it went fine."

"Oh God," Clare said, clapping her hand over her mouth. "He's angry."

"Well, it must have been a bit of a shock," said Rose. "Can't say I'd have not slapped Gloria myself, if I was in his shoes. At least it shows a bit of character."

"Shut up, Rose. He didn't actually strike me. Maybe we can try to have a calm conversation" asked Gloria, "without you making barbed comments? This has been a difficult evening, and emotional. I don't think any of us need your running commentary."

"Oh mum," Clare stood up, "tell us what happened."

Gloria sat down in Clare's armchair. Clare perched on the coffee table in front of her. Rose watched from the couch.

"Well, he's shocked. When he was here this morning, Miranda came in. I think he guessed. But he was still surprised when I confirmed it tonight."

"Then why did he want to slap you?" asked Rose.

"Well, I told him first about Miranda. Well, he guessed about Miranda. And I think he was excited by it. Shocked but excited."

"But he was angry when it came to me…"

"Sweetheart, I think he was just shocked and angry but only with me. He just looked wild and left. I mean the whole thing was so farcical. I don't know." She looked at Clare who looked bewildered and across to Rose who was just staring at her.

"You know, girls, I used to be in love with Simeon. He was never interested in me, other than as friends and the occasional fling, but I was determined to try and entice him. I have always been proud that two of my wonderful daughters are his. Neither of you were a mistake. Rose, that doesn't mean you are not wonderful. You are. You are my first. You and I belong to each other. You are much more me. We have a special cord"

"Not so sure that is so wonderful," Rose muttered.

"No, maybe not, but I'm trying to explain something. I'm proud that two of my babies were from the one man that I truly loved, and maybe still do. You were intended. And then, when you wanted to start looking for him, Clare, I didn't know what to do. In a way, I wanted you to find him. I wanted to show him what I had done for him, what he had done for me. And I thought, maybe, just maybe, he might be interested in setting up a life together, now, if he wasn't married. Now, after all these years.

"Jesus Christ, you're crazy, Gloria," said Rose, standing up. "How do you think that little speech makes me, the rapist's daughter, feel? And you say it's wonderful that I'm like you. I hope not. What about Clive? Does he know about this infatuation?"

"Is he married? Does he have other children?" asked Clare.

"Clive knows, and Simian is getting married. No other children, as far as I know."

Rose turned away from her and took another sip of wine. Gloria continued

"God, what a mess. I'm sorry. But at least you know the truth about me and Simeon."

Clare stood up

"Truth! Jesus, Gloria! You make truth fit whatever you want. Do you ever consider anyone else? I am not interested in your feelings about Simeon, except that it makes him my father. I just want to know that I have a father who cares, even if it is after 17 years. Does he want to know me?"

Gloria looked at her daughter.

"Of course, he does, Clare. He wants to meet you as soon as possible."

"Good. I'm going to bed."

Left alone, together, Rose and Gloria stared at each other in silence.

"She'll be okay," said Rose. "she and I are chalk and cheese, don't you think?" said Rose. "I wish I was more like her. Different genes. See, they make all the difference. I'll go to bed too," said Rose. "Enough truth for one night"

Gloria sprawled back in her chair.

"Good night, mother."

"Good night Rose, I love you."

The sitting room door opened. They both looked up, surprised Clare had come back. It was Miranda.

"I can't sleep."

"Ok, sweetheart, would you like some hot milk? You go back to bed and I'll bring you some down," said Gloria.

Miranda looked around the room.

"Where's Clare?"

"She's gone to bed," said Gloria. "Go on, back to bed. I'll bring you the milk and read you a story."

Miranda looked at Gloria and Rose, nodded and disappeared. She padded down the stairs and opened the door to Clare's room. Clare was lying on her bed in the dark. She raised her head to see who it was.

"Come on, poppet. Come and have a cuddle," Clare said. "Can't you sleep?"

Miranda ran across to Clare. "Can I sleep with you?"

"Come on then, in you pop."

Fifteen minutes later, Gloria found them both asleep in Clare's bed and her heart flooded and sank at the same time. A thought occurred to her. What if she lost them?

Chapter 18

The next morning, Gloria and Margaret were having coffee in the kitchen.

"Margaret. There's so much going on here at the moment. If we ever need a pair of extra hands around, to mind Miranda or do some extra cleaning, would you be willing? I'll pay you, of course."

"Is it Rose?"

"It's everyone! You know us…always drama, but I think Clare is feeling pressure."

"Clare? You mean with her exams?"

"Her exams? God, yes, that doesn't help. They start next week, don't they? I had forgotten. She is definitely in need of TLC."

"I thought it was Rose who needed a bit of attention?"

"Well, Rose is always looking for attention."

She still doesn't know, thought Margaret. Jesus. What is going on then?

"Is Clare at school today?"

"Yes."

"Ok. Well, let me know if there is anything I can do. You said to clean and hoover downstairs today."

"Yes, if you wouldn't mind. I am going out. Rose is here now but working this afternoon, I think, so, if possible, could you look after Miranda this afternoon?"

"If you need me this afternoon, I'll have to go and get James from the childminder. Is it okay if I bring him here?"

"Of course. Margaret, you can bring him any time. You don't need to pay a childminder. I don't mind at all. Where is Miranda now?"

"I've given her crayons. She's drawing a picture for her new school."

"Aah, how sweet. I'm taking her to get her school uniform next week. I've been promising a while now."

"Yes. She's very excited."

The phone rang. Both women jumped.

"It's probably cold calling. That's all who calls on the landline these days."

Gloria got up to answer it.

"Gloria?"

She recognised his voice instantly.

"Hello, Simeon."

Gloria looked pointedly at Margaret who got up, emptied the slops from the cups, put them in the sink and left the kitchen, closing the door. After Margaret closed the door, Gloria half whispered into the phone.

"Simeon, I want to apologise for last night. I'm sorry. It didn't go so well."

"Well, yes. I'm sorry too. I reacted badly but Gloria, I'd like to meet the girls, both Clare and Miranda. I want to know how you thought it best to do that."

"Well, I don't know. If you came here, they'd be on home territory."

"I would prefer if it was a neutral space. Maybe it would be better if I met Clare first? Without Miranda?"

"Maybe, yes, for Clare, probably. Will we have supper together? Tomorrow? I can get a babysitter. I think Rose is working, but Margaret will take her."

"No, I think it would better if it was just Clare and myself."

"Oh."

"I just wanted you to know that also, I will be making formal contact and seeking access."

"Seeking access? Simeon, they are *my* girls. You can't come in and start asserting paternal rights. Your name isn't on their birth certs."

"But you have told Clare that I am her father, and Miranda's?"

"Well, yes, you are. You saw Miranda, Clare is her spit, just older."

"So, I have rights, Gloria. I would like to be on their birth certificates. I am prepared to have a DNA test, if that's what Clare would like. I will discuss this with her. However, Gloria, if I am her father, and she is interested in spending time with me, I *will* be asserting my paternal rights. Please be assured of that."

"Simeon, I think it would be better if we could keep this amicable. There is no need for all this formality. You're an old friend. We have been close. I'd hate to think that we can't be friends."

"Of course, that is what I would wish, Gloria, but I would like to see everything above board and processes put in place. I want to take my paternal role very seriously, despite being denied this for seventeen years."

"But why and what is your fiancé and family going to say?"

"I'm sure when I explain, Minoo will understand. Anyway, that is none of your concern. I was ringing to seek your advice as to how best to meet the girls. We are agreed that first I meet Clare and then Miranda when Clare is more at ease?"

"Well, yes, I suppose."

"Good, I will email Clare now. Good bye, Gloria."

"Simeon?"

The phone went dead. Gloria shuddered. She had better think about this carefully. Maybe she should encourage Clare to go travelling for the year after her exams.

The Favourite Café was full of students, drinking tea and coffee, eating plates of chips smeared with egg yolk and ketchup. Rose was flying around between tables, with her ponytail swishing. It was raining again and there was steam and condensation everywhere. Wet coats lay on chairs, on hooks and there was a constant babble in the air. A couple of tables were giving Rose grief, bantering about the shortcomings of the staff. Clare could see Rose doing her best to smile and take it in good spirit, but she recognised the sharp glint of annoyance in Rose's eyes. After five o'clock, business slowed down a little. Students began to leave for home.

"Rose, take your break. I'll bring you and Clare some tea and toast in a moment," said Nancy, "You've been run off your feet. I don't want to overburden my best waitress."

"Your only waitress," Rose grinned. She liked the praise. Clare realised she hadn't seen that grin of Rose's for a long time. "Thanks, Nancy." Rose slid into the chair opposite Clare.

"You're good at this," said Clare. "I wouldn't be able to keep up with all the orders. I'm sure I'd get things wrong."

"Actually, I don't mind it."

"It's not too tiring for you?"

"No, just my feet at the end of the shift."

"How are you feeling today? Any further on in your thinking?" Clare asked

"I don't know. I feel like I need to know more about where I come from before I bring a child into the world."

"You need to talk to Gloria. She's the only one who can help you."

"I know. I'm just trying to work out the questions before I sit down with her. I need to be calm. You know how easily she winds me up. I don't want it to turn into a slanging match. I have to curb my tongue."

Clare nodded and smiled. "That sounds eminently sensible."

"I know, but often, I pop before I even know it."

"And have you decided to tell Finn?"

"I will tell Finn when I know more about how I feel and what I want to do. But, you know, Clare, I am veering towards having the baby. I don't think I want an abortion. Mind you, it's good to have the choice."

For once, Rose's face looked in one piece, like it belonged to her. Clare felt a surge of jealousy. She was the one who wanted the family. Rose would be a terrible mother. Immediately, Clare also knew that wasn't true. Rose would probably be great, like the big sister she'd been to Clare.

"It wasn't long ago you said that you hated family. A baby will change your life."

"I know, I know. I just keep going around in circles. Maybe I'll move to the States. I'll talk to Finn. It would be exciting, wouldn't it? You'd have a niece. Jesus, Miranda would be an aunt, too. How cool would that be? Anyway, let's talk about something else. How are you? Have you spoken to Simeon? And how's the study going with all these distractions? I never see you anymore."

Clare stared at Rose.

"I spend a lot of time in the library and studying with Angie. I guess, I'm trying to avoid being at home."

Nancy bustled up with a pot of tea and a plate of toast, "Here you go, girls." Clare looked up and smiled at her. "Thanks, Nancy."

Clare waited until Nancy was back behind the till. "Are you thinking of going to the States? To live? That would be awful. Rose. You don't have to live there. If you want to have the baby, I'll help you raise it. I know mum will too."

Rose smiled. "Thank you, Clare, and there, exactly, is the problem. Gloria would probably want to adopt it. Now, please, enough of me. What brings you here? Have you heard from Simeon?" She poured the tea and pushed the cup across the table to Clare. Clare picked up her cup and leaned back in her chair, she took a sip and looked across at Rose.

"Yes, I'm so excited. I'm meeting him on Saturday. We're meeting at Camden Lock for lunch, and then he suggested we might go for a walk." She put the cup back on the table for fear of spilling it. "I am so scared. Supposing he hates me?"

"Of course, he won't. Did he phone? Email? What did he say?"

Clare passed Rose a folded piece of white paper.

Dear Clare,

Obviously, the news that I have two daughters has been a shock. But first I want to say how grateful I am that you took the initiative to find me. Thank you. I would be so pleased if you would meet with me so that we might get to know each other a little and if all goes well, maybe you could introduce me to Miranda soon after. I understand you are very close. I think she would be more relaxed if you were there and we would both be more relaxed if we had already met.

I would like to invite you for lunch at the Camden Brasserie. Do you know it? Would Saturday at 1pm suit? Then, afterwards, we could maybe have a wander around Camden Lock. If this time isn't convenient (I know you're studying for exams), do say, and I can fit in with your timetable. I have spoken to Gloria already and she agrees this is the correct approach.

I look forward to hearing from you, Clare
Very best wishes

Simeon.

"Clare, wow! What a charming letter. I am so happy for you." Rose handed her back the paper. "You look like the cat that got the cream, and it suits you." She wanted to add bitch but held her tongue.

"It feels strange. But really, suppose he doesn't like me?"

Rose laughed and took a bite of toast. "Don't be silly. I have to say he sounds great, straightforward, like you. Gloria's men have never been awful. Clive, well, he's a bit boring, but he's not awful."

Clare laughed and picked up the other piece of toast. "You shouldn't have told mum that you thought he was a paedo."

"Well, to be fair, he did look at Miranda oddly. Anyway, I didn't really mean it."

Rose raised her cup to toast her sister. "Well, sis, I think we are both on the brink of real change in our lives. This is grown up stuff."

Clare put down her cup.

"You know, Gloria is not going to like it."

"She'll have to get used to it."

"Rose, you need to look at it from her point of view too. If we want to make this work for us, it would be better if it worked for her too. If she's happy, we're happy, or happier."

"Jesus, Clare, you can be very irritating, you know. And anyway, I am really not sure that is true."

"I just don't want her to feel hard done by. Or for her to hate Simeon. Or to feel that she has to act to save her own interests. It won't be good for us. So, Rose, it's really important you think before you speak."

"Clare, you have one very mature head for them young shoulders."

Clare leaned back and smiled.

"You can thank Jane Austen, George Elliot and Bronte Sisters. You should try reading them, get a little wisdom."

Rose laughed.

"I'll stick to PD James, thank you. By the way, what does Simeon do for a living?"

"Gloria said he was an academic. She also said that he was into poetry and he was obviously politically interested as a member of the ANC."

"Hum, that's interesting. He's where you get it all from then. That's why I have to know more about my father.."

Chapter 19

When Gloria woke up, she lay in bed, listening to a light rain spattering against the window, pulling her duvet up to her neck. Today was the day Clare was meeting Simeon. God what a week, she thought. She now wished she hadn't told the girls about how much she had loved Simeon. It had sounded so childish. How often had she woken up in this bed with the wish that she'd kept her mouth shut? Gloria smiled and stretched, at least, for once, Rose wasn't the problem. Gloria supposed she should be grateful for small mercies. She decided not to be scared of Simeon. He would be a wonderful father, probably a better parent than her. That was the problem. She hated that idea. How dare he think that it was now ok for him to land in and start being a magnificent father. Is that why she hadn't told him before? Because even then, if she was honest, she had been fearful that he would have been the better parent? Fuck. What did it matter? It was all water under the bridge. She had kept them, reared them alone, they were good girls. They were hers. If Clare liked Simeon more than she liked her well, there was nothing she could do about it. But the thought kept niggling at her. He's going to take Clare away, and Miranda. Gloria pulled herself into a sitting position. She had better be sure of her rights, she thought. Gloria rolled across the bed and picked up her address book by the phone. Citizens Advice

Bureau. If Simeon wanted this, she was going to be prepared to battle. As she dialled the number, it occurred to her who might be an ally in all this. Rose. Rose was unlikely to want a stranger taking away her two sisters. She was a fighter, like her mother.

From the kitchen Rose could hear her mother was talking on the phone. When she heard the conversation finish, she called out

"Gloria, would you like tea?"

"I would love tea! Thank you, Rose."

Rose opened the door, pushing down the handle with her elbow and came in with two steaming cups. Gloria shifted along, plumped up the pillows and patted the bed beside her.

"Do you want to get in here with me?"

Rose looked doubtful. She wasn't sure how clean the sheets were. She perched herself at the end of the bed and handed Gloria a cup.

"Thank you, Rose. How is working in the cafe? We haven't talked for ages. All the focus has been on Clare."

"As it should be. After all, she has found her father."

"Yes, yes," Gloria said hurriedly. She didn't want this turning into a row. But Rose smiled.

.   "We should be happy for her," said Rose, trying to keep her promise to Clare to be nice.

"You have to tell her you're pregnant," Clare had said, "it will deflect a little of Gloria's attention from me. But be gentle. Don't be defensive. Try asking about your dad and his family. Explain that you'd like to know more. Margaret is taking Miranda and James to the zoo tomorrow, so you and Gloria will have the place to yourselves."

Rose wasn't sure she and Gloria were fit for mother daughter time, but she had said to Clare that she would try.

"I was wondering," said Rose after sipping her tea, "if we shouldn't do something together, if you're up to it. I'm not working today, Margaret is taking Miranda and James to the zoo. Are you free?"

Gloria could barely believe her ears.

"I'd love to do something. I need to be distracted. What were you thinking?"

"Maybe plan a meal, go shopping for the food and then cook it."

"I thought you didn't like cooking."

"Only because I don't know how. We could do a new dish or two together. Learn how to cook."

"Are you saying I don't know how to cook?"

"Well, Gloria, you're not exactly Nigella. I just thought it would be nice to do something together."

Gloria laughed.

"That's a great idea. Will we look at cookbooks?"

"Alright. Have you ever cooked from that South African one I bought you years ago?"

When they set off to the supermarket, the sun was making a feeble, watery yellow effort in the sky. It wasn't cold but a little breezy. The front gardens were struggling in the wind as they passed. There were more plastic bags knocking about than flowers in the gardens. They had decided to cook a few South African dishes; Bobotie, a beef, bread and spice dish and vinegar pudding which just seemed to use simple ingredients like jam, ginger, eggs, flour, butter, sugar. Rose was intrigued. As they walked up the street, Rose asked Gloria how Jo'burg was different to London.

"I haven't been back since '85, and of course, apartheid ended after that, so I don't know any more. It is a big city, like London, with beautiful buildings. And like most cities, it has its very wealthy areas and a lot of poverty. Before the end of apartheid, the city was surrounded by a ring of townships, like Soweto. You know about Soweto? Of course, you do. It was dangerous then and I hear it still is.

You know, in the 1880s it was a gold mining town, so, Jo'burg has always had a rough and ready atmosphere. My family lived on a farm out on the high veld. Summer days were fine but the nights were very cold. The climate is completely different to here, sub-tropical. As a young girl, I wasn't allowed into the city, but I was always sneaking off, hitching lifts, trying to attend ANC meetings. I hated our white farm life. Maybe it was my natural inclination to be different. Looking back, I was definitely a little wild. I fought with my parents and my teachers all the time, about everything. I used to wonder where I came from because I seemed so different to everyone else around me. I hated the way I was made to feel scared of everything, white men, black people. I didn't want to fear anyone. I wanted to be free. I wanted to be able to say what I thought. I wanted to be a real person, a real woman."

"And do you feel like a real woman now?"

"Well, yes, I guess. I don't know. Maybe not. I was a teenager. They are always difficult and having children definitely changes one's life. Children change everything…for the better of course. But then, I was a young woman with dreams."

"So, Pieter was my father's name. Pieter what?"

"Goldstone."

"So how did you get involved with civil liberties and everything over here?"

"Aunt May was a member of the ANC in London and was active during the eighties. It was a good way to meet people. The ANC were always stuck for meeting places. I had come over and the first thing I did was buy this house. My grandfather had left me 50k which in those days was a lot of dosh. Auntie May helped me a lot, but I was a little lost in London. Anyway, I joined the ANC and offered my house for meetings. Then I found out I was pregnant. I thought about an abortion, but I couldn't go through with it. I did want you, Rose, and May was very supportive. She felt more like a mother than my own mother. I really loved her and when she died of breast cancer, I missed her a lot. It was sad you never knew her. Anyway, by then the ANC had become my family, as well as you, of course."

Gloria laughed. "I'm talking way too much."

They walked in silence for a moment. Rose waited. After a minute, Gloria continued.

"We used the playroom as an office. It worked well. And, I could continue to be active after having you. Everything operated out of home. As you know, it became my life. I met loads of people, and felt I belonged to something. But then, when apartheid ended and Mandela was freed, well the movement fell apart. Over the last twenty years it has all petered out. So, I got involved with other organisations.

"When did your parents die? You didn't go back to the funeral."

"No. I was ashamed of them and they were ashamed of me. They both said they never wanted to see me again. They were proud and stubborn, like you. Like me. Can you believe it? I never forgave them. They didn't cut me off though. It's how we've lived. On their money. It's been an issue for me, living off their wealth. That's why I do what I do, all the volunteer stuff. It's a way of paying back."

Rose had never heard her mother open up like this. She wondered that she had never asked Gloria more. It must have been a very hard coming over here, starting afresh in a strange country.

"Gloria, that's some story. I never knew. I'm sorry."

"You know what, Rose?" Gloria looked at her daughter, her blonde, sharp featured daughter who looked like Gloria's grandfather. "I'm really glad you have South African roots. It gives me a tie to the country." She squeezed Rose's arm. "It gives us a special bond."

Clare wouldn't believe this if she could see it," Rose thought, smiling, the two of us like this. They arrived at the supermarket.

"Trolley or baskets?"

"Oh, I think a trolley," said Gloria.

The vinegar dessert was out of this world, and so easy. Rose wasn't sure about the Bobotie dish. It was a bit bland. Gloria had been on a roll, talking about the veld, telling Rose how suffocating the lifestyle was despite the beauty, the vastness of distance, the expansive open skies. They hadn't mentioned Clare once. Margaret came back with Miranda and they put her to bed. She wanted lots of animal stories, but ended up telling them about the hippopotamuses, and the elephants at the zoo. She liked the monkeys best and gave a hilarious impression of a penguin's walk.

"And the monkey zookeeper said I should go to a tea party there, with the monkeys. I thought he looked like a monkey himself."

"It sounds like it was a lovely day."

Miranda looked up Gloria and Rose, one on either side of her bed. She couldn't remember that before.

"A lovely day," she repeated and fell fast asleep.

Gloria suggested opening a bottle of wine to celebrate.

"Not for me, thanks," said Rose.

"Have you given up drinking?"

"No, just slowing down. Tell me more about Pieter, Gloria."

"Oh Rose, there is nothing to tell. He went to my school in the veld and was a neighbour. He was three years older than me. His father was in the police and he followed him in there. He wasn't particularly bright, never questioned anything. But he hated blacks. I used to needle him, tell him I was going to marry the coolest, blackest, eye rolling nigger that I could find."

Rose laughed. She recognised the temptation.

"So, what happened? In the police station?"

"I was arrested. They threw me into the cell on my own. Even the cells were segregated. I was proud. It was like a badge of honour. I was screaming and shouting about racist bastards and all the rest when suddenly Pieter came in with three others, smiling. He said, 'always think you know best, don't you, Gloria, nigger lover?' I suddenly knew what was going to happen. That was it. The three held me down and he raped me. Just him."

"Didn't you struggle?"

"At first, but then I realised there was no point. I just let it happen, pretended to be bored, above it all. They let me out after, with no charge. I went home. Then there was were three days of the most horrendous rows, as I said, with my father calling me slut and nigger lover and accusing me of lowering the family name. My mother didn't even try to stop him. Then on the fourth day, I went to the airport and caught the first plane to London. After three months, I discovered I was pregnant."

"How old were you?"

"Nineteen. One of those three days was my birthday."

And you never saw your parents again."

"No. I never saw them again." Gloria turned away. "They died seven years later. I inherited the farm, the land, everything."

"Why didn't you ever tell us?"

"Sometimes life is harsh, Rose. But that part of my life is over and finished. It's in the past. I I need another glass. Are you sure I can't persuade you? We ought to celebrate our day."

She's going to get drunk. I don't want her getting drunk, Rose thought.

"Okay, just the one glass."

"So, what do you know about Pieter's parents? Were they rich too?"

"God, yes."

"But they didn't know about me?"

"No."

Gloria poured out the wine. They were both silent

"Rose, what do you think about all this Simeon stuff? I am a little anxious."

"What about?"

"Well, Simeon was pretty upset with me. I don't know, but I think he might try to take Miranda and Clare away from us."

"Away from us? Don't be ridiculous. How would that happen? Clare is nearly 18."

"Well, he could look for custody of Miranda."

"Don't be absurd. How could he do that?"

"Well, he says he is looking for access. I have a meeting with the Citizens Advice Bureau on Monday just ascertain my rights, be sure of them. You don't know Simeon. He is as sharp as a meat cleaver. And clever."

"What does he do?"

"He's lecturer, he might even be a professor, in politics and, or, radical literature, I think, something like that. In Mumbai university with regular semesters here at London School of Economics."

"Very high brow. Well, Clare is nearly 18. It's up to her what she does."

"Well, he's not fucking well having Miranda."

"I'm sure it won't come to that, Gloria, stop drawing battle lines."

"If he tries to take Miranda from me, you'll help me."

"That is not going to happen. This is her home. Don't be ridiculous. She's starting school soon. Anyway, where would he take her?"

"India."

"Gloria, he can't possibly take her to India. I wouldn't let him. Clare wouldn't let him."

"Thank you, Rose. It's comforting to hear you say that. And thank you for today. I had a wonderful time. I didn't even think about Simeon until just now. Vinegar pudding ay? I wonder what the girls will think of it. Next time, let's try Karoo Lamb!

Gloria looked at her watch.

"Shouldn't Clare be back by now? It's 8.30pm. It must be going well."

Rose's phone went off. She picked it up.

"Oh, she's texted me. She and Simeon have gone to the South Bank. Gloria, talking of family. There's something I need to tell you. Mum, I'm pregnant."

Gloria heard someone shouting, there in the sitting room. She could see Rose, but it was as if Gloria was floating three feet in the air. She saw the cat jump up and prowl under the sofa. She saw Rose's face turn from shocked to sullen. The voice she heard was shrill. A heavy South African drawl. Like her mother.

"You are joking? How did I raise such a clot? After all that I have done for you, Rose, given you. You piss on it. You think you are so great, but you know nothing. You have no fucking idea."

Suddenly, Gloria understood it was herself. She put her hand to her mouth and looked at Rose's shocked face.

"God, I'm sorry," said Gloria, shaking. "That was my mother. Jesus, after all this time. I'm sorry, Rose. Truly. It came from nowhere."

"Jesus, Gloria. You didn't even look like you. And there was I thinking you might be pleased, being so fond of babies yourself."

"Please, Rose. I didn't mean it."

Gloria tried to speak with a level voice, but there was a quaver.

"Are you planning to keep it? It will change your life. It really will. It's hard work. I do know, Rose. What about college? You've only just registered. Have you told Finn? Is it Finn's? You could have an abortion. You are so young."

"Not as young as you when you had me. And yes, it is Finn's."

"Look at me. No college, no degree, nothing but a string of babies. Rose, this is not a game. I love you and Clare, and Miranda but I made you my life. I love babies and I hope to have another one because it is too late for me to start a different life now. But not for you. You're just starting out. There is so much ahead of you. Please, don't throw it away."

"Gloria, I can do both. It's a different world."

Gloria said nothing. She stared at Rose. She knew she had to be careful.

"Okay. Let's talk about it. If you want to have it, I'll help as much as I can. Miranda will be very excited. And if I have another, it will be like brother and sister. A whole family."

Wow, thought Rose, quite a turn-around, from harridan to mother hen. She had never heard her mother quite as violent as the first of her reactions had been. Was that truly what Gloria's mum had been like? Was that the true Gloria? That's what they said. You end up like your mother. Rose had always thought of her baby as a girl. She caressed her stomach. It might be easier if it was a boy. Do they say boys end up like their fathers? She hadn't heard that.

"That's why I want to know more about my father," Rose said. "I need to know more about my family."

"I don't know a lot. I didn't like him. He just followed the crowd. Well, you don't take after him in that way. He was good looking. You have his rose bud lips. I told you that. But he had a violent streak, like his father. But that came from having power, not some family gene or something. His father was chief of police. They could do what they like, with impunity, with no fear of retribution."

"So, did he have brothers, sisters? What happened to them? Gloria, you must know. How can you just have walked away? Do you really have no-one there?"

"It was easy, Rose. You have no idea. He was an only child, spoilt."

"I need to know more. You might want to deny your history and heritage, but I don't."

"What are you talking about Rose? You have no idea of the violence, injustice and hatred that existed in South Africa. That's why I left."

"To build your comfy lifestyle here," said Rose. Gloria stared at her daughter. Why was Rose so resentful? She had given up everything for Rose.

"Rose, let me tell you something: whatever you do to smooth over, change, ameliorate, improve yourself…that baby will find your one weakness, and milk it for what it's worth. That's been my experience. I wish you luck with that."

Gloria stood up, her eyes flashing.

"Thank you for our day together. I did have a lovely time, for most of it. We'll talk tomorrow."

Gloria went to her bedroom. She picked up the landline and phoned Clive.

"Clive, will you come over? I need some TLC. I've had the most ridiculous day, just when I thought it couldn't get any more absurd. Let yourself in."

Rose swore at herself. She had done so well and then fucked it up. Who had that woman been?

Chapter 20

Simeon stared at Clare across the table. She seemed very composed, unlike Gloria. Like Miranda, she reminded him of his sister. He noticed her brown eyes were slightly askew, like his. Her black ringlets reminded him of Dorothy in the Wizard of Oz.

At the same time, Clare stared at Simeon. He was tall, had a slight bump in his nose, smooth skin, a light brown colour, darker than hers. He had dark stubble, tiny black splinters across the lower part of his face. She could see herself in him, sort of. She could feel it.

"We're both staring at each other," Simeon laughed. "It is odd, this, don't you think?"
Clare nodded.

"It's a relief for me," she said. "But maybe not for you."

"A surprise, but not a problem, Clare. At least I hope not."

"Do you have children? I mean other than me and Miranda."

Simeon laughed.

"Other children! How odd to think I have children! No, other than you and Miranda, not yet. But I hope to. I am getting married in three months. In India. You will be a shock for Minoo. I hope you will like her."

"What a strange name." Miranda might think he is marrying a cow, Clare thought and smiled to herself.

"So, I'll race through my family. You have aunties and uncles," Simeon continued. "I have two sisters and two brothers. The girls are in India, both married, with young children. What would they be to you? Cousins, I guess. One brother is in Australia and one is in Leeds. They look after the family business which is the import and export of spices. My parents died five years ago, one after the other. My father was English. He lived in India, met my mother and they got married. They set up the business when they came over to England forty years ago. He wanted to raise his children here. I was born in London, in Ealing. I'm the youngest. I teach on a course at the University in Mumbai and on a course here at LSE. As I say, I'm due to get married in three months, in India. Maybe you and Miranda will come? Anyway, it is early days yet. God, listen to me babble. Sorry, I am nervous."

He laughed. Clare noticed the lines around his eyes.

"No, I'm interested. It's exactly what I want to know."

"But I want to hear about you."

"Uncles and aunts. I hadn't thought about extended family! Mum's an only child. It's just me, mum, Miranda and Rose."

"I remember Rose. She was a scavenger! Always rooting around, like a wild red squirrel."

"Yes, I can imagine. She's even wilder now, more like a ferreting fox. We are chalk and cheese. It is weird, the thought that I have family in India. It's hard to get my head around." Clare tailed off, then started again. "I'd love to go to India."

"What about university? Are you planning to go?"

"Yes, but I'm taking a gap year. I want to do English. I love reading."

"Me too. What's your favourite book?"

"Oh, I couldn't say. I love Jane Austen, well, all those nineteenth century female writers. I like thrillers. I love Graham Greene, and, this probably sounds pretentious, but Shakespeare too. But I wouldn't say that at school."

"Your secret is safe with me. Have you applied anywhere?"

"Bristol, but I have to see what grades I get."

Simeon nodded.

"And Miranda, and Rose. Are you close? Are you a 'happy family?'"
He made quotation marks with his fingers.

Clare looked at him and thought of Clive describing them as dysfunctional.

"I am very close to Miranda, and Rose, well, of course, I love her, she practically raised me, but she's a challenge. She

156

surrounds herself with drama. And, mum, well, she and Rose rub each other up the wrong way. They are very alike. So, it can be a rumbustious family. I tend to be the peace maker."

Clare looked Simeon in the eye, feeling guilty, maligning her mother and sister. "We are really close," she added. "I guess we're maybe slightly dysfunctional."

"That's perfectly normal. You should see mine in India. My mother used to say she was Anapurna, the nourisher, my father was Vishnu, the preserver. Both are very respected Gods. She describes my oldest brother as Matangi, the dark one. He is the intelligent one, living in Leeds. He doesn't say much but is wise in a quiet way. I am Hanuman, the monkey king…"

"That sounds naughty."

"A little. Hanuman is strong and courageous and very loyal. Of course, my mother aligns us with only the interesting Gods. My oldest sister is named after Durga Devi, who is a rather frightening Goddess who fights to restore moral order. My younger sister, who is a little spoilt, is Lakshmi, the Goddess of good fortune.

"Wow, fancy having the titles of Gods and Goddesses as your nick names. Gloria only gets as far as 'bitch'. I know very little about Hinduism or the Indian Gods. I'll have to do some research."

Clare was beginning to feel out of her depth. He was so clever. She began to worry that he would find her too silly.

"You will be Saraswati."

"Who is that?"

"The Goddess of learning, wisdom, music…culture."

"I'm not learned or cultured. Not yet. Tell me is the monkey king full of devilment?"

Simeon laughed again.

"Sharp girl. Let's order."

They ordered lamb's liver. When their plates arrived, the sliver of meat lay there on the white porcelain plate, bloody, the red veins slightly stringy, with black charred sides. A big basket of French fries was placed in the middle of the table alongside a shimmering green lettuce.

"That looks fresh, I wouldn't be surprised to see a caterpillar crawl out!" said Simeon, "dig in, Clare. What's your favourite food?"

Simeon kept the conversation easy going, but Clare wasn't hard to talk to. They kept returning to books and films, and India.

"I know nothing about India, as you can see."

"I think you will love it."

"I loved the Raj Quartet. I watched that with Gloria that on TV. But it's all about the Brits. I don't remember any Gods."

"Yes, the BBC is good at period drama. Clare, when we've finished here, shall we go into town. Have you ever been to that 30's cocktail bar in Piccadilly? The Creighton. It's got fabulous décor, very 1930s. They do mocktails too.

"Mocktails? I've never had cocktails of any type. I do drink! Not much, but I do drink the odd glass of wine."

Keep it light, Simeon thought to himself. She's lovely. Let us just get to know each other, nice and slowly.

Clive was driving to Gloria's down the Seven Sisters Road. He was wondering if he could he was making a mistake. The drama Gloria wove around her might be less amusing if he couldn't walk away. He needed to spend time with her outside the house. but she hardly ever went out. The other night in the Chinese, she seemed really uncomfortable. He had to inveigle her to the pub. He couldn't recall her ever talking about holidays. She must have taken the girls away, but he couldn't remember, maybe a trip to Wales, once. Maybe that's what they should do. Go on holiday. A trip together. No girls. No drama. Just him and Gloria. Maybe, South Africa. She could show him where she came from. As he stopped at the pedestrian lights, he saw Clare coming out of the tube station. Wow, he thought, she was literally gliding along, as if she were two feet above the pavement. Clive pulled up beside her, unwound the passenger window and called out

"Clare, Clare, do you want a lift? I'm going up to see Gloria."

She stopped and laughed.

"Oh, Clive! Okay. Thanks."

"Get in."

Clare lowered herself into the car.

"How did it go with Simeon? Gloria told me you were meeting him tonight."

"Yes. He was brilliant. I had the most amazing time. We didn't stop talking. He is so interesting."

Clare glanced over at Clive while he was driving. She suddenly realised how little she knew about him, and yet he and Gloria were supposedly getting hitched. What would it mean? Was Clive going to be her father? No! she thought, with frisson of pleasure, I have a dad now.

"Clive, did you know Simeon back in the day??"

"Not really, just met him once or twice."

Clare hadn't realised Clive had been around so long.

"He seems super intelligent. I can't believe he's my father."

"You got on well then. What did you do?"

"We had lunch in the Camden Brasserie, wandered around the market, had cocktails in The Creighton, what an amazing place, the glass, the art deco. It was a perfect day." She laughed.

Clare remembered what Gloria had said about him being the only man she ever loved and shivered. The thought of Simeon and Gloria appalled her.

"He invited Miranda and I to India for his wedding."

Clive pulled up outside the house.

"Gloria will be on tenterhooks."

"How come you're only coming over now?"

"Gloria and Rose spent the day together. Shopping and cooking, I believe." Clive looked across at her. She smiled at him.

"Great. Happy families, then."

Both of them laughed. As they went up the steps together, they both fished about for keys. Clive found his and went forward to open the door.

"Oh, you have a key." said Clare. "Yes, Rose told me you and mum are thinking of becoming an item. I hadn't really taken that on board, what with all the excitement of my dad."

Clare waited while Clive fumbled with the lock. Clive looked at her as held the door open and let her go first. This *was* a big decision. Maybe he had made it too lightly.

"We are trying to keep it low key."

"Low key?" Clare laughed, "you must be having a good influence, then. Low key is so not Gloria's style."

"Well, we're all getting older. And, Clare, you seem to be the one in the lime-light. Literally, there's an aura around you."

Clare smiled. You obviously don't know about Rose, she thought, and almost felt sorry for him. She pulled off her coat and threw it over the bannister. She peeked into the sitting room which was empty. Gloria called from her bedroom.

"Clare! How was it?"

Clare walked into the kitchen and put the kettle on. Clive stood at the Gloria's bedroom door. Gloria put out her arms to Clive.

"Clive, I need a cuddle."

Clare frowned. It was unusual for Gloria to be openly affectionate.

"Hi mum," Clare called from the sink, "It was a brilliant day. I can see why you liked Simeon so much."

Clare looked at Clive disappearing through the doorway and added quickly, "way back when, I mean. We had dinner, went into the West End."

She walked across to the Gloria's bedroom. Clive was now sitting beside Gloria who was already in bed. "Will I tell you all about it in the morning.".

Clare wanted to hug it to herself just a little longer, revel in it.

"Yes, you go to bed," Gloria said.

Clare was surprised. She had expected Gloria to be all over her.

"Is Rose in?"

"Clare, do you know? About Rose?"

So, Rose had told her. Clare suddenly felt deflated. She couldn't do this now.

"You know what?" Clare answered in a flat voice, "I'm wrecked. I'm going to bed. Good night Gloria, good night, Clive. See you in the morning."

Clare went downstairs. Clive looked at Gloria. She too looked exhausted.

"What's up?" said Clive, "What has happened?"

"Get yourself a drink and get me another. I need it."

Chapter 21

The following morning, Clare woke up, leapt out of bed, and pulled back the curtains. The red and yellow tulips she had planted in her window box were glorious. They stood tall, erect, majestic, red heads held high. Enjoy them, she thought to herself, because they won't last long. They would wilt. She hated dead tulips and cut them down as soon as they showed signs of drooping. Later in the summer, it would be the fuchsia bush. Fuchsias were her favourite. She loved the delicate, bell shaped blossoms in summer with their pretty stamens like bell ropes. Across the road, the sun was smacking the front windows of the houses, glinting. What a beautiful day! Clare watched Mr Arden coming out of his front door, whistling and tossing his keys in the air. His cheeriness raced across the street. She wondered if Rose was around. Last night Simeon had suggested a picnic in Regents Park next weekend with Miranda. She thought it was a brilliant idea. Miranda would love that. She prayed it would be warm enough. Sometimes it was warm in April. Look, it was lovely today. Simeon would bring interesting things to eat. Samosas and Indian snacks. Tea. She wanted tea. She would see if Rose was awake. Gloria would not be up for ages. It was Sunday and only 7am. Clare pulled on her dressing gown and opened Rose's bedroom door gently. The curtains were still drawn. She could see Rose's red head and shoulders hunched into the white bed covers, her knees drawn up tight. She tip-toed over.

"Rose, Rose,"

Rose opened her eyes and saw Clare. "Ugh, Clare, what time is it?" She shut her eyes again and tried turning over.

"It's early, but I want to tell you about yesterday. It was brilliant."

Rose's voice was muffled from under the duvet.

"Tell me all about it. No, make tea then tell me. I can't wait."

Rose stuck her head out.

"Sorry, Clare, that didn't come out right. You know I'm not great in the mornings. Go make tea and I'll wake up."

As soon as Clare left the room, Rose sat up. She ran to the bathroom, getting there just in time. After being sick, she still felt nauseous. The last thing she felt like doing was wallowing in Clare's happiness. Make an effort, she thought. She got back into bed just as Clare arrived with tea. Rose sat up.

"You look pretty rough, Rose. Are you okay?"

"Morning sickness. I can't believe it. It's grim. Anyway, tell me all. Have you and Miranda got a fabulous father?"

"Rose, don't sneer. I'm not going to let you spoil it Yes, he's wonderful!"

Clare took Rose through the lunch, the conversations, the cocktails.

"Rose, you know, I think I am going to enjoy having an Indian family."

"Ah yes. maybe we will discover that Simeon is really a raj."

"Rose, why can't you be happy for me? And Miranda?"

"Sorry. I am pleased for you, I'm just a little jealous. You got the great man. I got the dead wicked rapist. Seems unfair. You know, Simeon's presence is going to shake things up around here a bit."

"What do you mean? Shake things up? It just means Miranda and I have got a father. Nothing is going to change."

"Of course, it will change, Clare. Don't be so fucking naïve. Do you think Gloria is just going to let Simeon sail in? She said as much last night. She is convinced that Simeon is going to drag you away."

"Drag me away? Where?"

"God knows. Deepest darkest India, I suppose. Anyway, be warned. Gloria is preparing for war." Rose yawned.

"Gloria and I did a lot of talking yesterday. We cooked Bobotie and Vinegar Dessert."

"You what?"

"South African dishes."

"Really? You and Gloria cooking? Together? I can't imagine. Did you tell her?"

"I did. She went loopy. Sounded like a fish wife, not that I know what a fish wife sounds like. After she had calmed down, she said it was her mother coming out. Freaky. Then she tried to be rational, said she wanted to sleep on it. So there, all the secrets are out. But, before all that, she did tell me quite a lot about South Africa, if not my father about whom she knew very little."

"Wow. So, what happens next?"

"Who knows?" They were silent for a moment.

"If you have the baby, if Clive and Gloria get hitched, if Simeon becomes our father…"

"Your father. Not mine."

"You know, Rose, he and I seem very similar. We love the same things. He told me all about Indian Gods. He wants me and Miranda to go to India for his wedding in a few months."

"Ah Miranda. I wonder how she's going to fare in all this." Rose took a sip of tea and grimaced.

"It's wonderful for her, to have a father."

"Will it be, though? A lot more people for her to take on board. And, really who has her best interests at heart? Simeon? Clive? Me, You? Gloria?"

"What do you mean?" cried Clare. "We all do."

"Do we though? If I have this baby, it will be my priority, and Finn. I may even move to America. You say Simeon is getting married. He will have his own babies with his new wife who I am pretty sure won't have much truck with babies from his past. Will they even be living here?"

"I don't know."

"And Clive and Gloria…well, that could work for Miranda. She knows Clive. How is Simeon going to be any addition? Two fathers! And, what about you? What are you going to do?"

"What do you mean?"

"Well, now your natural father has turned up, are you going to stay here or are you going off? Does India beckon?"

"What you are talking about, Rose. I am not running off anywhere. I don't want to leave London, except to go to uni."

"And what, remind me, is family? Mothers, fathers, stepfathers, stepsisters?"

"Stop it, Rose. You're just like Gloria, reactive. Unless it's about you, you have to find fault."

"Maybe, it seems I don't have Simeon's karma. I'm all Gloria and some South African rapist. Let's hope my baby picks up some of Finn's more palatable characteristics."

"Rose, stop it. Why are you doing this, being so horrible?"

"Clare, I don't have to 'do' anything. I can let the Gods do it all for me."

"What on earth are you talking about? If anyone is in charge, Rose, it's you."

"Me? So, Gloria has nothing to do with it. Our South African heritage has nothing to do with it. Our crazy up-bringing in a left wing, anarchist environment because our mother was reared in a right-wing apartheid regime has nothing to do with it? The Gods that be have nothing to do with it.

"Rose, I don't understand you."

They stared at each other for a minute in silence.

"Clare, if I go to America, to raise my new baby with its father, it won't be running away, will it? Not like Gloria did."

Clare couldn't imagine Rose in America.

"I don't know. I haven't thought about it. You're way ahead of me.

"You're right. I need to start thinking about what I do. How what I do will affect the world. Butterfly wings and all that. Think how all of this will affect Miranda. Me having a baby, you meeting your father. You could end up in India. If I have this baby, I might be having the world's next Hitler."

"Butterfly wings, Hitler! My God, Rose. You're demented."

"Think strategically, Clare, I'm pregnant. Clive is joining our family. Simeon is serious about his paternity rights. Gloria is mad. Thank God, the rapist is dead. No, I mean it. Pieter did not sound nice."

Clare cocked her head. Was Rose hormonal? What was she talking about?

"I can hear Miranda getting up. I'll bring down more tea and breakfast.

"Just black tea for me. I still feel sick."

"Okay."

Clare got up and went to the door.

"Clare, I meant what I said about Miranda. We do have to think about her. She's going to need us. There's a lot of change going on and more is coming. I booked a flight to the States last night. I've made my decision. I think I want the baby, but I need to talk to Finn to see how he feels about it."

Clare turned around

"Rose, are you sure? I don't think you should make snap decisions. Margaret said…"

"I haven't made any snap decision, and I'm big enough to make decisions on my own. I don't need Margaret and Gloria telling me what to do. I'm just letting you know, I leave in two weeks."

Clare went upstairs. Fuck Rose, she was ruining everything. Surely, having a father would be good for both her and Miranda. If Rose wanted to go and live in America, fine. If Gloria married Clive and had more babies, fine. It wouldn't make any difference. But, suddenly, deep down, Clare could feel the disturbance below the surface. Jesus, typical of her family! Her one chance at happiness and suddenly Rose is pregnant, Gloria decides to get hitched. Fuck them. She would plough her own furrow – with Miranda.

Chapter 22

Gloria snuggled under Clive's plump white freckled arm. The curtains were open, and they were staring out into garden which was dappled with morning sunlight. Clive kissed the tip of her nose. She looked up into his face and leaned up to kiss his lips which were warm and dry.

"I've been on a bit of a rollercoaster with the arrival of Simeon and discovering Rose is pregnant," murmured Gloria, "It's been a relief having someone to share it with. I know I said the girls were mine, and of course they are, but I like that you are going to be a member of the household."

"Going to be?"

"Sorry, are a member. Yes, I like the feel of that, I think."

"Me too," said Clive. "You know, it occurred to me last night that despite being here so often, I have hardly ever been downstairs. It's like two worlds. Upstairs and downstairs."

"I had to do that for mine and the children's sanity."

Clive prodded her.

"Sanity? I'm not sure many people would agree about that!"

Gloria laughed.

"I've always pushed people away, been independent, because that way I keep safe. But you seem to have wormed your way in. Rose is similar to me. Clare not at all. Rose has a better head on her shoulders. Despite all that impetuousness, I think she has a better grasp of reality."

They were silent.

"You know, Gloria, I think it's about perspective," Clive responded, "it's how you look at things. We are always affected by our environment. I wonder did you bring the violence you experienced in South Africa, both through apartheid and being raped, into your household here? I don't mean, consciously. I think we only understand the impact of our upbringing when it's too late. When we are young, we fight to change what we think is wrong. It seems simple. The hubris of youth leads us to believe that we can change our world for the better. We believe we can square the circle, make a difference. But we can't. All we can do is shape the people we live with. We only begin to understand that when we are older, wiser with more experience or perspective."

"That's some philosophy. Is it Buddhist? I'm not sure I understand."

Clive chuckled.

"Maybe, sort of. I think I'm trying to say that a long term perspective, less reactive response is important. For instance, what do you think you have taught the girls?"

"Taught them? I don't know. I hope the importance of humanity, law, compassion; that it's necessary to do stuff, action is important. But did I teach them that? I don't know. Maybe they learned more about loneliness, and self-protection instead because I was lonely and always trying to protect us all."

"'Families, they fuck you up.' That's Philip Larkin. How right he was but they're good kids. Rose is a bit hot headed, like yourself. You know, it's sad we don't live with our elders anymore. If we did, we might benefit."

Gloria leaned up on her elbow and looked at him.

"I can just see the girls' faces when I tell them that we want to shack up with them for life so they can benefit from our wide angled lens experiences."

Clive smiled, and pulled Gloria tighter to him.

"A lot has happened in the last few months. But everything that has happened is good."

"What do you mean?"

"You and I getting together is good. Finding Simeon is good. Miranda and Clare having a father, if we are all calm, all will be well. And Rose getting pregnant. It is exciting and could be good. If we approach these events in the right way, they can be positive. Change is frightening but it can be positive. Gloria, I have an idea. I was thinking maybe you and I should go away together. I thought South Africa. Maybe we could do some rooting. You could show me where you lived. Wouldn't it be interesting to see the new South Africa? Explore it together?

We could maybe see what's happened to Rose's father's family.
I can understand how she feels she needs to know."

"Go to South Africa?"

"Yes, take off for a month."

"How? What about the girls? Miranda?"

"Miranda has her sisters to look after her and Margaret.
And now she has Simeon. Gloria, it would be time for
ourselves."

Gloria nodded slowly. "Everything will be very
different."

"Won't that be a good thing?"

"Maybe. Rose might like to join us."

"That wasn't the sort of trip I had in mind. I wanted it
to be us."

"Just for a part of it. After all, she wants to know more
about her roots. But, do I want to leave Clare and Miranda with
Simeon? Do I want him here? Maybe he won't be here. He is
going to India, to get married in July."

"Well, maybe the girls will go with him. For a holiday.
Then we could go to South Africa."

Clive moved on quickly as he saw the frown cross
Gloria's face.

"Gloria, don't worry about losing the girls. You're their
mother. And think how this journey could help Rose. We can
find out about her grandparents. Come to think of it, Gloria, if

Rose has her baby, we are going to be grandparents. Imagine, a grandfather and I'm not even a dad...yet."

"Jesus, I hadn't thought of the grandmother side of it."

"It's going to be a whole new family...with Finn and his family too. You always liked Finn. And then, isn't it great that Clare and Miranda have found their natural father who is a good man and reasonably well off. If Simeon wants to be involved with Miranda's up-bringing, let him, Gloria. We can be friends. You like him.

"One big happy family, ay? Clive. I'm not so sure. Maybe I like Simeon too much."

"You used to, but Simeon is not for you."

Clive leaned over and kissed her hard. She pulled away, laughing.

"We're going to be great parents, Gloria. Miranda is a lucky little girl. As, indeed, I hope our own child will be. Come on..." He started to caress her and pull her dressing gown open. "I would like to try for our own baby, a little sister or brother for Miranda."

"Jo," said Gloria. "Jo is where this all started."

They were silent for a minute. Clive was caressing her. She put her hand on his shoulder.

"You are such a good man. I don't want to hurt you."

"Gloria, we've made our decision. We simply need to get away together, to explore each other."

Clive kissed her and Gloria wriggled out of her dressing gown.

"I haven't been back to South Africa since I left. It would be very strange. I don't know anyone there."

"Aren't you interested to see the changes? We can travel. We don't have to stay in Jo'burg. I'd like to see Cape Town too. We could go on a Safari, have drinks in the sun, by the pool."

Someone entered the kitchen next door. Gloria recognised Clare's footfall. They listened to her fill the kettle and light a match to the grill. Gloria pushed Clive away.

"She's making toast" Gloria said and called, "Clare, come in for a minute."

Clive pulled himself upright. Clare popped her head around the door. She eyed them both in the bed.

"Good morning."

"Are you making toast? Will you make us some? Why don't we have a big family Sunday brunch…everything eggs, bacon, waffles, black pudding, tomatoes, mushrooms. A family breakfast!"

Clare looked at her mother. The room felt fetid and smelt of stale sex and cigarette smoke. Clare had to stop herself recoiling.

"You might need to open a window in here. I'm not sure Rose is up for breakfast. I think she is feeling a little sick."

Gloria leaned up on one elbow and looked at Clare.

"Okay, let's all have breakfast together a little later. I," she looked at Clive, "we have some exciting news."

"Oh, God, Gloria. I think there is enough going on for us all to deal with at present."

Gloria laughed, a tinselly, happy laugh.

"No, it's good, Clare. I'll cook for twelve noon. Is Miranda up?

"Yes, I'm just making her toast. She's playing with Rose in my room."

Clare brought down a tray of tea to her bedroom. Rose and Miranda were reading Babar in Clare's bed. Rose didn't encourage children in her own white mecca.

"Gloria wants us to have a family breakfast. I didn't know it was a meal she knew about," Clare continued. "Now that Clive is on the scene, maybe she is trying her hand at homely family life."

"There is no way I can eat breakfast. I'll just throw up."

"Well, come up for a cup of tea."

"Christ."

"It'll be fine. She seems to be in a good mood. And she says she has news."

"You have got to be joking."

"Do you want to play with my sick beanie babies, Rose?" Asked Miranda.

"No, thanks, Miranda. I'm sick enough."

Chapter 23

Towards midday, the smell of bacon, and burnt toast tripped down the stairs. They could hear the chink of plates and tinkle of cutlery being gathered. Billie Holiday was singing 'What a Wonderful World' and Gloria was joining in, in a rather flat key.

"Really?" asked Rose.

They heard Miranda calling

"Mum says breakfast is nearly ready."

"Coming. Come on Rose."

The table was set. Gloria was serving up scrambled eggs, burnt bacon and grilled tomatoes. The smell of coffee devoured the kitchen.

"Good morning, girls. Come and sit down. Clive, it's ready."

She put the plates in front of everyone with a flourish. Rose turned pale.

"Just tea, for me. Black tea."

"Oh Rose, I'm sorry. Are you not feeling well?" Gloria asked

Rose shook her head.

"Well, I have some news that will please you," said Gloria. "Clive and I are thinking of going to South Africa in the summer, August, maybe. Check out family roots and all that. I thought you might like to come, Rose, for at least for a part of it. I'll pay. I have a flat in Cape Town in Bishops Court, a suburb in the South of the City. I rent it out."

"Really?" said Rose, staring at her mother. "You have a place in Cape Town? You never said."

"I have never been there. I bought it when I sold the farm. I wanted to have some investment in South Africa." said Gloria brightly. "We can go."

"Where is Cape Town?" asked Miranda

"It's in Africa, darling."

"We have another home? Is it like here?"

"Not really."

"What about school?"

"Sweetheart, you'll be going to school here. But who knows? This would be a holiday, but, in the future, it could be our second home."

"Well, here is a fly in the ointment," said Rose. "I've just booked my ticket to the States. I need to talk to Finn."

"Donners! When?" said Gloria, "You might have mentioned it. How long for?"

"I'm going in mid-June. The ticket is open ended, a couple of months, maybe. Or maybe two days. It rather depends on Finn's reaction to the idea of a baby. What's 'donners' mean? Can't you just use English expletives?"

"I thought you wanted to know about your father, Rose. This is your opportunity to find out more. We're not going until August. You'll be back by then."

"Gloria, I don't know what I'm doing. I need to talk to Finn about the baby. Maybe if you had discussed it with us first…even told us that we had a house in South Africa."

"Is this Baby Jo?" asked Miranda

"No, it's not baby Jo, Miranda. It's complicated," said Clare.

"Miranda, I'm having a baby," said Rose," so you are going to have a nephew or niece very soon."

Miranda looked at Gloria and then at Clare who shook her head slightly. Miranda looked down at her plate.

"I am discussing it," continued Gloria. "It's you that booked the ticket to America, Rose, without any discussion."

"Why don't we all relax and enjoy breakfast?" suggested Clive. "We haven't booked our flights yet. We can work this out."

"Has mummy given the baby to Rose?" asked Miranda

"No, sweetie. She hasn't," answered Clare

"Is Africa near India?"

"No, darling. It is a separate continent."

"Is America?"

"No, it isn't either," said Gloria. "Miranda, don't worry, no-one is going anywhere for the moment.

A cold fury crept over Clare. This whole meal was ridiculous. Her mother was mad. Rose was impossible.

"You know what?" said Clare, "I'm also making travel arrangements. Maybe I should let you know. Simeon and I are thinking of taking Miranda to India in August to meet the rest of family and go to his wedding. So, if you want to go to South Africa, that could work quite well."

There was a minute's silence then Gloria burst out

"Simeon and I! What is this Simeon and I? There's no way you can go to India. And certainly not Miranda."

"Gloria, girls, why don't we discuss this after breakfast. I don't think there is any need for anyone to get upset," said Clive. "It's all about perspective." He looked meaningfully at Gloria, hoping she would take the hint.

"Don't start on again about fucking perspective," snapped Gloria.

"And who the fuck are you to tell us when we can get upset or not?" said Rose.

She turned to Clare.

"Are you sure about this, Clare. It seems a big step to take. Going to India? I mean you don't even know Simeon. And I agree with Gloria, you can't take Miranda. She starts school in September."

"Jesus, Rose. You're planning on having a baby and going off to America. Maybe living in the States. Mum's planning to get married and take off around South Africa. I think I can decide on whether I can stay with my father or not for a few months, with my sister."

"You have no right to decide what's best for Miranda," said Gloria, slapping down her knife against her plate.

"Oh, I'm not sure I'd agree with 'no right'," said Rose. "She has been more than a mother to Miranda and Simeon is Miranda's father."

"How dare you? None of you have any idea. Anyway, I'm sure Miranda doesn't want to go India. She wants to start school, don't you sweetheart?"

They all looked at Miranda.

"Will Margaret be in India?"

Clare pushed away her plate and stood up and lifted Miranda up. Clive was staring at his plate. Rose was pale but her cheeks burned red. She looked like a scrawny chicken, not blooming at all. Clare could see Gloria was weighing up her options.

"Clare, you realise that there is no way you can take Miranda to India without my agreement, don't you? She's too young, she is about to start school and she needs security. I would have thought you would understand that."

Her voice was shrill. Clare lifted Miranda's plate of food and walked out. Gloria poured another cup of tea from the pot and took a sip.

"What the fuck is it that we cannot have a calm meal together?" Gloria said. "What is wrong with us? Maybe we need therapy. Is that it? I'm going to ban people leaving the table."

Clive and Rose were silent. Rose looked at her mother over her cup.

"Maybe we should all go to India for Simeon's wedding."

Gloria started to laugh, hysterically.

"What is so funny?" Rose asked

"I'm just trying to imagine Simeon's poor wife's face if this family piled into the church or is it a mosque? God, the poor woman."

Chapter 24

Margaret and Gloria were sitting at the kitchen table, drinking coffee. Margaret had just finished cleaning. It is a lovely house when it is clean, Margaret thought. If only she could get rid of that cat. She was sure it sprayed everywhere, and those disgusting hairs.

"This household has been a little hectic recently, actually, mad would be more accurate," said Gloria. "I hope all this isn't too much of a distraction for Clare. Her exams start tomorrow."

"Yes. So, Gloria, are you and Clive going to get married?"

"I don't know. If it works out. We're planning a holiday to South Africa later in the summer. It will be time together. We'll know more then, how we get on."

"South Africa? Wow. When are you going?"

"Possibly late August, early September, for a month. Clare should be here, and Rose hopefully will be back from the States. She's going to Montana to talk to Finn about the baby. But I would like you to be around, Margaret. Would that be okay?"

"I got no plans. So, Rose wants to keep her baby?"

"I think so. She needs to talk to Finn."

"Does he know she is pregnant?"

"Not yet."

"When is she due?"

"November, I believe."

"And this Simeon…what is he like? You say he is the father of both Miranda and Clare?"

"Yes. He's very nice. I had a thing for him back in the day. He's smart. He commutes between here and Mumbai."

"Commutes between here and India? Jesus."

"Yes. He teaches at LSE and in Mumbai university."

"Clare tells me he is getting married too. It's certainly happy families all around in this household."

"Yes, to a woman called Minoo, in Mumbai, in August. Clare wants to go to the wedding."

"Oh. Is Simeon a Muslim?"

"A Hindu, I think."

Margaret sat still for a minute.

"Well, well, I better be getting on. Maybe I'll take Miranda to feed the ducks in the park."

"Sit down a while longer, Margaret, have some more coffee. Miranda is fine. There's an idea I want to run past you."

Margaret nodded, sat down again, feeling a little uneasy.

"So, what do you think, Margaret?"

"What do I think?"

"Yes. I can't think straight. You are someone who knows us all. Maybe you can bring an outsider's perspective. Ha, Clive is getting to me.

"I beg your pardon?"

"Sorry, nothing. Clive keeps talking about perspective."

"You want to know what I think? Honestly?"

"Yes, honestly. Please be your usual direct self."

"I think you're all crazy."

"But why? Clive and I getting hitched isn't crazy. Ok, maybe Rose having a baby is a little crazy, but that's nothing new. Clare and Miranda developing a relationship with their father isn't crazy, is it? Going back for a holiday to South Africa isn't crazy. Rose going to America to discuss the future with the father of her baby isn't crazy. Simeon getting married isn't crazy. It's just that they have all happened within the space of four months. Yes, that's a bit crazy but it's not like I could do anything about that."

"No. I guess not, but, Gloria, what about Miranda? She must be a little confused."

"She must be. It's Miranda I am worried about. At least you are a constant for her. For all of us. Actually, that leads me to what I wanted to ask you."

"What?"

"The flat upstairs is empty. I need to rent it. Would you and James be interested? It would mean you wouldn't have to

189

travel every day to collect Miranda when she starts school. The rent would be the same as you pay now. It would be brilliant to have you and James here. Miranda loves James. You're almost one of the family. Of course, I would understand it if you weren't interested. I mean, you're right, things seem to happen in this household, but, you wouldn't have to get involved."

Margaret was surprised. Move in! Jesus, she spent enough time here as it was. Whenever Margaret pulled that front door shut behind her after leaving, she felt a shiver of relief. She was escaping a mad house. That's what it was, a mad house. Live in the same house as that cat? If she had her way, she would have it drowned. And the goings on. The shenanigans! She could never work out what was happening. And now, Gloria getting married at her age, to Clive of all people. And Rose having a baby. She was so young. And poor Miranda. An Indian for a father. Yes, that poor child. Shifted from pillar to post. Mind you, the upstairs flat was fancy. Nice. She had cleaned it after the last tenants left. Light and airy. James could go to the same nursery as Miranda did. She knew people on the street, well after skivying for years here. And, she was fond of them all, really. If she kept her boundaries, it might work very well. She was fond of the girls. After all, she had nearly reared them.

"Would you give me a few days to think it over?"

"Of course, Margaret. Take your time. Just know, it would make us all very happy. But I want to be honest, given that Rose and I will be away at the same time, it would be really great to have you here, to help Clare with Miranda."

Chapter 25

In the early summer months, Clare and Simeon spent a lot of time together, though he had been very careful to make sure she studied. He had even been happy to test her. Gloria and Clive were planning their tour of South Africa and Margaret had moved in. Clare was delighted at that. Since Rose had gone to the States, the household seemed calmer.

Today Clare, Simeon and Miranda were going to the zoo, to celebrate her exam results. It was August and Clare had hoped at this point that they would be in India, but Simeon's marriage had been postponed, though Clare didn't know why. He had said they simply needed more time to prepare. The spring picnic in the park with Miranda had been successful, though they hadn't told Miranda that Simeon was her father. It seemed such a hard thing to explain. In the meantime, they had taken her to the movies, and been on a few trips to the park and Hampstead Heath. But while Clare and Simeon always had a good time, Miranda never seemed very relaxed. She wouldn't talk, nor hold Simeon's hand. Simeon said to leave it until she was ready, but Clare was irritated. She wanted to tell Miranda so that Miranda could be as happy as Clare. Maybe a trip to the zoo would be good. Miranda loved the zoo.

The three of them were sitting on a bench in front of the cage watching the baby monkey bounce around the adult. It crawled on to its back and clung around its mummy's neck. It patted its head and swung itself round to the front and clambered down, pawing at the enormous chest. The mummy swiped it away, but it just ran up her arm, like it would a branch of a tree. The adult monkey wasn't big. Her fur was long and thick around the head, chest and shoulders. There was a patch of flat brown hair on her head, above sunken dark eyes which stared sullenly out of her bony head.

"Why are her legs less hairy?" asked Miranda

"I don't know. It looks like they've been shaved," said Clare, "but I don't think they have. Isn't she lovely? She looks like a hairy human."

"The baby is so sweet. It looks just like my Beanie Baby, not much bigger."

Simeon went off to get ice creams from the kiosk. Clare leaned back on the bench. The sun was warm. Miranda was standing near the fence, trying to entice the mother monkey and baby over towards her. Clare pulled her back.

"Not so close, Miranda. Here, sit on my lap."

They both stared at the monkeys.

"Miranda, do you like Simeon?"

Miranda nodded. "Yes, he reminds me of the panther in Jungle Book, Big Hera."

"Bageera. Yes, he does, doesn't he? Well, I'm glad because I have some news. Simeon is our daddy, Miranda. Yours and mine!"

There was a silence. Then Miranda said

"I thought so but then I thought I must be wrong."

"Why did you think so and why did you think you were wrong?"

"Mummy said his name, remember. And then I thought I was wrong because he doesn't seem like your father and she said we had the same father."

"Why doesn't he seem like my father? Oh Miranda, aren't you excited? Don't you like him? I think he is wonderful."

Miranda nodded. Simeon returned with the cones, sat down and gave Miranda hers.

"Vanilla for you."

Miranda thanked him. She eyed him suspiciously, staring into his face. "Clare says you are my daddy. I guess that means I have two fathers because mummy told me Clive is going to be my daddy. But that's okay because I have two sisters, and two mothers, so that makes it even. Are you moving in, like Clive?"

Simeon glanced quickly at Clare. He raised a questioning eyebrow. Clare loved how he did that. He squatted in front of them both. Miranda stared at him while licking her ice cream.

"No, Miranda, I won't be moving in. Is it alright with you, that I am your father?"

Miranda nodded. She pointed at the baby monkey. "Does she have a father?" she asked.

"Yes, daddy monkeys play an important role in how the baby is reared."

"So, they all live together?"

"Yes, and they all look after each other."

Simeon patted Miranda's head and got up. He walked up to cage and rested his hand against it. He leant into the bars.

"Be careful," said Miranda. "The monkey zookeeper told me that the monkeys like to steal ice-creams."

Simeon laughed, and turned around. Clare smiled at him. There was silence while they licked their ice-creams, staring at the antics of the baby monkey who started swinging around and around on the bars until he fell off and scampered away into the arms of his mother. Clare envied how easy life as a monkey seemed to be.

Clare walked up to the Tube station with Simeon after leaving Miranda back at home. They had left her telling Gloria all about the baby monkey and how the father looked after it as well as the mother.

"The father banged his chest and tossed the baby monkey away," said Miranda.

"That's why we don't like fathers," Gloria had said pointedly. "Come and give me a kiss."

"I'm sorry about announcing it just like that," said Clare. "I just wanted to share the news with her. It feels like finding my father is so momentous. I feel there should be trumpets, and bells, and headlines and there's nothing. Everything is still the same when really I want to climb all over you like that baby monkey."

Simeon smiled.

"Not sure how I'd feel about that!"

"Not really, of course," Clare said, suddenly thinking she might have offended him. "It suddenly felt right, at the monkeys. I just wanted her to know."

"That's fine, Clare. Do you think she was pleased? She didn't say much. When Gloria first told me, I didn't know what to think. I felt angry, angry that she hadn't told me that I had two daughters. But afterwards, I was excited. I think I had an inkling because I had seen Miranda and she looked just like my sister. But you were a shock. I hope I can live up to your expectations."

"I don't want us to be a burden" said Clare.

"Of course not!"

Simeon stopped walking and turned to her. "Clare, you are a joy. But these things take getting used to and Miranda probably is too young to understand."

He looked at her and continued,

"Clare, I should tell you, Minoo is not as happy as I am. It's been a bit of a shock for her. That is why we have postponed the wedding. I am planning to go over soon. But let's not talk of that. Will we go ice skating next weekend before I go? Do you think Miranda would like ice skating? They say you should start young."

The following Friday morning, Miranda clutched Clare's hand going down the endless spiral of steps. The air smelt stale with a whiff of rubber. The steps got narrower so she kept close to Clare. Her feet just fitted the width of the step. Margaret always caught buses if they went out. she liked to clamber up the steep curved bus steps, her wobble as the bus took off, having to clutch the bus poles as the bus moved off until she got to the front where she could sit and lean forward to see out the window. Miranda wished they were on a bus and that Margaret was with them.

"How far down does the tunnel go?" Miranda asked

"Not much further, now."

There was a rumbling noise, then a heavy wheeze. Miranda tightened her grip of Clare's hand.

"It's ok, Miranda. That's just a train coming in. There'll be people coming up now. Just go one step in front of me, hold the rail tight, and don't move. Let them pass you."

Miranda heard a stampede of footsteps and felt a rush of wind. She looked back up at Clare's face. Clare's ringlets were flying back in the wind.

A young man led a crowd of people. Behind him two schoolgirls in uniforms were laughing and talking. A trail of coats and boots followed. A morass of people. They barged past the two girls.

"It's like a herd of giraffes," said Miranda, and hid herself in Clare's legs. The hoard of people thinned out and the girls started off downwards again. At the bottom of the spiral staircase, they met a woman with a buggy and a little girl Miranda's age. She was standing, staring at the stairs.

"How many stairs?" The woman asked Clare.

"Hundreds."

"Damn. What do they expect us to do?"

"I don't know. The lift isn't working."

They heard another train come roaring down the tunnel. Miranda clutched Clare's hand.

"Come on, Miranda, we are late. Can you run? We need to catch that tube."

They arrived on to the platform just in time to see a silver train flashing in. It was wedged with shadowy figures. It slid to a stop and the doors opened with a wheezing sound. Clare picked Miranda up. People teemed out around them, bumping them as they passed. Clare held Miranda tight, planting her two feet firmly and bracing herself against the flow. When the exodus eased a little, she pushed her way through and she put Miranda down by a pole. Coats and jackets, faces, arms and legs were standing up around her, holding on to whatever they could.

"Hold tight to the pole, Miranda," said Clare.

The train moved off with a jerk and Miranda fell back against Clare's legs. She was surrounded by trousers and shoes, briefcases. She held the pole tight. The tube picked up speed and hurtled along. Miranda could feel the vibration running through her shoes and up her legs. There was a sudden jolt as a brake slammed on. She grabbed Clare's leg to save herself from falling and looked up. It wasn't Clare. It was a man wearing a suit. She could feel his hard muscle and knee beneath the material of his trousers. He looked down at her and raised his eyebrows.

"Hello, little girl."

Clare pushed her face down amongst the people and lifted Miranda up. The train jolted and they both fell back. The man whose leg she had held grabbed them both.

"Whoa, careful now."

A blonde-haired woman scowled.

"Sorry, sorry," said Clare, "sorry."

A woman sitting down stood up.

"Sit down, love."

"Thank you!" Clare said gratefully.

She plonked herself down in the seat, pulling Miranda on to her lap.

"It's okay, Miranda," she said, "it's just rush hour. I should have thought about that. I'm sorry. We're okay now. It's going to be great. Ice skating! You'll love it."

"Shouldn't bring a child on the tube at morning rush hour."

A heavily jewelled man with tattoos and a bald head looked down at her. Miranda nestled further into Clare.

"I don't like the tube and I don't know how to ice skate."

"Nor do I, sweetie. We are going to learn."

Simeon met them at the entrance to the station at Queensway. He was wearing his wide brimmed felt hat which he took off his head. He bowed graciously. Clare laughed. He bent down to Miranda. His dark face loomed up. His brown eyes were amused and gentle, but his eyebrows were bushy and a little wild, and his eyes were red rimmed.

"Are you ready for ice skating, Missy-anna?"

Miranda shook her head, shyly and clung on to Clare's hand.

"This way, girls. Now it will be very cold in there, Artic in fact."

Simeon pushed open the rink doors and they entered a massive, cold, dark, pink room with strip lights. There was a horrible smell of feet, sweat and loud music. In the distance Miranda could see a circle of white with a few people holding hands and others scrabbling around the edges.

"We hire skates over here."

The tiny white skates on Miranda's feet were heavy. When she stood up from the bench her ankle gave way and she immediately fell over. She grabbed Clare.

"I can't walk!"

"I will carry you over, Miranda," said Simeon. "All you have to do is relax."

He lifted her up high and smiled. His teeth were white, and he smelled of something strange. Everything here smelt odd, a strange mix of unpleasant cat and old socks.

"It's going to be fun. Are you ready, Clare?"

Miranda watched Clare stand up and wobble precariously. Clare grabbed Simeon's arm to stop herself falling. She smiled nervously.

"It is difficult to walk," she agreed.

"You'll find it easier to skate on the ice. Now off we go."

They hobbled to the edge of the ice rink which was packed with people leaning and hanging in odd positions on to the side of the rink.

"Now watch me for a moment, it's about balance. You push off, slide on one leg, then push off on the other. Use your arms to balance."

Simeon pushed himself off into the circling crowds.

"Doesn't that look fun, Miranda?"

Miranda said nothing and held Clare's hand, tight. She lost sight of Simeon in the crowd, but he returned quickly.

"Clare, you start. Come with me just to get the feel of it, and then I'll take Miranda. Miranda, can you wait here?"

"Without Clare?"

"We'll only be a minute. Hang on to the wall here and watch. You stand just here. We'll be just two minutes. Don't move. Come on, Clare."

Clare gave Simeon her hand, and they launched into the circle of people, Clare bent over, almost falling back, but Simeon caught her. Miranda hung on to the rail. Her feet hurt and she was cold. She didn't want to skate. Clare and Simeon came back laughing and smiling.

"Miranda, it's great. You'll love it. Have a go? Simeon take her, and I'll try on my own."

Simeon bent down, holding her hand.

"Come on, Miranda, I won't let you fall."

She hesitated. Looked at Clare.

"I don't like it," she said.

Miranda looked at the ice. It was covered in scars and lines. As people whizzed past, bits of ice flew up. It was very noisy, and very cold. Scarves and legs flew past.

"I don't want to go." Miranda started to cry. "I don't like it."

"Oh Miranda, try! It's fun."

Miranda shook her head.

"Clare, you keep trying, I'll look after Miranda."

Simeon came off the ice and lifted Miranda up.

"Don't you worry, cherub. Let's go and get our shoes on and get hot chocolate. We can come back and watch Clare make a fool of herself."

"Hah! Just you wait and see!" Said Clare, "I'm a natural."

Half an hour later, Clare got off the ice, she walked all funny and they left the ice-skating rink and went to McDonalds. They sat down to eat burgers and chips.

"Miranda had to walk down hundreds of steps at the tube this morning. The lift wasn't working at the tube at Belsize Park. I bet you're tired aren't you, sweetie?"

"I wonder if that lady with the baby is still stuck at the bottom."

"No, someone would have helped her."

"We didn't."

Clare was taken aback.

"Well, there wasn't much we could do. We couldn't climb back up the stairs with her."

"I was going to suggest a walk in Hyde Park." said Simeon. There are lots of paintings on the railings. I thought you might like them and a stroll in the Italian Gardens, or maybe a boat on the Serpentine. Would you like that, Miranda? What would you like to do?"

Miranda looked at them both. They looked at her and at each other, smiling.

"Go home"

Simeon and Clare looked at each other.

"Okay. Is Margaret at home?" Simeon asked

Clare nodded.

"I think so."

"OK. Let's get a taxi home and maybe take some ice-cream for Margaret."

As she fingered the plastic tiger that had come in the Happy Meal, Miranda decided she didn't like having a new father or sharing Clare with Simeon. She could see Clare liked him. Miranda didn't like anything at the moment, except her Beanie babies, Margaret and the Zoo

Chapter 26

Miranda twirled in front of Gloria and Margaret in the sitting room in her tartan school uniform.

"Slowly, darling, let me see." said Gloria. Miranda turned on tippy toe extra slow and Gloria Clare, and Margaret clapped.

"You look so sweet, Miranda," said Gloria. "I wish I was going to be here for your first day."

"I want to show Rose."

"You can when we skype her, later," said Clare.

"Gloyia, will you bring me back a Beanie Baby from South Africa? A lion?"

"Of course, I will."

"I'll have learned lots in school by the time you come home."

Everyone laughed.

"I'm only away a month, darling. And when I'm back you will be able to teach me everything you have learned." answered Gloria, pulling Miranda on to her lap for a hug. Miranda struggled off, straightening her school uniform.

"But you went to school already. You know where America is and Africa."

"Aren't you a slim Klompe? Clever clogs. So do you. We showed you on the map. On the globe. Remember?"

Miranda had been disappointed by the globe. They had ordered it on-line and there had been a lot of excitement when it arrived. They had all been there to unpack the big box to show Miranda where all the countries on the earth were. But, the only thing in the box was a large circular blue ball painted with different shapes and colours. It was hard to imagine people living on it. Clare said that was what the world looked like. Miranda didn't understand how people didn't fall off. Gravity, explained Margaret. It helps us stand up. Miranda had suggested they get some gravity at the ice rink and everyone had laughed. Last week, on skype, Rose had taken her on a tour of Finn's house and garden in America. There was Rose walking around in America but she wasn't sideways, or upside down. Her house had a wooden veranda, lots of trees in the garden and snowy mountains in the background. It looked like a picture. The sky was blue with white floaty clouds. Inside the house looked similar to her home, except much cleaner and brighter. There was a kitchen, a cooker, a fridge and stairs, a living room with a fireplace, with a deer's head over it. Rose had said it was Miranda's home too, and that she would love it. Miranda decided she wouldn't like animal heads on her wall.

"Margaret and Clare will take me to school tomorrow, won't they?"

"Of course, we will, and James will come." said Margaret.

"You're going to love school, Miranda, I did," said Clare.

"I really wish I was able to take you, Miranda," said Gloria. "I thought you started school on the 1st September, not the 7th. That's why I put the trip off until 6th September, so I would be here to take. I'm sure Rose and Clare always started on the 1st."

"We never did," said Clare, "you always got it wrong."

"You can wave to me from the aeroplane. I'll wave to you, Mummy."

Gloria fumbled with her cigarettes and lit one. Why on earth had she agreed to go away? What had she been thinking? She got up and stared out the window. The woman from number nine walked past with her dog on lead. Gloria didn't know many neighbours. She had been to one Christmas party in her twenty years of living here, but she had had a few drinks too many and had never been invited back. She didn't mind, they were all a bit stuck up. Years ago, Rose had a friend a few doors down, but they had moved, and to be honest, Gloria hadn't really got to know the parents very well. She turned back to Miranda.

"I'll be back before you know it, sweetie but somehow, I think you and Clare are going to have a wonderful time."

"We will," said Miranda and did a jig. "Listen my heels click."

Later that night, Clare helped Gloria lug her blue suitcase into the hall. It was all strapped and buckled up.

"I don't know why I agreed to go. I don't want to."

"Gloria, you're going to have a wonderful time. You and Clive deserve some time together. Find out as much as you can for Rose. She is desperate to know more about Pieter's family. Be happy. Rose is happy. I'm happy. Miranda is happy. She can't wait to start school."

"Is Rose happy? Did she tell you how Finn reacted about the baby? She hasn't said anything to me."

"He was gobsmacked. Gloria, stop worrying. Clive will be here at 6am with the taxi. I'm going to bed. Good night, and really, don't worry. You didn't come with me to school on my first day all those years ago. Rose and Pindi took me. It never did me any harm."

"Pindi? Oh, the minder. No, I'm sure I took you."

"No, you didn't."

Gloria hesitated.

Clare?"

"Yes?"

"I'm worried about you too. You're thin and you've lost wait."

"There's no need to worry. I'm fine."

Gloria felt as if she had lost touch with Clare and wasn't sure why. Was it because of her own relationship with Clive? Or the arrival of Simeon? Clare used to be gentle but seemed distracted recently. She wasn't rude, just cool. Funnily enough, it reminded Gloria of how Simeon had behaved when Gloria had been desperate to hold on to him. She had forgotten Simeon's way of appearing kind when she found his reserved manner rather cruel. At least Rose was transparent in her feelings, like herself. You knew what you were dealing with, even it was a lightening temper.

"Will you be seeing much of Simeon?"

"He and I are going out to dinner Saturday night."

"To dinner? You do nice things together."

"We have a lot of catching up to do."

"Maybe we could all go out to dinner together when I get back."

"Don't be jealous, Gloria. South Africa is going to be wonderful. Forget about us. We'll be here when you get back. I'm going to bed. I'll see you in the morning."

"Clare, I want you to know, I'm not in love with Clive."

"Gloria, don't be ridiculous. You are very lucky to find someone at your age!"

"Clare! I'm only 45."

"Gloria, give yourself and Clive a chance. It will be a great month. You won't believe how fast it will go. I'm sure you'll be wanting to take us all back there next year."

Jesus, Clare thought, talk about role reversal. She leaned across to kiss her mother who grabbed her and hugged her close.

"Oh Clare, I'm sorry. I just feel like this is the end of something. I don't know why."

Clare could feel her heaving slightly.

"Stop it, Gloria. This isn't like you."

However, Clare also felt anxious, as if she was a thousand fragments glued together. Thank God, Gloria was going. She would get Miranda to school, and, unbelievably, she would have the house to herself. And she would do nothing but sleep for days. She was exhausted but she didn't know why.

When the alarm went off the next morning, Gloria opened her eyes. I'm going to South Africa, she thought and jumped out of bed. As she got washed and dressed, she thought about her panic the night before. Yesterday, she had been so upset about missing Miranda's first day. It was odd, today she didn't feel bothered, not really. After all Clare and Margaret would be there. Clare was right. She shouldn't worry so much. Her life was just beginning. Clive was with her. As she put her make up on, she saw how she had lost weight. It was good. She could tone up while in Africa. She would get fit. They would go on Safari. The colours, the skies, the bush. She was looking forward to seeing the sunshine! She smiled at herself in the mirror. She waved good bye to Miranda and Clare, got into the taxi, and tried to look sad.

Chapter 27

After dropping Miranda off at school (she had marched in without a turn of the head), Clare shut the front door behind her. She heard Margaret chatting to James as she carried him up the stairs to the top floor flat. She leaned back against the door, taking stock. Miranda was a funny little girl. She was very self-contained, very accepting of what was going on around her, but Clare had a feeling that something was hardening up. Not once had she ever heard her question all the coming and going of the last months. It was as if she was impervious to all the friction going on around her.

The house was quiet. Bliss. Clare couldn't remember when she was last alone in the house. Had she ever been? Gloria was always such a strong presence, even if she was shut away in her bedroom with a migraine. The fridge hummed and rattled. A click, click of claws as the cat crossed the kitchen floor after picking at its bowl. A ray of sun coming in the hall window caught the dust - a highway of mites. She took off her coat and threw it over the bannister, the mountain of coats. There must be ten years worth. She could smell them, the rain, the muskiness, the tobacco, the alcohol. Clare made a mental note to throw some out. Gloria wouldn't notice. She walked into the sitting room, around the couch in the bay and stared out the window. She was so used to this scene. The pink fuchsia was in blossom. It hid the tiny brick wall of the front garden. Back in the day, she and Rose used to run along the wall when sent out to play by Gloria. They used to try and get along as many garden walls without touching the ground. When they were seven, they used to roam the neighbourhood looking for adventure, usually finding it in dark underground carpark of the flats behind the house. They would play there, running to hide when a car lumbered down the run to the basement. She felt a burning coal in her stomach. It was a lump not a flame. It was heavy not light. Why did she feel so anxious? She had got into Bristol to do Politics and History next year. Now, here, with the house to herself, she had time to read. Time and peace. She wanted to read into the Indian Caste system and find about the Hindu Gods. She could also have some time with Simeon alone. Rose would have her baby in November, Clare was planning a trip to India in the Spring as Simeon thought his wedding would take place then. After that, she would travel around the country herself. Maybe Simeon and Minoo would join her for a bit. Then, she would come home and start college. She had everything to look forward to…so why was she depressed? Clare looked at her watch. She had five minutes before she was to skype with Rose.

Rose looked flourishing. She had put on weight and her face was almost soft looking. She had lost her angular edginess.

"Rose, you look … like an American soap character."

"Is that supposed to be a compliment?"

"I guess. You look well, anyway. How are you, what's happening? Have you and Finn decided?"

"Yes! We are going to stay here in Red Rock, have the baby, and get married. What do you think?"

Rose sat back, face shining, very satisfied with her announcement. She was also speaking with a slight American twang. How ridiculous thought Clare. She's only been there a month or so.

"Jesus. Get married! Have the baby! Is that what Finn wants?"

"Yes, we've gone over and over it. We want to be together, so why have an abortion.

"And, what do you mean, live there??"

"I mean live here. Clare, I love it. Red Rock is another world. You need to see it to believe it. Also, if we have the baby here, it will have American citizenship which will give it opportunities later in life. And, Clare, when we get married, I'll get citizenship too. Can you imagine it, Clare? Me, a married American citizen, living the Dream? Ha! What do you think?"

Rose giggled at Clare's shocked face.

"I know, it's unbelievable, isn't it? Honestly, Clare, America is vast and beautiful, well, Red Rock is. You'd love it. Well, you'll see it when you come for the wedding. The sky is gigantic and melodramatic. The mountains, lakes, forests are like nothing you have ever seen. The Glacier Park is amazing. The river! The weather is wild. So dramatic. It puts you in your place and puts life in perspective, to borrow Clive's phrase." Rose laughed again. "Finn is a reporter on the Carbon County News, which is the local rag. You know, people do real life things here, like fishing, hunting, skiing, playing sports. That's what people do. You just head out and go hunting. Really, you wouldn't believe it. People have antlers and animal heads on their walls! Really. Everyone knows how to shoot. It reminds me of the Waltons. Maybe I'll call the baby, John Joe, if it is a boy."

"But, Rose, it's so far away! What about London, and your journalism course? What about us? Anyway, you don't know how to shoot."

Rose laughed. "I can learn. That's what I mean. This place is full of 'can do'. I'm going to have a baby, and this is a place to raise children. Anyway, aren't you going to India? You're not staying in London either. You're moving to Bristol, so it makes no difference to you."

"Yes, but I'm only studying there. I'm not planning to move for ever."

Clare examined her sister's face for a sign of irony. Is this what happiness did? Softened the mental faculties. Clare had never heard her sister sound so affable, happy, uncritical.

Clare almost wished Gloria was with her to witness this. Was Rose on some sort of medication or was this America?

"Tell me about you. How is Simeon? And how was Miranda's first day at school? I bet she loved it. School will be the making of her. Get her away from all of us. God, Clare, remember, just nine months ago we were depressed and arguing in London, watching The Magic School Bus, and now I'm living on the prairie…under the biggest sky you can imagine. The stars at night here make me delirious. Can you believe it? Have you heard from Gloria yet? Did they arrive safely?"

"Rose, you don't even like Americans. Don't make any major decisions. And, yes, Miranda went off without a by your leave. She seemed very stoic."

"Stoic. Five year olds can't be stoic, or shouldn't be! Yes, of course I have thought it through. I've done all the pros and cons. To be honest, it's mostly pros. And, I can always come back if it doesn't work out. Clare, you'll see for yourself. We went pig racing the other day, with real pigs. The Grizzly Bear is our State animal. Miranda would love it: all the animals. Oh God, Clare, I am so happy, I'm scared it's all going to vanish!"

"Rose, you have gone crazy. When are you planning to get married?"

"Soon, before the baby is born. Having babies out of wedlock is frowned on here. We've been looking at a place downtown to rent. A condominium. I was hoping Gloria might help me put down a deposit. I thought I might start a blog, a Londoner's Diary and, hopefully, start a syndicated column. I'll be able to write. Clare, be excited for me!

"I am. I'm just getting used to it."

Rose's face might have put on weight, but it still dipped and zipped: big smiles, the nose flashed. Her hands danced and gesticulated. Clare saw Finn in the background, his face loomed up in the camera. He looked…bonny was the word that came to Clare's mind. He seemed to be as happy as Rose. They chatted a little more. Rose wanted to get married in late October. They discussed dates. Finally, after lots of shrieks and air kisses (that would never have happened if they had been in the same room, Clare thought), Clare clicked on the red hang up button and stared at her desktop. Red Rock, Montana. It was Hicksville, wasn't it? Rose living amongst the Waltons? How long would that last? Well, she thought, at least I'll get to see the world this year, America, India and Bristol.

It was Clare's first taste of running a household and at the end of Miranda's first week of school, she was exhausted. Every morning she had to get Miranda dressed, make her lunch, give her breakfast and take her to school. After Rose left, Nancy had given Clare the 10am til 5pm shift at The Favourite so she could get back for Miranda in the evening, though Margaret picked her up and gave her tea at 3.30pm. Thank God Margaret lived in the house with them. Credit to Gloria for organising that, Clare thought, wiping the last of the tables down in The Favourite before she left. When Clare got home, she cooked both her and Miranda supper, though occasionally Nancy gave her the last of the dish of the day to take home. She tried to find out what was happening to Miranda in school but Miranda said little. She didn't seem to have made any friends. Clare hadn't realised how time-consuming children were. While, on the one hand, she liked playing mother, and keeping house, Simeon was not keen to visit it there, so she wasn't seeing as much of him as she hoped. Overall, she thought, to her surprise, it would be a relief to have Gloria back. Clare rang up to Margaret to ask if she would babysit Miranda Saturday night.

"No bother, Clare. She can stay over up here too so you can sleep in Sunday morning. In fact, bring her up in the afternoon. She can play with James. Any news on Gloria?"

"Yes. We skyped. She's having the time of her life. She is going on some kind of garden tour or something tomorrow. She looks and sounds great. Kind of young. It makes me feel guilty."

"Guilty?"

"That she was so Gloria-ish for the last twenty years. As children, we must have been a terrible impediment to her."

"What nonsense, Clare. Your mother has always done exactly what she wanted. No need for guilt as far as she is concerned, you mark my words."

Clare was a little taken aback.

"Oh, right. And…" she hesitated

"Yes?"

"Good news about Rose too. She's having the baby, marrying Finn and they're going to live in Red Rock!"

"No! Are you serious?"

"Yep, the wedding is next month. Expect an invitation."

"Jesus, she's just like your mother. Doesn't think."

"Yes, they both seemed to have gone mad."

Chapter 28

School was a maze of corridors and classes with a host of different smells: milk, polish, dust, disinfectant, body odours that all mingled in the air. Miranda was surrounded by confusion, talk, shouts, jeers, and running footsteps. Her class room was in the front of the building and she had been given a window seat which she was staring out of, watching a robin hopping about. Suddenly, out of the corner of her eye, Miranda noticed a forest of arms and hands rise into the warm stale classroom air. The boy next to Miranda was lifting one cheek of his bottom of the chair thrusting his arm so high. Miranda took a last look up at the sky, trying to see an aeroplane, but saw nothing. She turned her attention back into the classroom. She noticed a ray of sunshine, flooded with dust mites milling above the heads of hair in front of her. Miranda remembered what Clare had said. Dust mites are bits of us that have fallen off, spinning, flying around. She shivered. Maybe if she kept perfectly still, she would remain whole. Miranda held her breath and tried not to move, not her fingers, not her toes, her head. Then she became aware of laughter. Her name was being called.

"Miranda, what does your name begin with?"

She had been so focused on being still, Miranda found it difficult at first to understand what the teacher was asking. She shook her head. Everyone laughed.

"M for Miranda," the teacher said.

"Do we have another name beginning with M?"

There was silence.

"Michael, where are you?" asked the teacher.

A small black boy wearing a red cap slowly put up his hand on the other side of the class. He reminded Miranda of the robin. Hesitant but curious.

"Michael, and Miranda. Michael, where do you live?"

"I live in the flats in Royal College St."

Michael's voice was quiet.

"Who knows Royal College St?"

Hands soared.

"Miranda, do you know the name of the road you live on?"

She shook her head.

"You don't know where you live?"

Miranda felt the eyes on her and heard muffled sniggers. She felt a burning sensation in her cheeks. Miranda looked at the teacher who appeared to be talking to her, but she wasn't sure. It looked as though teacher was looking slightly to the left of her, at Ollie, the boy next to her. Ollie thought so too.

"I do, Miss. I live next to the Greek church on Albany St."

"I'm asking Miranda, Ollie."

"I live on a Place," answered Miranda. "A small street near the station."

"Good girl."

The teacher looked down at a list on her desk.

"That's right, Wilmot Place, does anyone else know where that is?"

No hands went up. Miranda felt as if she wasn't giving the right answers.

"I also have a home in South Africa, and in Red Rock," she added, feeling slightly desperate and remembering what Gloria and Rose had said.

"Oh," said the teacher. "Where is Red Rock?"

"America."

"I see. Well, that is a long way. Now, Ollie, did you say Albany St?"

"Yes, Miss. I live with my mum and Dad and my big brother. He goes to this school too. I am Greek."

"Very good. Does anyone know where Albany St is?"

Another flock of hands went up.

"Now, do we have someone whose name begins with P?"

The girl directly in front of Miranda put up her hand.

"I'm Polly. And I live in Holmes Road."

"Good girl, Polly. Who knows where Holmes Road is?"

Another forest of hands stretched out.

"South Africa, Miss!" shouted a boy called Alexi with a giggle. Everyone laughed.

Polly turned around to look at Miranda. She had shoulder length hair and her skin was a little flaky. She turned back.

"I only have one home, miss, but I like it. It's next to the police station. My dad is a policeman."

Miranda felt snubbed.

"I have two dads…" she said loudly, "well, I'm going to have two dads. One is an Indian. My mum is in South Africa with the other one.

"Does your father live in South Africa, Miranda?" asked teacher.

"No, my mum has a home in South Africa. My sister in Red Rock and my father in India. So maybe I have three homes. Well four if you count where I have always lived, in …the Place.

"Gosh, that sounds complicated, Miranda. Who do you live with?"

"My sister and, Margaret. Margaret is like my second mum, but my real mum will come back soon."

"Okay."

The teacher made a mental note to find out more about this little girl. She was probably going need special attention and the special needs budget had been cut this year.

"Let's find out about the others. Sadie, what does your name begin with?"

"SSSS for slithery snake, Miss. We all have slithery snake names in our family. Sadie, Susie, Sophie, Simon, Samuel."

"Oh, my goodness, this is quite a class!"

Chapter 29

On Saturday afternoon, Clare and Miranda knocked on Margaret's white flat door and went in without waiting for her to answer. Miranda tugged a pillowcase full of beanie babies and her night things along the floor behind her. Sun was shining in through the sitting room window. It glinted on the mirror, and the glass red, white and blue Venetian animals that Margaret collected. Stripy colourful rugs were spread across the dark wooden floor. There was a TV in the corner and two colourful boxes of toys. A smell of baking came from the kitchen where they could hear Margaret pottering around.

"You've made this place lovely, Margaret," exclaimed Clare.

Margaret came through, wiping her hands on a tea cloth.

"Yes. Thank you. Actually, we all often come up here after school rather than downstairs. It's easier. James has all his things here and Miranda seems happy. Now Miranda, go and put your overnight stuff in James' room and see if he is awake. He took a nap. I've baked shortbread. Do you want have some?"

Miranda grinned a gappy smile, nodded, headed into James' room.

"Wakey wakey, James…it's me! Time to get up, time to get dressed, time to look your best!" James was standing up in his crib, laughing and cooing.

"She adores him," said Margaret, "she's such a little mother. I wanted to suggest, Clare, why doesn't Miranda stay up here for the rest of the time Gloria is away? She can share a room with James and if she needs anything she could pop down. It would take the pressure off you a little, too and I would be only delighted."

"I don't know," responded Clare, frowning. Her first thought was whether she herself wanted to be alone downstairs with just Sasha. It was bleak down there without Rose and Gloria. She could understand why Miranda preferred being up here.

"Of course," Margaret, continued "you could come up here anytime too, eat here, watch TV, do whatever you do. I'll be cooking every night."

"Oh Margaret."

She had not realised she was feeling so vulnerable.

That evening, Clare and Simeon went to the Camden Brasserie on the off chance of getting in. Clare thought of it as 'their restaurant'. The manager knew Simeon and squeezed a little round table for two in behind the door.

"I'm impressed. Do you come here a lot?" asked Clare.

"Yes. The manager and I went to school together."

"Really? I still have so much to learn about you. I want to know everything."

"I don't think children are supposed know so much about their parents. It is I who needs to discover things about you."

"You don't feel like my dad."

"Really? What do I feel like?"

Clare felt herself blush.

"I don't know."

Simeon smiled at her and put his hand on hers. He had a charming smile. He always looked so cool in his hat. Clare turned his hand up and looked at it, as if she could read it and find it more. She played with his fingers. They were long and straight. He had nice nails. They didn't feel like the hands of a father.

"Do I feel like a daughter to you?" she asked.

Simeon laughed. He paused

"I don't know, Clare. My experience of daughters has been rather sudden. I do want to be a great father, but something has come up which may take me away for a while."

"Take you where? India? What's happened?"

"Minoo has broken off our engagement."

"Oh no, why?"

Clare looked directly into Simeon's face. She noticed for the first time that his ears were a little like dried apricots. An imaginary image of his mother popped into her head. She saw a tiny brown woman, with apricot ears wearing red ruby earrings and pendant, and a colourful sari. She had a red spot on her forehead. This was her grandmother. It was hard to believe. Clare tasked herself with finding out what the red spot on the forehead symbolised. She noticed that the skin under Simeon's eyes was darker and engraved with little lines.

"It's nothing to do with me and Miranda, is it?"

"I think she is struggling with the fact that I have two daughters. To be honest, her parents are probably finding it hard as well. The family is quite conservative and traditional."

"But if you're in love…then surely it doesn't matter?"

Simeon laughed and the lines around his eyes deepened. Buried in his brown skin, they gave him a distinguished look, but he looked tired.

"Ours is an arranged marriage. Well, not arranged as such. We were introduced, and we liked each other, a lot. Over the year, I think we came to love each other. We were well suited."

"An arranged marriage! That's awful!"

"It often works well. It is normal in India, it's …well, regular." He smiled, "… traditional."

"Oh, I'm sorry!" cried Clare, "I didn't mean to offend you. I just mean, well, it seems better if people fall in love. Maybe marriage would have more of a chance, then. And, well, I'm sorry about Minoo. Are you upset?"

"Yes, I am. I am hoping I can change her mind. And her parents' mind. There is a lot depending on our marriage, my family business. I will have to go back to India. I will go and woo her." He laughed. It sounded hollow.

"You're going away? But we're still getting to know each other."

Simeon laughed again. She wished he would stop laughing. None of this seemed very funny.

"And what a pleasure that is, Clare. Come on, let's order our food. There is so much to discuss and plan - for instance where you might travel in India next year. Maybe I can join you for a while. Will we have some wine?"

Clare nodded. There was nothing to worry about. He was her father, after all. No one could take him away, but, she wasn't sure. Something felt wrong. She suspected Miranda did not like him, and was vaguely impressed that was possible, that Miranda had her own likes and dislikes. Anyway, what did it matter? If Minoo didn't get back with him, she and Simeon might be able travel together next year; that would be brilliant. She flashed a picture of them hiking through Indian tea plantations.

"Miranda is staying with Margaret upstairs," she said. "You'd be very welcome to come and visit during the day, if you'd like.

"Really!" Simeon answered. "You're all alone downstairs, now?"

"I sleep down there, but Margaret says I can eat and hang out up there with them. She has made it very nice. It's a bit odd downstairs without Rose and Gloria."

"I wonder what Gloria will have to say about that"

Clare hadn't considered what Gloria might say. She suddenly realised Gloria would probably not be happy about Miranda living upstairs.

"How is Miranda getting on in school?" Simeon poured her wine.

"I'm not sure. I don't think she has made any friends. She mentioned a Polly and an Alexi and a Michael but they don't appear to be friends. She says she prefers the animals in the zoo!"

"It is hard to get to know Miranda," Simeon leaned across the table. His teeth were even and white. She and Miranda had his teeth. Gloria's were awful. "It's been easier with you! But she is only five and I don't have much experience with children. With you, I'm talking to an adult, and an intelligent young, attractive woman. So, it is not hard. Indeed, it is a joy."

"Well, Miranda is not used to men, really. So, when are you going to India?"

"Next week, I think. But whatever happens with Minoo, Clare, it will not impact on us. Already, you mean so much to me." He took her hand. "You do believe me. Whatever happens, I will love you."

Clare nodded. She closed her fingers around his and smiled with joy.

Chapter 30

Two nights before Gloria's return, Clare lay in bed, unable to sleep. The streetlamp cast a gloomy light across her room. She stared up at the cracks in her ceiling. There were two fine parallel cracks, a little like a highway, with smaller off shoots. Ever since she was a child, she had created an imaginary village with the cracks serving as paths and the damp patches as houses. The large darker patch in the bay window was a lake, like the Serpentine in Hyde Park that she and Simeon had walked along earlier this summer. Now, Simeon's face presented itself to her, fleetingly with that enigmatic smile of his but she couldn't pin it down. It kept shifting. Clare turned over on her side to face the wall but couldn't get comfortable. She turned on her other side to face back into the room. She hated it when night time Clare was on the prowl. She tried the relaxation exercises Gloria had shown her when she was a child, but she couldn't get past her knees before forgetting what she was doing. Simeon's face kept popping into her head. In Hyde park, that time they walked along the lake, he had thrown off his t. shirt and collapsed on the grass. Clare had stared at the way it glistened with sweat, like beads of gold on chocolate brown. They had walked hand in hand and she had felt so proud to be on the arm of this tall dark man.

Should she feel like this about her father? She tried to recall the initial excitement she had felt when Gloria had told her about Simeon. It wasn't the same feeling. She felt obsessed by him, but it was understandable, surely. He was her father. That thought made her uncomfortable. Clare ached to see him and she wasn't sure that was right. She wondered if she had ruined his life like she had ruined his marriage. Simeon made her feel like a princess...a Goddess! Saraswati! Clare smiled in the darkness. She was so proud to belong to him. His mother, her grandmother, she reminded herself, was right about him being, Hanuman, the monkey king. He was fun, strong, courageous and devoted. She hated Minoo for upsetting him. Should a daughter be jealous of her father's fiancé? Simeon had said a father daughter bond was inextricable. Why hadn't he contacted her recently. He wasn't returning her calls. Had he gone to India without telling her? Did he love Minoo? How could you fall in love with a stranger? An arranged marriage. Maybe he was being polite to her in the same way as he was to Minoo. Was Rose right? Was this what family meant? Trouble, anxst? That's what Rose had always said. But now Rose was having a baby and she seemed to have forgotten all the rough edges of family. Recently, she hadn't mentioned her racist father either, or family genes. Thank God, Clare thought. She was jealous of Rose. I want babies, Clare thought. I've always wanted babies, like Gloria, she thought. That was how all this started. Gloria had wanted Simeon's babies. Yuck, that was disgusting. Clare wanted him to hold her, embrace her, to tell her what to feel. He made her feel special. She had to stop thinking like this. It was just night terrors. Clare tried to put him out of her mind. Gloria was coming back – the day after tomorrow. Everything would be back to normal. Tomorrow Clare had to make the house to look welcoming. Do the shopping. What would Rose say about all this? All what, Clare thought. What do I mean? She wasn't sure. Clare closed her eyes. Oh, how to stop these night terrors!. She felt as if a white whale was flipping inside of her, like the red fortune fish in crackers flipped in the palm of the hand, but huge. Breathe deeply, she told herself. She realised that this is what she had been saying to herself for the last few months. How stupid could she be? Not to know how she felt.

At about four, she heard the diesel engine of a taxi drive up. The headlights rolled across her ceiling. She wondered who it was. The street was a quiet one. A door slammed. She heard a familiar loud voice.

"It is so good to be back!"

"Gloria!" Clare leapt out of bed, grabbed her dressing gown and ran up the stairs. She threw open the front door.

"Mum! What are you doing here? You're not due for two days!"

"Clare, liefling."

Oh, God, she's going to have more Africaans, thought
Clare.

"Mum!"

Clare ventured down the steps, pulling her robe around
her. She was mentally checking the state of the house, the
things that needed to be done still. Miranda was at Margaret's.
Gloria wouldn't like that. Could she creep up and get her in the
morning before Gloria realised, she wondered. Gloria came
around the taxi and hugged her tight. Clare threw herself into
her neck.

"Well, it's lovely to see you too, sweetheart. Is
everything regso?"

Clare stepped back and looked at her mother who wore
a wide brimmed hat, white trousers, with a colourful African
shirt tucked in.

"What does that mean? Speak English."

"Is everything alright?"

Yes, fine. Mum, you look great." Gloria had put on a
little weight, but she looked great.

"Let's get off the street. Clive, bring in the suitcases.
Clare, go put the kettle on. No, we brought back some South
African wine. It's not too late. I guess Miranda is asleep or have
I woken her?"

"Er yes, well actually, she stayed up with Margaret tonight. I was out. It was easier. We thought you weren't coming back for another two days."

"Ok, then, come on, let's have a night cap. And I can tell you all about it. We caught an earlier flight, didn't we, Clive? We'd had enough. Or rather, Clive had had enough of me."

Gloria gave a tinkly, unnatural sounding laugh. She looked fit and tanned, like an ageing super model. Clare turned to Clive and gave him a kiss hello. He looked tired.

"Welcome back, Clive. Did you have a good time?"

"I guess. Gloria, I'm going to take the taxi back to my place."

"Okay, whatever you like, Clive." said Gloria. "Clare, can you manage those three small bags? Come on sweetie, I want to hear about everything. Does Miranda like school? How is Simeon?"

Gloria turned her back and heaving her big bag, disappeared through the front door."

"Is everything alright, Clive?" asked Clare

"Not sure. Take care, Clare, nice to see you."

Clive got into the taxi, slammed the door. He slumped back into the seat. Clare picked up the three bags and followed Gloria into the house. She dumped the bags in the kitchen. She could hear Gloria in her bedroom.

"Mum, why has Clive gone home?"

"There's a lovely bottle of south African red in the small red bag you brought in. I got it in a vineyard. I went on a wine tasting tour. Get some glasses. I want to get into something more comfortable. Have we any crisps or anything? I'm starving. Were you in bed, darling?"

Clare peeped in through the door. Already, her mother's room was a mess. Gloria had had already thrown clothes and plastic bags across the bed.

"Well its four o'clock in the morning so I was, but not asleep. There's nothing to eat, except cereal but there's no milk. I was going to shop tomorrow."

"Oh, not to worry. I'll be out in a min."

Clare heard the shower running. She found some crackers at the back of the cupboard. She laid out glasses and crackers on the table.

"Oooh lovely, darling. It's very tidy in here."

Gloria was her dressing gown and her hair in a towel. Her face was brown, and her eyes shone. She looked like a different person.

"You look fab, Gloria. You dyed your hair. It's lovely."

Gloria twirled. "I'm a blonde! What do you think? Fresh air, exercise, good food and wine. I swam every day. On safari, I walked five miles a day. And I used the gym in the hotel. I feel like a new woman."

"Great! What about Clive?"

Gloria looked at Clare and pulled a face.

"It didn't work out brilliantly. He was so 'geaffekteer'. I don't know what the translation is, namby-pamby. He didn't want to do anything but tourist tours. Tourists tours! We flew up to Jo'burg to see the old house. It was gone. They've built a massive housing estate, on the veld!. Really weird. I couldn't find much out about Pieter. His parents apparently moved to Canada but died in a car crash. There were cousins in Zimbabwe, so that might be a trail Rose wants to follow up. Anyway, Clive was a disaster. It made me see him in a whole new light."

"I don't really understand namby-pamby, either" said Clare

"No sense of adventure. Okay, both Cape Town and Jo burg have a reputation for muggings etc, and everyone is very security aware, so he would not go out after 9pm, unless there was a guide. He kept saying I was taking unnecessary risks. God, so irritating."

"So, are you no longer together?"

"We'll see. Now, I don't want to talk anymore about it. Tell me all about you and Miranda, and Simeon. Is everything okay? Pour us some wine, sweetheart, let's have a good old chin wag. Tell me, how is Miranda settling into school?"

Clare explained that Miranda seemed happy, but she didn't seem to have made friends. Gloria wasn't over perturbed.

"It will come. Its early days. Miranda is a very self-contained child."

"What do you think about Rose getting married?" asked Clare

"It's very exciting! I think they are going for a wedding date at the end of October. I don't know if it is the best thing, but I like Finn. He's a good boy. America though. Red Rock! Anyway, it seems like she has made up her mind…for the moment."

Gloria caught sight of Clare's stricken face.

"Don't you think it's a good idea?"

"I don't know," said Clare. "Will she be happy living in the States?"

"Ah, she'll be back, I know my daughter."

"But don't you mind?"

"Clare, what can I do about it? You know Rose. She won't listen to me. Anyway, it could be for the best. Finn seems to have a solid family around him. They might be able to exert a more positive influence than me."

"Wow, that's very reasoned of you. What's going to happen to us?"

"To us? Well, you have your life mapped out, don't you? Travelling, India, college. It's all ahead of you. It's me who should be worried. My daughters leaving home. But I still have Miranda. And, well, who knows. Maybe it is time for change. Maybe I'll go back to South Africa. It's a fascinating place."

"South Africa?"

"I don't know, Clare. Everything is changing. Anyway, nothing is going to happen immediately. The property market is shit, at the moment. We wouldn't get a decent enough price for the house."

"You mean sell this house? But this our home. You can't do that."

Gloria couldn't possibly be serious. Selling their home. Where would she go? It was her home. She couldn't imagine London without it. What about Miranda? And Margaret. Where would Rose go? Where would she go in college holidays?"

"You can't sell this house," Clare faltered.

"Darling, you are going to be leaving! You won't feel like that for too long, I promise. Anyway, I won't, not immediately. Now, tell me about Simeon. How is he?"

"I want to know more about your holiday."

"I'll tell you all about it tomorrow. It was great. It really invigorated me. It made me realise how drab my life had become. Now, tell me about you and how is Simeon? When is he getting married?"

Why did she keep asking about Simeon? Each time Simeon was mentioned, Clare felt as if her stomach had been stabbed. She didn't trust Gloria, but she also wanted to tell Gloria how she felt and to know if it was normal to feel so anxious.

"Not much to tell. I haven't seen him too much though he and I did go out to dinner a couple of time and had a couple of walks. But the engagement is off. Minoo isn't very happy about me and Miranda. He's going back to India to try and persuade her."

"The engagement is off? Well, well. Hardly surprising. I warned you, Clare. The appearance of two daughters is going to be slightly off putting to anyone, even if they were madly in love."

Tears begin tipping out of her eyes before Clare had a chance to choke them back.

"Mum, I don't know what's happening. Everything is so upside down. I feel so confused."

"Clare!"

Gloria pulled her daughter towards her and hugged her tight.

"Don't worry, we'll get him back. Just you wait and see. Don't worry." Gloria yawned.

"God, I'm more tired than I thought. I must go to bed, darling. Let's talk in the morning. Did I mention, I've given up smoking and cut back on the old vino!"

"Wow, really? Mum, it's great to have you home."

Was it? Clare wondered. She had missed her and felt lonely, but as soon as Gloria walked in the door, Clare wasn't sure.

Chapter 31

The bedroom was bright when Clare opened her eyes the next morning. Yellow sunshine flooded across her carpet. It must be after ten. She heard the front door bang, then the radio came on in the kitchen upstairs. Her heart jumped. It was good to hear someone in the house again. She leapt up, grabbed her dressing gown and ran up-stairs.

"Good morning, Clare."

Gloria was dressed in grey slacks and a figure-hugging t shirt. Her dyed golden hair was tied back. She was unpacking shopping bags on the kitchen table.

"I've been shopping and bought food. There was nothing here. Have you been eating?"

"Of course."

"Do you want to go and get Miranda while I get breakfast?"

"Okay."

"Then why don't we go to the zoo? Miranda seems to love it so much, and I want to spend time with her. You know, I think Miranda would just adore safari. But first, after breakfast, let's Skype Rose. We can all do it together and hear about the latest wedding plans. We'll need to book flights."

"I'll go get Miranda now."

The doorbell went as Clare stepped out into the front lobby to go upstairs to Margaret. She opened the front door. Simeon stood there, hat in hand.

"Simeon! What are you doing here?"

Simeon raised his eyebrows. He was wearing a suit, with a black polo neck jumper underneath. He looked very debonair. Clare noted, still a little tired. His brown skin reflected a shadow of grey. Gloria came hurrying out.

"Simeon, hello! How nice. You are just in time for breakfast."

She leaned up and gave him a kiss on his cheek.

"Clare is just going to get Miranda, she stayed with Margaret last night. Apparently, Clare was out. Darling, you never did say where you went last night."

"Just out with Angie, nowhere special."

"Good, well come in, Simeon, throw your coat there. Oh, Clare, you cleared the coats. That's great. Go on, Clare, go and get Miranda. I can't wait to see her. Coffee is on."

Simeon smiled at Clare, shrugged his shoulders and followed Gloria inside. He threw his coat on the bannister, balanced his hat on top and disappeared into the kitchen. Clare went upstairs to Margaret to collect Miranda. She wondered how she was going to sneak down all Miranda's stuff without Gloria seeing. Gloria, it seemed, was changed into a battery charged rabbit. It would have been easy before, she never got out of bed. She hoped Miranda was up and dressed. She wanted to get back to Simeon as soon as she could. She shuddered with a thrill of pleasure. Finally, he had come to see her. He'd have got a shock to see Gloria. Poor Simeon.

"Well, I think this is the first time we have all been together, en famille!" Gloria grinned at them all. "The family breakfast! Whomever would have thought. Even the bacon isn't burnt." Cheerily, she waved a piece of bacon on her fork. "What do you all think?"

Simeon smiled. He had been quieter than Clare knew him since he arrived. It was Gloria who had been doing all the talking.

"I like bacon," said Miranda. She waved her fork too and the rasher flew off. It landed on Simeon's shirt, leaving a smear.

"Miranda!" said Clare, "don't wave your fork about!"

Simeon and Gloria laughed. Gloria began to tell stories about her safari trip. She had seen real monkeys in the wild. Miranda was hooked. Simeon began to tell Miranda about elephants in India, like Babar. Clare began to feel a little excluded. Simeon hadn't talked to her at all. They seemed to be playing happy families. Well, it wasn't a happy family. Clare stood up

"Ok, thanks for breakfast. I'm afraid I've got to go."

"Where are you going?" asked Gloria. "I thought we agreed we would go to the zoo."

"Sorry, I forgot that I said to Angie I'd go out with her today."

"Oh! Wouldn't she understand…I mean I'm only just home. Don't you want to spend some time with us? I asked Simeon specially. Quality time."

Clare's heart kippered in her chest. Gloria asked him? When? Had she called him? Why had he come when Gloria called but not when she did?

"Sorry. I can't." Clare turned to Simeon, and summoning as much dignity as she could muster, she kissed him lightly on the cheek.

"If I don't see you before you go to India, keep in touch, Simeon, bon voyage, and good luck. I'm going to get dressed."

"Clare, it's Miranda's birthday tomorrow," Gloria reminded Clare. "I thought we might go to the London Eye. Would you like that, Miranda? It's a massive big wheel that turns high in the sky. If the weather is anything like today, we will see the whole of London. We could all go. Simeon could you make it?"

"Yes, yes," shouted Miranda.

"That might be fun," said Simeon.

She had momentarily forgotten Miranda's birthday.
Clare was appalled at herself. It was usually Clare who
reminded Gloria. She forced herself to smile.

"That would be great. Now, I've got to go."

Clare left the room, head held high. "I'm sorry,
Simeon," she heard Gloria say. "Clare isn't usually so rude."

How dare Gloria apologise for her like she was a child,
and to Simeon. He was her father! Clare held the bannister tight
as she forced herself to go slowly down the stairs. If there was
anyone who needed to be apologised for it was Gloria! Clare
threw herself onto her bed. Sobs started to choke her chest.
Why, oh why was she crying? She could feel the warm rays of
sun move on to her back and felt silly. She stopped crying and
sat up. Suddenly it occurred to her what Gloria might be trying
to do. She was trying to set them up as a family. Well, that
wasn't going to work. She didn't want Gloria and Simeon as
her mother and father. Clare prayed Simeon would come down.
She wanted to warn him. Clare got showered and dressed. She
would have put a stop to Gloria's stupid game. When she was
fully washed and dressed, Clare listened carefully, but couldn't
hear anything. Clare checked herself in the mirror and was
happy with her reflection. Her hair was glistening, and she
looked cool in her jeans. No trace of tears. She would show
them how level-headed she was. The house was silent as she
went up. Where was everyone? Had they gone into the garden?

No, she would have heard them pass. No one was in the kitchen. The new Gloria wasn't that new: she had left all the dishes on the table. Clare walked into the living room. No one was there either. She checked Gloria's room, peering out of the window at the garden, but she knew there would be no-one there. She went back to the hall. Simeon's coat and hat were gone. On the front door was a note.

Clare. Gone to the zoo. Text if you want to join us. We plan to go to the Camden Brasserie for lunch too. Do come. Love you. G x

Clare felt a surge of bitterness. The Camden Brasserie was their restaurant. Hers and Simeon's. She couldn't bear the thought of Simeon entertaining Gloria there. She'd go and see Angie. She looked at her watch. It was 8 o'clock am in Red Rock. She would call Rose now before leaving. Typical, Gloria had forgotten they were to skype Rose. No, Gloria hadn't changed at all.

Chapter 32

Rose still looked well. Her ponytail was thick and glossy. Instead of bouncing around her head, it lay sleek and fat on her shoulder. She had put on more weight. Her blue eyes were shining. Her rosebud lips glistened. She looked so different.

"You're putting on weight. You look lovely," said Clare. Rose looked like a golden slug, she thought.

"Too much weight, I think," moaned Rose. "I never thought I'd have to worry about fat. I'll have to work hard at taking it off after the birth. It's the food here. There's so much of it." Rose peered into the camera. "You're looking well, sort of. Have you lost weight? Actually, Clare, you look a bit peaky. Are you alright?"

"I'm fine. Is all well with the pregnancy? Finn? Are you all playing happy families too?"

"Too? What are you talking about? Yes, everything is fine. We have set a date for the wedding on Saturday, the 30th October. The night before Halloween. We are going with a horror theme. It seems appropriate!"

Rose laughed, a brittle laugh. That sounded more like her, Clare thought.

"I'm going as Rosemary!"

Clare smiled. This was definitely more Rose.

"As in Rosemary's Baby?"

"Yes! Isn't it fun? I love the idea of a Halloween wedding. Finn is dressing up as Dracula. I want his dad to be Frankenstein and his brother, The Joker. Cool, isn't it? What do you want to come as? I thought Gloria could be a cool wicked witch! Maybe Miranda should be Dorothy."

"But this is a wedding, not a fancy-dress party."

"It can be both. It'll be real fun."

"Oh Rose," Clare started to smile. "You don't change! I'm so glad. Gloria has changed. She looks great; got lots of new clothes. She's toned, dyed her hair, tanned, stopped smoking. She even gets up and does things. Still left a pile of washing up, though."

"Is she back already?"

"Yes, came back early. It seems Clive wasn't 'man' enough for her. But she loved South Africa. She says she is thinking of moving back."

"Like living there? Leaving London? Forever?"

"Maybe."

"Wow!" Rose thought for a moment, "nah, I'm sure it won't happen. You know Gloria. Its one of her madcap fantasies. How's Simeon? Will I invite him to the wedding?"

"No, he won't be able to come, he is going back to India to court Minoo who has broken off the engagement."

"Oh, Clare. That's a lot going on."

"Yeah, but I'm fine. When is the baby due exactly? I'm thinking of going to Thailand with Angie, but I don't want to miss the birth."

"What happened to India? The EDD is 10th November. But I guess it doesn't matter if you are in England, Thailand or India. They have the internet, don't they? Has this broken engagement changed things?"

"I don't know. Angie is going to Thailand in early November. I don't see the point of hanging around here anymore, why wait until Spring for India? God, Simeon was here today with Gloria and Miranda. In fact, they have gone to the zoo."

"Why haven't you gone?"

"It just sickens me to see Gloria, the new, beautiful, stylish Gloria sucking up to Simeon like that, pretending all is okay with the world."

"I would have thought you would be happy. I mean, you are one family, mother, father, two daughters. Isn't that what you always wanted?"

Clare felt tears bubble up in her eyes. Rose frowned

"Clare! What's wrong?"

Clare tried to smile. "I know, this is ridiculous. I feel like Gloria is trying to take Simeon away from me."

"How?"

"She wants him. I can tell. You remember all that stuff about him being her only love. Now, she is using me and Miranda to get him back. Between her and Minoo, I don't think I have a chance."

"Have a chance of what?"

"I don't know, him loving me."

Clare watched Rose carefully for her reaction. Rose leant back in her chair and slid her ponytail off her shoulder. She looked around the room.

"Clare, this can't be easy for Simeon. To suddenly be foisted with two daughters…it must have been a terrible shock…"

"Thanks, Rose, it's nice to know that he was 'foisted', that I'm a 'shock'."

"Clare, you know what I mean. It'll take him time to even realise what it is to be a father. I don't quite understand what you want from him."

"I want to do things together, talk about life, politics. I want to plan our future together. I want him to look after me… and Miranda."

Rose stared at her sister and leaned forward into the camera.

"Clare, 'plan our future together,' that sounds weird!"

"How is it 'weird'? Doesn't a father help his daughter plan her life? Anyway, who are you to be suddenly so reasonable? Listen, I have to go. Angie is expecting me. We'll talk later in the week. Send my love to Finn. And look after yourself but ease up on the carbs. You're turning into a blob! We need to know when you want us over. The exact dates."

"Clare!"

"Love you, big sister. Got to go. Bye."

Clare clicked on the red receiver and rested her head on her arms on the desk.

Chapter 33

Sitting on the same bench that they had before, Simeon stared at the monkeys. Life seemed a lot easier on that side of the cage. He watched Miranda and Gloria crouching up at the bars, the child telling Gloria that the monkey family groomed each other for fleas, that they picked them out and squashed them dead. She was sweet, he thought. She was his. What was he going to do? Minoo had been very clear. He wanted to be involved with Clare and Miranda, but daughters were one thing, Gloria was another. Miranda looked back at him.

"Look, Simeon, look at the mummy picking out the fleas."

The baby monkey wriggled out of its mummy's grasp and swung away, scrabbling up a twisted, bare tree and flung itself head over heels back onto the monkey mother who slapped it and tossed it away. It landed on all fours and scarpered away to the back of the cage. Miranda laughed.

"Look, they are playing but the mummy monkey doesn't look very happy."

Simeon got up and walked over to them.

"You're a little monkey!" he said. Miranda squealed with delight. He lifted her up and tossed her on to his shoulders.

"Is it time for lunch? Where are the bananas? That's all baby monkeys get, baby bananas whereas your mother and I are going to have steak and chips and jelly and ice cream."

"And trifle, or what about crème caramel? Or I might have a chocolate éclair," laughed Gloria following behind, "let's see what about banoffee pie? Or a big mac followed chocolate éclair? Mmmmm yummie!"

"Yes, yes!" Miranda began bouncing on Simeon's shoulders.

"Only a banana for a monkey. I will ask the zookeeper if he has spare one. Do you remember him, Miranda, from our last visit?"

Miranda stopped bouncing as Simeon made a beeline for the zookeeper.

"Hello. Do you have a banana for this little monkey up here?" Simeon asked.

Miranda wriggled, trying to get off his shoulders. The zookeeper looked up at them

"Oh, my Goodness! How did she escape? She's a terrible one, always wanting to go home with the children. Here, give her to me and I'll pop her back in with her mum."

"I'm not a monkey!" yelled Miranda as she half slid, half fell from Simeon's shoulders.

"Oooh! No. I can see you now. Of course, you're not. You're a lovely little girl. I remember you. Miranda, isn't it? My mistake. Lucky escape, missy. My poor eyes. Not what they used to be."

"I'd like to go into the monkey cage though."

"I'd like some of that steak and chips you were talking about, Simeon," said Gloria, taking his arm.

"Can I go into the monkey cage?"

"As you know, Sir, we have a monkey lover here," explained Simeon.

The zookeeper was red faced and wore a cap. His forehead loomed over his eyes which were deep set. Simeon wondered if keepers grew to look like the animals they look after.

"Well, you're in luck. It's just about feeding time. Do you want to help me, Miranda?"

"Oh yes! Can I? Can I?"

"Is it safe?" asked Simeon.

"Oh yes. They're more likely to be more scared of her than she of them."

Gloria put out her hand. "I'm Gloria, Miranda's mum. Pleased to meet you."

The zookeeper shook Gloria's hand, he pointed to his name badge, Stephen.

"Well, Miranda, aren't you a lucky girl?" Gloria continued. "What do you say to this kind man?" She didn't wait for an answer. "If you are sure that it's alright?, Stephen," asked Gloria.

"Thank you, mum, thank you."

Miranda jumped up and down on the spot. The zookeeper put out his hand.

"Come with me, Miranda, and if your parents want to go to the café, I'll return you there rightly in half an hour."

"Don't you want to feed the monkeys?" Miranda asked, looking up at Gloria and Simeon. She looked so innocent, Simeon fell in love with her again.

"Excuse me, young lady. Not every Tom, Dick and Harry can feed the monkeys," said the zookeeper. "It's a privilege allowed only to a few and I seen you at the monkey fence a good few times this summer."

"We're not far, Miranda. Simeon and I will be in the café just over there. Thank you very much. That is so kind of you. She will be over the moon. Thank you!"

Gloria gently pulled Simeon's arm and led him off to the café.

"Are you sure she's going to be alright. Shouldn't we have gone with her?" Simeon said in a low voice, looking behind him. Miranda was dancing off holding the hand of the zookeeper. She reminded him of Pooh Bear holding Christopher Robin's hand.

"No! She's fine! It's her dream come true. She's in safe hands, for God's sake, you even know his name."

"I guess. We were chatting the last time we were here, but he could be anyone."

"He's the zookeeper for the monkeys."

"I think we should go to the monkey house and watch. She'd like that."

"She's fine, Simeon. You know, as a father, you'll have to learn to be a little less protective. He obviously knows her and she's happy. Come on. Let's get a coffee. We only have a half hour grace. Now tell me, what is going on with Minoo? Clare says the engagement is off."

Simeon allowed himself to be pulled away. "Minoo says it's off. She doesn't even want to see me. I thought I'd go back. But she's told me not to bother."

Gloria took his hand. "Simeon, I'm sorry, but maybe it is for the best."

Simeon disentangled his hand from Gloria's fingers. He had no intention of discussing his engagement with Gloria. However, she continued,

"I know it's an arranged marriage. Who arranged it? Do you love her?"

"My brothers. Her family is a good one. The two families were going to go into business together."

Gloria stopped walking and turned to Simeon.

"Simeon, did you want to marry her? Live in India?"

He didn't answer and tried to walk on. Gloria grabbed his arm and changed tack.

"What does your mother think about you having two daughters?"

Simeon swirled around, angry.

"Both my parents died a few years ago."

Gloria was taken aback, but she stood her ground.

"I'm sorry, Simeon, but I'm sure your mother would have wanted what's best for you. London is your home. I mean, you were raised here. And what is the family business to you? You're an academic."

Simian looked at her. He wanted to hit her. He wondered why he felts so reactive? Gloria did that to people.

"I have responsibilities to my brother…"

"And now you have responsibilities here. I'm sorry. I should have told you before about the girls. But, in my defence, when we met five years ago you were so wrapped up in your thesis and your work. You clearly weren't interested in me."

"I wasn't interested in settling down. If I had known children were involved, then I might have reconsidered."

"I didn't want that to be the reason."

Gloria started walking again. Simeon followed her.

"Gloria, you should have told me about Clare then."

He put his hand on her shoulder, as if to make her turn around. She stopped and did.

"You didn't want to know."

"How do you know?"

"As you said, you didn't want to settle down, and children have a habit of making you do exactly that."

Gloria walked off again. He stood still. She stopped and turned around to him.

"Let's stop this, Simeon, all that is history. You have to decide what you want now." She changed the subject. "Look at those giraffes. I love the grace of giraffes. I saw them on safari too. I want to take Miranda on safari. She will love it."

"What did Clive think of South Africa?"

Gloria put her arm in Simeon's and started to walk again.

"Clive and I didn't see eye to eye. I guess it was lucky we went and discovered sooner rather than later that we are not compatible."

"What do you mean? You seemed happy before you left."

"I wasn't sure. South Africa was vibrant and full of energy. I used to be like that but then London sapped me. You remember me when I was first over, don't you?

"Yes. I'd never met anyone like you. You were explosive…every which way. You were determined, ruthless. Like a lion, with all that red hair.

"Well, I evolved into a rhinocerous, grey and fat, wallowing in mud. Gloria laughed. "I may not be up to being a lion again. But I wouldn't mind being a giraffe. Poor Clive. The whole experience was a bit of a shock. I wanted to do everything: visit places, go on expeditions, sail, climb the Sugar Loaf, explore every neighbourhood, do safari. Honestly, Simeon, it was as if the sun, the spirit, the music of the country reached into me. It was wonderful. I didn't even have to work on it. In the mornings, I ran. I swam in the sea. I got fit. But not Clive. He thought we would be mugged every time we went out. He worried if I left the hotel alone. And if we ventured into a dodgy area, he would tug me to go back. Like a child! Or a mouse!"

Gloria lapsed into silence. They were at the gates of the café.

"What animal would you be?" She asked.

Simeon thought for a minute and made a self-deprecating noise.

"I feel like a mole. Here's the café. Do you want to sit outside?"

Gloria giggled. She leaned up to his face and kissed his cheek.

"Ha, ha a mole! That's good! Didn't you once tell me you had a nickname, something about a monkey king God? That was a great chat up line. I fell in love with you on the spot! Here, you get the table. I'll get the coffee and cake."

Simeon chose a square table at the edge of the café and sat down. It was a bit chilly, but much nicer to be outside than in the noise inside. Gloria brought out a tray balancing dishes of banoffee pie, chocolate éclair, carrot cake and two steaming cuppucinos.

"Look, beautiful milky foam hearts. Miranda would love these. She is constantly squirting that awful cream foam stuff she makes me buy into the shape of a heart on top of whatever she is eating." She handed Simeon a coffee. "Rose says it looks like an arse more than a heart. Miranda has obviously inherited my poor drawing skills."

Gloria cut the éclair and carrot cake into two and put each half on a plate and passed it to him. "Let's hope the same doesn't apply to her love life. By the way, you seem to be getting on with her very well."

"Yes, I must confess, I am a little surprised. It's not usually so easy." He took the plate, splashed a serviette on to his lap and bit into the éclair.

"Hum, delicious. To be honest, at first, I thought Miranda didn't like me. She clung to Clare and usually wanted to go home. But today seems different."

"Maybe because Clare isn't here. By the way, Clare seems upset. She mentioned you didn't text or email for the last while."

"Actually, to be honest it all became too much. Dealing with two new daughters, a broken engagement, trying to decide the direction of my life, weighing up the different responsibilities and dealing with cards that I didn't know I had been dealt. I needed to work it out. I needed a bit of time to think, just doing ordinary things, work, reading. I hope she isn't upset."

"The thing about daughters, they generally forgive you. As a father. You'll learn."

"And no doubt, you are happy to be my teacher." Simeon, laughed. This was bantering he felt familiar with. Gloria smiled and bowed her golden head briefly. He noticed the greying roots. Then, she tumbled on to one knee, put her hands on Simeon's legs, looked up at him smiling and said

"Simeon, marry me. Our family is already made!"

He had to laugh. She'd always made him laugh.

"Gloria, you are mad. Some things don't change!"

She laughed back, pleased. She had planted a seed.

"Mummy, mummy, what are you doing?"

Miranda came running up, the zookeeper not far behind. Gloria stood up.

"Miranda! How were the monkeys? We have banoffee pie for you."

"I fed them bananas and held the baby. He was soooooo sweet."

"You got a natural here," the zookeeper said, "she definitely has a way with animals. Couldn't believe me own eyes."

"Can we go back? Pleasssse."

Gloria looked at Simeon and smiled

"Ask your father, Miranda."

"Simeon, pllllleasssse."

Simeon smiled. He put his hands up in surrender. "Why not? Come and eat your banoffee pie."

He pulled her on to his lap. He turned to the zookeeper

"Pull up a chair, Stephen, sit down, I'll get you a coffee. I think we are going to be seeing a lot of each other!"

Chapter 34

Clare read Simeon's text. For privacy, she had gone to the bathroom.

> Had to spend the whole day at the zoo! Please, join us at Camden Brasserie for dinner. I've booked! 7pm.

She re-read it. Why did he have to spend the day at the zoo? 'Join us'. 'Us' presumably was Gloria and Miranda. She wanted to see him, but, not if Gloria was there. She wasn't prepared to buy in to all that 'family' stuff. And while she did want to see Gloria and Miranda, she didn't with Simeon. How dare he try and inveigle his way into her family? Clare, you wanted to find him, a little voice whispered from her shoulder. She could see it, a tiny figure, like Tinker Bell in Peter Pan. You didn't take Gloria into account, the demon on the other shoulder said. The irritation Clare felt was flooded by a wave of jealousy. She, Clare had found him. Simeon belonged to her. Typical now that Gloria would surf in and try to steal him. It was entrapment. No, she wouldn't go to the restaurant. You can't hate your mother, the little voice said. You can, said the demon. After all Gloria doesn't care. Rose has always said she was a crap mother. She composed a text to Simeon.

> Eating with Angie. Maybe a walk tomorrow? Talk? After the London Eye. Supper maybe?

Clare reread the text. It sounded fine, grown up. Then she texted Gloria.

Hi, eating with Angie. May stay over. See you tomorrow.

That would show her that she was independent and could do what she liked. She felt a tide of sadness flow through her. Actually, she wished that she was at home, curled up watching TV and that none of this was happening. She flushed the toilet and re-joined the girls. Julie was jiggling at the computer. Angie and Julie were planning their trip to Thailand. Angie had got pissed off with Clare and all her changing plans and agreed to travel with Julie.

"Oh my God, Kop Pha Ngan looks fabulous. Let's go there," said Angie.

Clare looked over her shoulder at the screen. It did look quite a beach. Maybe she should go with them. That would show Gloria and Simeon. Clare felt a rise of delight at the thought. Yes, she would travel with Julie and Angie. She needed to get away. A new perspective.

The next morning was chilly for early October, but fresh, bright and dry. Clare and Miranda sat on the steps of their house wrapped up in scarves and mittens. They were waiting for Simeon and Gloria who were unloading the dishwasher in the hope of finding Gloria's car keys. Miranda was clutching Bongo and Clare was holding Topper, the Giraffe. Miranda was nudging Topper with Bongo.

"Topper, you're going to see the whole of London and you'll be able to see more because you are so tall." Miranda spoke in her squeaky Bongo voice.

Clare manipulated Topper's long neck so that she nuzzled Bongo.

"I can't wait" Clare growled in response. Clare wondered whether that was a right tone for a giraffe.

"Won't it be very cold in the big wheel?" asked Miranda

"The London Eye is closed in. In fact, on a day like today we should be able to see for miles. How was the zoo yesterday, Miranda, did you have a good time? It wasn't so cold yesterday."

Miranda looked at Clare, her eyes shining and nodded.

"Clare, I went into the monkey house with the zookeeper. He is called Stephen and he is a really nice old man. The monkeys love him."

"Do you like Simeon better now?"

Miranda lowered her eyes and nodded shyly.

"How come?"

Miranda shrugged. "He's just normal. He and mummy are just normal."

Clare felt her face flush despite the cold. She stood up.

"Bongo and Topper must be freezing. I am! Let's go and see if they have found the car keys."

As she spoke, Gloria flung open the front door, flourishing her keys in her hand.

"We found them. In the cupboard, next to the tea caddy. I remembered seeing them when I made tea before booking our flights to America this morning, and thinking, I must remember the keys are by the kettle. Then I must have put them away with the tea. I do that so often, these days. But, I guess, it's not every day you book flights for your daughter's wedding. Three weeks and we'll be in the States and I'll be giving my girl away. God, I can't believe it."

Simeon appeared behind her, grinning. He gesticulated into the air as if to say, 'what will we do with her'. Clare watched from below. Simeon was at ease with Gloria. She turned around and took Miranda's hand.

"About time. We're freezing."

"What a lovely day for it." Gloria put her hand through Simeon's arm. She started singing

"*Oh, what a beautiful morning. Oh, what a beautiful day. I've got this wonderful feeling*

Everything's going my way'. I'm so excited.

"Yippee," said Miranda, "Let's go." She tugged on Clare's hand.

Chapter 35

Blue, sunshine and black night. White sunshine. Now, milky vapour filled the aeroplane windows. Miranda sat back. She had expected to see the whole world flashing past like the pages of a book, but the window was dirty, and there was nothing to see except white.

"Only another half an hour, Miranda."

Clare's tone was flat and seemed to have been for ages. Miranda missed hearing the music in her sister's voice.

Rose stood out in the arrivals hall, her red hair piled high, green handbag on her arm, wearing a short white coat, an emerald green scarf, her stomach bulging with baby, Miranda heard Clare gave a little yelp. Gloria was hollering and waving.

"Rose, Rose."

Gloria picked up Miranda and sat her on the trolley of suitcases and she was pushed through the milling people, to Rose who hugged and kissed them all, though her tummy got in the way. Clare started crying. Gloria was laughing.

"Rose, you look like Grace Kelly."

"Gloria, that is the nicest thing you've ever said to me. Miranda, you brought Bongo!"

It was a long, straight black road and it seemed to go on forever.

"I need to go the toilet," said Miranda.

"We can stop at the Last Chance Café," said Rose.

"Is it really called the Last Chance Café?" asked Gloria.

At the café, Clare got out of the car. Mountains loomed all around them. Some rounded peaks were capped with snow, but others had pointed nibs of slate grey that scrawled their features across the deep blue sky. They rose, grey ridges, out of a still sea of green pines. The sky was so vast, so blue, it felt unreal. Nothing wavered. It was beautiful, but felt out of reach, as if it was behind glass. Clare put her hand on the roof of the station wagon, just to feel something solid. Gloria took Miranda into the Last Chance café to find the toilet.

"They call it the 'bathroom'. And get some coffees," Rose instructed. She got out of the driver's seat and went around to Clare.

"Stunning, isn't it?"

Clare shivered and pulled her Afghan tighter around her. It smelt of the coat pile at home.

"Unreal."

"Wait until you see the metropolis of Red Rock," said Rose. "Honestly, it's like living slap bang in a Western. They even have a rodeo. Thank God I'm pregnant, otherwise they'd have had me up on a horse lassoing cows."

"Who?"

"Finn's family."

"I can see you as a cow-girl,"

Rose humphed. "No Londoner worth her salt will be found lassoing cows. It is all very…American. You know, it makes me want to be more English than I am, just out of pig headedness. Ah, here they come. Good. We're late, and Americans are very prompt. Come on, everyone, let's get back on the road."

They all piled back into the station wagon, Clare and Miranda in the back, Rose and Gloria in the front.

"I'm hungry," said Miranda. "You should have seen the burgers in the café, nearly as tall the waitress. And they serve chips…"

"Fries," corrected Rose.

"Fries, on a separate dish."

"The burgers in the Red Rock Inn are gigantic too. You'll have to watch yourselves here, food portions are ridiculous.

"Drink your Coke, Miranda, that will fill the spot."

Gloria handed out beakers of coffee and a Coke for Miranda.

"She shouldn't have Coke," said Clare.

"She'll need it, to keep her going. The jet lag will kick in soon," said Rose.

"I can't wait to see cowboys," said Gloria.

"Sadly, the Rodeo isn't happening while you're here," said Rose.

Thank God, thought Clare. She could imagine Gloria trying to stay seated on a bucking bronco, wearing a suede and tassel jacket. Gloria had wanted to buy a cowgirl outfit to wear to the wedding. You're mother of the bride, Clare had told her, not a cow girl. Fortunately, Gloria had seen sense, and they had bought a smart, tasteful Fifties style wool skirt and long jacket, pale purple with a green trim.

"There's the pig racing track." Rose pointed at a low building around a track.

Miranda spurted Coke, "Wow, can we go?"

"I'm afraid, it's not the season, either. You'll all have to come back in the Spring, guys. However, we're off to Bear Tooth Cave for the pre-nuptial celebrations tomorrow. Maybe, we'll see a bear."

"At least, a tooth," said Gloria.

"Real bears?" asked Miranda in breathless awe."

Rose looked in the rear-view mirror at her little sister, leaning forward in avid interest, her face full of expectation. She wanted to show off America. But, at the same time, she didn't want to disappoint.

"I don't know, honey. I haven't seen one. Red Rock, Montana, the US of A is a great place, and I love it, but everything is slightly exaggerated."

"What do you mean, Rose," asked Gloria. "It is so beautiful. There is nothing exaggerated about those mountains."

"Yes," responded Rose, "but everything feels a little unreal, don't you think? It's like living in a dream."

"Well, at least you're sleeping beauty!" said Gloria

"Are you getting married in a bear cave?" asked Miranda

"No. I'm getting married in the prettiest little white Lutheran church. You are going to be flower girl, Miranda. I have chosen a beautiful posy of dried black roses for you to carry. They will match your hair which looks lovely, by the way, in that bob. You'll be pretty as a picture."

"Black roses and a Lutheran church. God knows what the world is coming to," commented Gloria with a sigh. "I never thought one of my daughters would be married in church, let alone a Lutheran church."

"I know," sighed Rose. "I'm doing it for Finn's dad, well, his new wife, Mel, really. She's done so much for us, for me, and she's quite big in the church, and it's no skin off my nose. In fact, it's such a pretty place to get married. So, keep the peace, Gloria."

Gloria turned to look at her eldest. Rose was blooming but she had also got a little fat. It was as if the baby had smeared itself across her face, tummy, boobs, chin, arms, thighs.

"Do I detect a ripple of irritation from you about the land of plenty, Rose?"

Rose swerved to the side of the road, stopped the engine, put her head on the steering wheel and started heaving with sobs. Clare leaned forward but was constrained by her seatbelts. She couldn't remember the last time she saw Rose cry. Gloria started to rub her back.

"Rose, is something wrong? Are they not treating you well? are you sure you want to go through with this. There's time to change your mind."

Rose turned and glared at Gloria.

"Jesus, Gloria, how can I change my mind? I'm getting married in three days. I love Finn. I'm pregnant. I live in America. For Christ's sake, it's probably just hormones or nerves, I just need a little encouragement. For God sake, you turn everything into a drama! I need some air."

Rose snapped off her seat belt, got out of the car door, and strode off up the road. Gloria and Clare stared after her.

"Well, that's more like the Rose, I know," said Gloria.

Clare went to get out of the car.

"Leave her," said Gloria. "I don't think there's anything you can say to her that will help. Give her five. I'll drive after her then."

They waited in silence. Clare wondered how Finn coped with Rose's tantrums. She wondered if Rose behaved the same in America as at home. Gloria got into the driving seat and followed Rose. She slowed up as she approached the white coated figure. Rose wasn't dressed for outdoor weather. She looked a folorn figure traipsing the highway. Gloria wound down the window, and said in an exaggerated American drawl,

"Hey, are we on the right road to Red Rock. We got a wedding to get to. A real special wedding." Gloria blew her a kiss. "I'm sorry, Rose."

Rose smiled. "Ignore me. It's definitely the hormones, I guess and having you all here. Makes me feel unsure of what I'm doing, like I'm playing a silly game. I keep having to remind myself this is real and when I do, I'm not sure it's for me. But I think that's just nerves." Rose patted her tummy. "Ok, let's go find some cowboys," she answered, and got in the passenger side, letting Gloria drive.

They drove into Red Rock slowly. The Main Street was wide and dusty. On either side of the road were wooden or brick two or three storey buildings, all different heights and colours, shapes and sizes. The pavement was raised, and the shops had different frontages, some with colourful awnings.

Pick-up trucks and station wagons were parked at right angles to the road. It was bright and busy. Miranda thought it was like Richard Scarry's Our Town.

"Wow, it's a busy place," commented Clare, glancing from side to side.

"Look, cowboys! Standing over there. See their hats? But I don't see horses. Shouldn't there be horses?" Miranda asked.

"Not these days, Honey. Look, there's Finn, outside the Red Rock Hotel."

Finn was leaning on a post, wearing his own cowboy hat. He smiled and waved as Gloria parked. He bounded over and threw open the passenger seat door, planted a kiss on Rose's cheek and, taking his hat off, stuck his head into the car.

"I thought you'd never arrive. The folks are already inside, having a drink. They're dying to meet you. Welcome! Did you have a good flight?"

Clare smiled and unsnapped her and Miranda's seat belts.

"Stiff and hungry. It's great to see you, Finn. Come on, Miranda, let's get out." They clambered out of the car and stretched their legs. Clare came around to Finn and kissed him.

"Congratulations."

Finn beamed. "Dandy, ain't it?" he said in an American drawl, "and I'm going to be a married man." He put his arm around Rose who had got out of the car. "Welcome, Gloria, or should I call you, Ma?"

"You'll do no such thing." Gloria looked around her. "Well, where have you brought us?"

"We can't wait to show you the place. What do you think so far?"

"It's very beautiful. And this," Gloria waved her hand at the town, "is like something out of Butch Cassidy and the Sundance Kid."

"Miranda, do you like it?" Finn knelt down. She stared into his friendly face, hat back on his head.

"Are you a cowboy now, Finn?"

Finn whooped and laughed. "Not really, Miranda. I am a newspaper man. Really, I should wear a trilby. Okay, let's go in and join Dad and Mel."

As Clare followed him and Rose in, holding Miranda's hand, she looked back. The light was fading. At the end of the street, the dark mountains rose, against navy sky. Stars were beginning to stutter into the light. The glow of the shop windows cast long stretching shadows. She looked at Gloria behind her. Gloria shrugged, raised her eyebrows and said

"I need a hot whiskey or is it bourbon here?"

"Mum, let's make it a wedding to remember. Let's make Rose happy."

"We need a drama then, don't we?" Gloria smiled at Clare, "but, I bet Rose is going to be on her best behaviour."

"Please, will you be too?"

After a slow start the next morning, and a breakfast of pancakes with maple syrup, Finn, Rose, Miranda, Clare and Gloria drove up to the Bear Tooth Hideaway in the woods and spent the day walking, eating, drinking and getting to know Finn's family who arrived in fits and starts across the afternoon. Finn's mum had flown in from London and Melissa's parents drove up with Finn's father and Mel from Red Rock in the early evening. A BBQ banquet was being staged in the main dining hall of the Hideaway in a mammoth log cabin with two huge open fireplaces, where flames wrapped themselves around tree trunks in a massive grate. There were black and brown sheep skin rugs scattered across the floor and Perspex cases of stuffed animals on the walls. On the deck outside, long trestle tables with red and white cloths were laden with towers of burgers and bowls of green salads. There were dishes of courgette, aubergines, peppers, coleslaw. In the centre of the yard, a big fire was burning in a pit. Their sleeping cabins were clustered nearby, in the trees.

"We can toast marsh mellows later," Rose told Miranda. "Now, I must go and practice my speech."

She left Clare and Miranda sitting on the bench outside on the veranda, wrapped up in thick shawls, Miranda swinging her little legs. They stared across the valley of dark shapes to the opposite ridge. A huge white circular moon stalked the tips of the trees themselves shrouded in black. The yard was cast in a shadowy silver light.

"So much black, gold and silver," said Miranda in awe, watching flames and sparks spurt out of the fire pit. "And in the fire, it's like the flames are trying to escape."

Clare put her arm around Miranda. "It's beautiful." She turned to Miranda. "Were you disappointed we didn't see a bear today?"

"I didn't expect to," said Miranda. "They hibernate in the winter."

"Oh yes."

There was a silence. Miranda was growing up, Clare was thinking. She looked at her little sister who turned and looked at her at the same time. They stared at each other and smiled. Clare wanted to say something poignant, profound, that Miranda would remember for the rest of her life. Instead, she asked

"Do you think Rose is happy?"

Miranda's small face flickered in the flame light. Miranda shrugged.

"Why wouldn't she be happy?" Miranda nestled into Clare. "I think we should all be happy. You, Rose, Clare, Mummy, and Margaret."

"What about Simeon?"

"You and mummy love Simeon, so he must be happy."

Clare said nothing.

After eating, the family gathered around the fire, toasting marsh mellows. Finn attached his Ipod to speakers, and soon people were dancing. There was a lot of whooping. One of Finn's brothers grabbed Clare and started twirling her. Gloria was dancing with Finn's dad. Mel was leaping around with Miranda. Rose and Finn were more gentile, given Rose's bump. Breathless, after half an hour's dancing, laughing and shaking her head, Clare sat back down on the bench. Rose joined her.

"This is amazing, Rose. Dancing in winter, in mountain woods, under a vast American starlit sky, what could be more romantic? Look at the shadows, leaping in the firelight. I wish Simeon could see this."

"These people, Clare," Rose waved her hands. "They're going to be my family, imagine that." Rose hesitated. "Why didn't Simeon come?"

"I don't know, he said he couldn't. Your family. That's a good thing, isn't it? Mind you, for a girl who couldn't stand family, you seem to be extending yours at a rate of knots."

"I know, everything has happened so quickly. I'm scared, Clare, it could go dreadfully wrong."

Rose slipped her hands across her bump.

"You mean with the baby? You're healthy, Rose. No drink, no fags. You've done everything right. I'm sure it will be okay."

"No, I mean with family. I can't quite comprehend that this is my new family. Everything is a little unreal. I feel like I am play acting. Oh, Clare, the baby's kicking. Quick, feel here."

Rose dragged Clare's hand to the side of her stomach. Clare felt the round of the bump and a movement in her palm.

"Oh my God, that's amazing, Rose. That's not play acting! Are you still worried about the genes?"

"No. I think where and how she is brought up is more important. However, I can't imagine rearing her here. I don't know the pitfalls, At least in London, I know the underground car parks, I know where the drugs are sold, I know the adolescent playgrounds. I know how life plays out. I would be able to protect her more."

"Her?"

"It's just a feeling."

They watched the dancing in silence. Soon, people were drifting off into trees, into log cabins, saying good night. Gloria came up and threw herself next to them.

"I am wrecked. It's suddenly hit me, the jet lag. I am going to take Miranda to bed. I think she has fallen asleep inside. Thanks for everything, Rose. You're taking on quite a family. They are lovely."

Rose didn't answer her. Silence hung. Clare watched Gloria wait for an answer. Were they all thinking the same thing, Clare wondered. Was this a perfect family? Is this how their life should have been? Gloria got up kissed Rose, then Clare. People came over to say good night and soon it was just Clare and Rose.

"Clare, what do I know about hunting, canoeing, horse-riding? Skiing. Her life is going to be so different to mine. Everything is rather over the top here, even the views. Sometimes I feel like I'm living behind glass and I want to smash it open and then all the beautiful stars will fall down. And, you know, Americans are quite conservative. Red Rock is republican. I'm scared of opening my mouth. Everything has to be just so, even down to the white picket fences. Sometimes, I feel like I cannot breathe, despite all this wonderful fresh air."

"Oh, Rose. What are you going to do?"

"Don't know yet. We'll see."

Finn came and offered his hand to Rose.

"Time to turn in?"

"I'll only be another few minutes. Promise."

"Keep warm. You're the last two up. Dampen the fires, will you?" He kissed Rose on the lips and Clare on the cheeks. They sat there in silence, watching the fire get drowsy.

"What's wrong with you, Clare?"

"Nothing."

"Why aren't you going to India, with Simeon?"

"Because I'm going to Thailand with Angie and Julie. Simeon's going through a lot. Splitting up with Minoo. Anyway, whoever heard of doing a gap year with your father?"

"You wanted to before. He's not like a normal father."

"No, he's not," Clare admitted. "He's pretty perfect. And I love him. But, I'm not sure it's right, Rose."

"What do you mean, 'right'. He's your Dad."

"He's a wonderful man. I can't tell you how I feel. It's a mix of stuff, pride, excitement. When he takes my hand, I'm so happy.

"Well, can't imagine any that with Old Racist Pieter. So, why aren't you happy? You've got everything you want."

"Have I? Anyway, I think I'm going to bed. I said I'd do the flowers in the church with Mel, tomorrow. They're not black roses, are they?"

"No", Rose sighed. "Black would have been nice."

"How do you dampen down a fire?"

Rose laughed. "I had to learn. The first time I poured water on it and it made a terrible mess. You rake it a little and then sprinkle drops on it. I'll do it."

"Good night, Rose. I'm happy for you. You'll learn together, you and your daughter."

"Good night, Clare. I'm happy for you. You're the one off for adventure in Thailand, then college. Your whole life ahead of you. That's pretty cool. You're lucky."

"I never thought you would be getting married and having a baby before me."

"Nor did I. Good night, Clare."

Chapter 36

Margaret and Gloria were chatting at the kitchen table. It was 4.30pm. and dark outside. Miranda was tucked up in the sitting room with Sasha, next door, watching a nature programme. They could hear the melodious tone of David Attenborough.

"Well," Gloria sipped at her coffee, "it's good to be home. It was such a fun week and the wedding was gorgeous, Margaret. Rose was disappointed you didn't come."

"It wasn't really my sort of thing, and I don't like flying. The short hop to Ireland is enough for me. I'm sure she didn't notice, with all the fancy people and excitement."

"You know, Finn's family kibboshed Rose's idea of a fancy-dress wedding, thank God. I think even Rose was relieved. She hadn't thought it through. She did insist on wearing green rather than cream, but she looked gorgeous, despite being eight months pregnant. Look, here's a photo of her and Finn coming out of the church. It was a very pretty, diminutive church which was charming. I think that church was the smallest I've ever seen. Lutheran. Honest to God." Gloria laughed, "no pun intended. My Rose getting married in a Lutheran church in America's Wild West. Well, yes, the wild west works. Doesn't she look fabulous?" Gloria swiped her phone. "Here is one of Rose, Miranda and Clare."

Margaret took the phone.

"Clare looks lovely, but rather sad."

Gloria looked closely at her phone.

"She does, doesn't she? Actually, Clare was quiet throughout the whole thing. I wondered if she was rueful of Rose in some way. You know how Clare loves babies. Mind you, we all cried like babies at the actual ceremony. I can't believe my Rose is married!"

"What are Finn's folks like?"

"Very nice, a little conservative in that American way. They all hunt and are very sporty but I guess that goes with the territory, I mean the Red Rock territory. It's amazingly beautiful. Mountains, rivers, forests. There's a glacial park. It's stunning. I can't see Rose fitting in long term but, for the moment, she seems to love it."

"Did Clare get off alright?"

"Yes, we put her on a flight to Denver yesterday or was it the day before? She seemed to be…stoic rather than excited. She had an overnight in Denver and was catching a flight to Thailand yesterday, arriving today, I think. I don't know. I'm confused. So many different time changes. I've had enough of travelling and airports for a while. I don't know what day it is, even."

"Well, I hope Clare enjoys herself. She needs a break."

"Yes," Gloria looked at Margaret, "The last year has been a bit of a roller coaster. For all of us. Thank you, Margaret, for being such a wonderful back up…for being here." Margaret stood up and began to clear away the few plates and cups.

"I've done nothing I don't normally do."

She rinsed out the dishes, left them to drain by the sink. Gloria continued

"Being here was enough. Anyway, hopefully, there will be a little less coming and going now. We can get into a routine."

Margaret took off her house coat and hung it on the peg behind the kitchen door.

"Right, well, I'm away upstairs, if that's ok."

The doorbell rang. Gloria jumped.

"Good Lord, I wonder who that could be."

"I'll see on my way out."

"Oh, I don't want to see anyone. Tell whomever it is to go away."

Gloria stretched in her chair. She heard Margaret talking to someone. She just wanted her bed. Hopefully, Margaret could get rid of them.

"Hello, Gloria, welcome home."

She turned around. It was Clive, slouching at the door. She hadn't seen him since they got back from South Africa.

Jesus, Gloria thought, I'd almost forgotten about Clive. Why doesn't he stand up straight? Gloria got up and kissed him on the cheek.

"Clive, how are you? I was just about to take a nap. You should have rung."

"I was passing. I wanted to find out how the wedding went and well, how you are. Also, I thought we might have a look at some photos of our South African trip. I got some printed. There are great ones of the Safari. Brought a bottle of wine, too"

"Oh, that's nice of you, Clive. But not now. Why don't you come around tomorrow night for supper? Simeon's coming too. We can show him and Miranda. Did you get any pictures of monkeys on the safari? Miranda loves monkeys"

"Gloria, I'd like to talk. About us. I mean, what's happening?"

"Happening? Nothing."

"Gloria, don't be obtuse. You know very well what I mean. Are we still an item? Are we going to get married!"

"Married! Jesus, I don't think so, Clive. We weren't such a good match. Everything has changed."

"What has changed?"

"Clive. We are the oldest friends and I love you. But didn't we go to South Africa to see how we got on and, well, it wasn't a huge success. I don't think we will work long term.

We're friends, Clive and I want to stay like that. Maybe we shouldn't push it. Come for dinner, tomorrow evening."

"With Simeon?"

Gloria looked at him.

"Oh, Clive. I'm sorry. I wanted to try but I should have known it wouldn't work. If it was going to work, it would have happened years ago."

"And it is working with Simeon? Is that what you mean."

Gloria forced herself to keep looking at Clive.

"I'm sorry, Clive. Please can we be friends. I don't want to lose you as a friend"

Clive looked at her. He straightened up.

"Jesus, Gloria, I can't believe that you are being so blind, selfish, and what is more, stupid. You must know Simeon is not for you."

"Clive!"

He turned away from her, took a deep breath, shook his head and turned.

"I'm going."

Miranda came in through the kitchen door, hugging Bongo.

"Mummy? Oh, hello Clive."

Clive crouched down to her.

"I'm sorry, Miranda. I shouldn't have raised my voice."
He looked up at Gloria, "I'm sorry, Gloria."

Gloria said nothing.

"Now Miranda," Clive continued, "tell me about the wedding. I'm just about to go but I do want to hear how Rose looked."

"She looked beautiful. Her dress was green and she wore a pointy hat like an elf, on top of all her hair. But she looked like an elf who had swallowed a football which had got stuck in its tummy."

"Hah! What a wonderful description. You're going to be a writer one day, Miranda. Well, if I come for supper tomorrow, will you tell me more then?" Miranda nodded. "And school. How is that?" Clive ruffled her hair.

"Fine, but I was on holiday in Red Rock, so I don't know," said Miranda and wriggled away from him. "Mummy, I'm going downstairs to play."

The following day Gloria woke up feeling fresher. She stretched. She must go for her run. She and Miranda would go to Sainsburys and buy food for dinner tonight for Simeon and Clive. Clive…honestly, she should never have agreed to them getting married. She didn't want to hurt him, but, if there was a chance with Simeon, she had to take it. Gloria looked out of the window. It was raining. She didn't want to run in the rain.

She would wake Miranda instead and they would have breakfast together. What time was it? Gloria looked across at the clock. Jesus, it was nearly noon. She leapt up, went into the kitchen and listened. There was silence. Miranda must still be asleep. On American time, still. She would make waffles and then go wake her up. Gloria switched on the radio and turned the grill on. She filled the kettle with water for tea and went downstairs to the playroom. Miranda wasn't there.

"Miranda?"

Gloria looked in Clare's room. Clare's bed had been slept in. Had Miranda slipped in there after Gloria had put her to bed last night?

"Miranda?"

Her voice echoed in the empty room. Gloria looked in the living room. It too was empty. She looked down the hall. The front door was open.

"My God!"

She rushed out and opened the house front door. The ivy rustled in the wind, but nothing else moved. No one was there. Bare branches were dripping, the road was shining. The cold wind whistled in. She shut the front door and opened the door to the flat upstairs.

"Margaret," she began to call. "Margaret!"

Margaret opened her flat door.

"Morning, Gloria. Are you looking for Miranda? She's up here."

"What is she doing up there?"

"You were asleep, so Miranda came up to me."

"I'm sorry. I was just so tired. She should have woken me."

"She's fine. She's playing with James. Come up."

Gloria climbed the stairs, pulling her dressing gown about her. She looked about the sitting room. It was lovely and homely. A fire was burning in the grate. The two children were playing on the floor.

"Oh! Margaret. I hope Miranda didn't wake you."

"No, we're early risers. Coffee?"

"No thanks, Margaret, it's kind of you, but I'll take Miranda and we'll go downstairs. I'm making waffles."

"I've had breakfast, mummy. We made porridge. Margaret said we could go to the park later."

Gloria felt as if she was the intruder, in her own house.

"Miranda, if you wake up, you must wake mummy. Not come and disturb Margaret."

"Margaret said I could come up whenever I want. I like it here."

"Of course, you can, sweetie. James and I are always pleased to see you."

"No, you can't," snapped Gloria. "Margaret needs her peace. Now come on, Miranda, we have things to do. I want to go shopping. Remember Simeon and Clive are coming over. You can help me. It will be fun."

Miranda looked at Margaret.

"Miranda, we'll go to the park after school tomorrow. Anyway, it's still raining. You go and help your mum. Say goodbye to James."

"Margaret, I know you've been great with the girls but, you know, I can look after my daughter."

"Of course, Gloria. It's just that Miranda is used to coming up here."

"This is not her home, Margaret. She is not to come up here unless it is agreed by me, in advance."

Margaret said nothing.

"Come on, Miranda. Now."

Margaret followed them to the flat door. Who did Gloria think she was, so high and mighty? If she kept that up, she might find herself looking for another lodger, she thought to herself. It was as much as she could do to not slam the door after her.

"See you later, Miranda, be good for mummy," called out Margaret. Hah, she knew that would kill Gloria.

Miranda didn't want to go shopping but Gloria was determined to make it an outing and promised Miranda a Big Mac for lunch.

"Clare says I shouldn't eat Big Macs."

"Clare isn't here, is she? Come on, Miranda."

"Why can't I play upstairs with Margaret and James?"

"You can't be with Margaret all the time. She needs some time with James alone. She doesn't want you taking up her afternoon. It's not fair on Margaret. Come on now. We'll cook a lovely dinner. What about shepherd's pie? You love shepherd's pie. And salad, and jelly and ice cream. Won't that be nice? You can ride in the trolley."

"Rose says I'm too big for the trolley."

"Well, Rose isn't here either, is she? Come on. We have to go."

"I don't want to go."

"Miranda, you have to. Stop this."

Gloria picked up Miranda who started to wrestle. Gloria marched out of the house and gripping Miranda tight in one arm, rooted for her car keys in her pocket. It was pelting rain. Miranda started screaming. It was loud, and high pitched. Gloria had never heard her make such a noise.

"Miranda! Stop this."

Miranda was flailing in her arms and kicking and hitting. She was spitting screams. Her face was contorted. Gloria slapped her. It shocked Miranda into silence. The rain was drilling into both of them. It poured off Miranda's face. Gloria prayed no one was watching.

"Miranda! get into the car. We're getting soaked." Gloria gasped. But Miranda started again. She pinched Gloria's arm. Gloria nearly hit her again but managed to control herself.

"Miranda, stop this right now." She opened the car door and tried to stuff Miranda's damp but rigid poker body into the car seat. She didn't dare look around her. She was scared neighbours would be at the windows. She knew Margaret would be.

"Miranda! What is wrong with you?"

She forced Miranda's body into the seat and clasped the lock. It was amazing how strong the child was.

"Now, stay there and calm down. I'm going to get shopping bags."

Gloria shut the car door and ran back up the steps to the house. She could hear Miranda sobbing. She felt like crying herself. Miranda had never acted like this before. Gloria got the shopping bags and went back out into the pouring rain to the car, holding them over her head. Mr Arlen was coming out of his house. She waved and got in. Aside from the rain, it was silent. She looked round at Miranda. She was fast asleep. Gloria bent her head on the steering wheel. After a few seconds, she straightened up.

After dragging Miranda around the supermarket, there wasn't time to stop at McDonalds and, though she had calmed down, Gloria didn't feel Miranda deserved a treat. She drove right past it. The big bright M shone out through the dripping light.

"You've driven past McDonalds!"

"Clare was right…you shouldn't eat Big Macs and we haven't time, not if I have to make jelly like you want. Jelly needs time to set. I bought jammie doughnuts, you can have one for your tea while you watch TV and I make the dinner."

"But you promised, and I promised Bongo and Bongo is sick."

"Bongo? Oh, your Beanie Baby. What's wrong with him?"

"He has a tummy ache."

"Well, a Big Mac won't help and a doughnut will just make him sticky. He probably just needs a cuddle. God, will it ever stop raining. Why did we ever come back to this godforsaken country? Look at it!"

Suddenly the hammering of rain on the car roof was ferocious. The windscreen wipers were blasting water across her windscreen. Rain was leaping on the street. It was so powerful, it leapt a foot back up the moment it landed on the road. It pummelled the car.

"I'm pulling over. It's dangerous."

Gloria sat staring out of the windscreen. No-one was on the street. There was a green tinge to the world. No cars, no people. Rain bounced off every surface and she could hear it on the roof but, aside from that, it was silent, spooky.

"Look at it! I always feel weather like this is a bad omen."

There was no answer. Gloria turned and looked at Miranda. She was asleep again. She had always gone to sleep in the face of adversity. Gloria suddenly felt a moment of panic. She had never really been on her own with Miranda. She waited for it to lighten and slowly drove home. After she had Miranda settled in front of the TV under a blanket with Bongo, a doughnut and a cup of hot milk, Gloria went into the kitchen. She poured herself a large glass of white wine. It was the last bottle from South Africa, a chenin blanc. The chef's glass of wine. She toasted the rain. It was her favourite glass, the chef's glass, while she prepared dinner. What was wrong with Miranda? All the recent upheaval? The weather? She stared out the kitchen window. When would it stop? The rain. She had never seen that behaviour from Miranda. Rose, yes. But Miranda, and Clare, never. She knocked back her wine and started chopping onions.

Chapter 37

At five o'clock the doorbell went, Gloria answered it, hoping it was Simeon. Clive stood there. He was wearing a plastic raincoat that was swarming with water. Rivulets ran everywhere. His hair dripped into his face. He looked miserable.

"Yuck, come in and hang that coat on my shower rail. I've never seen such rain. What happened to your key?"

"I left it at home. I'll give it to you next time. Yes, I am drenched."

"Quick, come in and put that in the bathroom, you are dripping over the floor. You can towel your hair dry in there."

She handed him a glass of wine when he appeared back at the kitchen door with a towel around his shoulders. Bits of his hair stood up on end where he had rubbed it dry.

"I came early because I wanted a quick chat before Simeon comes, just to clarify things," Clive said after taking a sip. "Nice wine. Is this what we brought back?"

Gloria nodded.

"Last bottle."

Clive nodded.

"Gloria, maybe, South Africa didn't work out quite as we hoped, though I think we got on better than you make out.

But, whatever, I don't think we should throw away a good friendship. Let's give ourselves time, not make snap decisions."

"I didn't say I wanted to throw our friendship away. I said the opposite. I want to keep it."

"Gloria, do you still want a baby."

"What I don't want is you coming around with a hang dog expression."

"I just want your word that should you ever think we could be happy together, you won't dismiss the idea out of pride. I know how you feel about Simeon, but if that doesn't work for you, I want you to know, I'm here."

"Well, if you can handle that, perfect. Friends it is. Pour me another glass. We'll finish the bottle, after all it is ours."

The front doorbell rang.

"That's Simeon," Gloria continued. "Clive, I want to tell you before he comes in that Simeon will be renting a room downstairs as from next week. It turns out that he is not getting married so now he needs somewhere to live. I hope that isn't going to be a problem for you, for us."

Clive almost laughed. Gloria was so transparent.

Gloria sat in her usual place at head of table. She had her hair up, and strands tumbled around her face which was slightly flushed, probably the wine, Clive thought. Conversation was awkward. Gloria was trying to regale funny stories about Red Rock, but no one seemed to be in the right humour. Her skin still looked healthy and tanned, but something, probably all the travel, he thought, was taking its toll. Clive noticed she was filling out the navy Abercombie sweat shirt she was wearing. Opposite him, Miranda also looked exhausted. She pushed the food around on her plate. Her hair, still wet from her bath, hung in damp ringlets about her shoulders, leaving damp patches on the red Little Princess dressing gown she was wearing.

Simeon, sitting next to Miranda, saw Clive looking at her. He pushed back his chair and lifted Miranda up into his arms.

"Bed for you, Monkey. You can't fall asleep at the table."

Gloria made a move. "No, it's alright, Gloria, I'll tuck her up. I won't be long. Come on, sweetie pie. We'll read a Babar story."

Miranda put her arms around his neck and rested her head and closed her eyes.

"She hasn't eaten much," Gloria worried.

"She's exhausted."

"Good night, darling."

Miranda murmured. Clive and Gloria watched Simeon carry her out.

"Gloria, is it a good idea? Simeon moving in, I mean? Doesn't Miranda need a little time to get used to him without him being in the house?"

"I'm sure she'll be fine. Simeon is her father after all." Clive shrugged.

"Clive. I've always been honest about how I feel about Simeon."

Clive nodded.

"I hope you know what you're doing, Gloria."

"Oh, for God's sake, Clive, stop."

Clive pushed his chair back.

"Ok, I had better go. I'll give you a shout later in the week. Say good night to Simeon for me and thanks for the Shepherd's pie. It was lovely."

"There's jelly and ice cream, I made it 'specially for Miranda. You don't want any?"

"No, no thanks, Gloria."

He collected his raincoat from the bathroom. Putting it on, he said

"At least it doesn't seem so vile outside now."

Gloria's mobile went off. She pulled it from her pocket and looked down to see who it was.

"It's Rose. Hello darling, how are you?"

Simeon came upstairs.

"You off, Clive?" asked Simeon, quietly so as not to disturb Gloria's conversation.

"Yep, Monday tomorrow, and I have a bit of marking to do. Good luck, Simeon." He held out his hand. Then he looked across to Gloria to salute goodbye. She held up the palm of her hand, smiling, indicating that he should wait.

"I don't believe it," she said to Rose.

Simeon and Clive looked at each other. It struck Clive that they were both wondering what richter scale of drama this might prove to be, and whether it was good or bad.

"A baby girl! That is wonderful. Are you both okay? Where are you?"

Gloria waved her phone away from her and squealed an aside.

"Rose has had a baby girl. Open the bubbly. It's in the fridge. Oh my God, I'm a grandmother."

She returned to the phone call. "How much did she weigh? Are you're both fine? Eight pounds! When did you go into labour?"

Clive went to the fridge and got a bottle of pro-secco. He waved it in front of Gloria. She nodded, her eyes shining.

"Have you decided on a name? Clara Rose? That's lovely, very sweet. Have you told Clare? Oh, Rose, this is wonderful." They watched her listen while Rose talked.

"Ok. Listen, I'll call you tomorrow. Send my love to Finn. I am so excited! Email me photos. I'll let you go, congratulations, baby."

Rose clicked her phone off and looked triumphantly at Simeon and Clive.

"I have a grand-daughter! Jesus. Isn't that wonderful? Named after her mother and aunt, Clara Rose. Very American don't you think? Clive, you must stay and have a celebratory glass."

Clive divested himself of his wet coat and hung it on the kitchen door.

"That's wonderful. Congratulations. Clara Rose? I like it."

"Gloria would have been nice, wouldn't it?"

She watched them look at her, aghast.

"I am only joking! Isn't this wonderful? Clara Rose is fine. The birth was fine. Rose had no gas and air. Typical Rose. She was born in only seven hours. Oh, my goodness, how perfect.

"It's great news," said Simeon.

"It is, isn't it? Gosh, I don't know what to do now. I wish I was there."

Clive toasted her "To the grandmother and new mother!"

They drank. Gloria turned to Simeon.

"Talking of good news, Simeon, did you get the research contract?"

"I did, but my news pales into insignificance in comparison."

"What research is that?" asked Clive.

"It's London School of Economics and Mumbai University research project. I've been given a nine month contract to research new Indian migrants in Britain. Young Indians come over to England on student visas and then work in appalling conditions in order to send money home. They are the new 'Irish', except they are even more exploited than the Irish."

"Well done, congratulations, Simeon. Well, let's toast…what? Good jobs and happy families!"

Gloria raised her glass again.

"To Rose, Simeon and Clara Rose," said Clive. "Now, I really do have to go into that dark night. Good luck, Simeon. Gloria, text me Rose and Finn's address in Red Rock. I'd like to send my congratulations."

Simeon watched him go, sat down and then stretched back in his chair.

"Congratulations, Gloria. To the grandmother." He raised his glass. "Thank God, I'm not a grandfather yet… am I?" He smiled. "You have a way of springing these things on me." Gloria laughed.

"No, though you never know with Clare. Don't you think she is the family type? Congratulations to you, about the work."

"Yes, I'm delighted. It provides me with a direction. I was feeling banjaxed after…everything recently. It buys me time, and it will be interesting.

"Are you sure it's okay if I lodge here for a while? It's a nuisance that my lease is up. It'll only be a couple of weeks.

"Of course. Take as long as you want."

"I just wanted to know that I had this contract before I look for something longer term. I can do that now."

"No, stay as long as you like. I'll appreciate the company, and it's an opportunity for you to get to know Miranda."

Simeon was quiet for a minute.

"No, I'll try to find somewhere quickly."

"It's fine. Stop fussing, Simeon. I feel so excited, here I am, a grandmother! At such a young age!"

Gloria looked at him, raised her eyebrows, clinked glasses again, lowered her eyes and took a sip from her glass.

"It's great. Right, I too am setting into that dark night."

"Are you leaving me on my own to celebrate? Please, don't."

"Yes. I've got to go. I've an important meeting tomorrow. Thanks for supper. Tell Miranda I'll see her next week. She didn't even wake up when I put her down. I'd say she is exhausted."

"Oh, Simeon, I meant to tell you. Miranda had a terrible temper tantrum today. I've never seen her behave like that before. I was shocked."

"I'm sure she is just a little overwhelmed. There's been a lot going on. She's just come back from a week in Red Rock at her sister's wedding, Clare is in Thailand, she's discovered she has a father, she's started school, and now she's an aunt. That is a lot to contend with. I'm sure she is just exhausted. Maybe keep her at home tomorrow, let her sleep."

"Yes, an aunt! I can't wait to tell her!"

Simeon put on his hat and coat.

"Poor child! Goodnight. Don't celebrate too much."

Gloria blew him a kiss and came with him to the front door. He gave her a kiss, perched his hat on his head. She watched him go down the steps and got ready to wave as he turned up the street but he didn't look back. He looked like an American gangster in the orange streetlight, with rain sparking down on him. She waited until he disappeared and went back in. She poured herself another glass and looked around her. Ugh, what a mess, she thought. I'll do it in the morning. She took her glass of bubbly to bed. Hum, she thought, getting undressed. I'll have to play Simeon slowly. A sudden clap of thunder startled her. Gloria tried turning on the bedroom TV to distract herself but watching TV when you had just become a grandmother seemed too trivial and lonely. She wanted to tell someone about Clara Rose. What about Margaret? Gloria remembered Margaret's cool tone from the morning. Maybe not, and it was after ten. She would wake Miranda. After all, she had just become an Aunt. She would want to know. Gloria put on her stripy dressing gown and padded downstairs to the playroom. Simeon had left the bedside lamp on. Miranda's dark head of glossy hair was spread out on the pillow. She lay on her back, her arms spread out, an angelic image of peace. Gloria was taken aback. Miranda's pale face glowed with innocence and well-being. She bent down to look closely. She had never seen Miranda so beautiful, innocent, so peaceful. Gloria crept out of the room feeling folorn. She didn't know why.

Chapter 38

The angle-poise lamp above Rose's hospital bed sharpened Rose's facial features and made her look pale.

"Hey Rose, it's the middle of the night, are you okay?"

Rose nodded and beamed into the camera

"Look."

Clare saw a hospital room swerve round and in the next second she was looking at a tiny scrawny face, full of wrinkles and blotches

"Oh Rose! You had it! Wow, amazing. What is it?"

Rose's disembodied voice laughed.

"A baby!"

"You know what I mean, a boy or a girl?"

"A girl! She's gorgeous."

The room flew round again and Clare was looking back at Rose

"Clara Rose. I've called her Clara Rose after you and me both, Clare."

"Oh, Rose. I wish I was there."

Clare's stomach turned. She wanted to be there, yet at the same time, she was glad she wasn't.

"I wish you were too. I even wish Gloria was here. It feels strange not having anyone here."

"Isn't Finn with you?"

"Of course, he's outside now phoning his family members. She was born two hours ago."

"There you are in Red Rock and here I am in Thailand. Oh, Rose"

"Show me where you are."

Rose couldn't see much. Darkness. Clare's face came back. Rose thought she looked weary.

"How was the birth?" Clare asked.

"A doddle. Nothing to it. She popped out in two hours. The doctors were amazed. It seems I'm a natural mother. Haha. Who would have thought? What do you think of Clara Rose as a name?"

"It's a beautiful name. I feel proud. Show me her again."

The room swivelled round again. Clare studied the face. Her niece. Thousands of miles away. It didn't seem real.

"How much did she weigh?"

"Eight pounds."

The room turned again. Rose came back into view. They stared at each other.

"I'm in shock," said Rose. "So, how are you? Having a good time?"

"Yep, fine. Lovely beaches. We've visited a million temples already, been to a national park. It is very beautiful.

We're going on a river trip for a couple of days so I don't know if I'll be able skype. Wifi can be a little patchy."

"You don't sound over enthused."

"It gets a bit tiring, traipsing around. Angie and Julie aren't keen on the food and so always want to eat in Western places. We ended up in MacDonalds tonight."

"Any boys?"

"Not really. Have you told Gloria about Clara Rose?"

"Yep, over the phone. She sounded over the moon and a little drunk."

"Clara Rose is lovely, Rose."

There was a further hesitant, awkward silence.

"Ok. Well, Clare, I'll let you go grab some sleep."

"Ok. Let's talk soon. I'll skype when I'm back from the river cruise. How is everyone at home?"

"I didn't ask, but I assume fine. Gloria clearly had people with her when I rang. But I don't know."

"Any news of Simeon or Clive?"

"No, I was caught up in my own news."

"Of course. I just wondered."

"Good night, Clare. Look after yourself."

"Bye, Rose, and send my congratulations to Finn too. Love you."

Rose clicked on the red skype button, frowning. The conversation was a little awkward. She thought Clare would have been more excited. It's difficult across such distances, she thought. Clara Rose began to snuffle. Rose leaned over and picked her up.

"Don't worry, little one, Clare'll love you when she sees you."

Chapter 39

Miranda was thrilled when Gloria told her about the Clara Rose the next morning. It had stopped raining, but it was cold. Miranda had her cream furry hoody blanket wrapped around her with the hood pulled up. She looked like a little Eskimo.

"A real baby? Can I see her?"

"It's the middle of the night now in Red Rock. We'll skype later this afternoon. But first, Miranda, I have an idea. Would you like to move into Rose's bedroom?"

"Doesn't Rose want it anymore?"

"Well, she'll come and visit but she lives in America now, with Finn. Her room will be too small for her and Clara Rose."

"Won't Clare want it?"

"Clare has her own room. No. If you want Rose's room, Miranda, it's yours."

Miranda cut up her waffle into four and dipped it into the pool of tomato sauce. She looked up at Gloria.

"Am I not going to school today?"

"No, I think you could do with the rest. Back to school tomorrow. We could move your room, if you like?"

Miranda put a forkful of waffle into her mouth.

"I can eat with a knife and fork now."

"I know, darling. Finish your breakfast and we'll get dressed. Then, we will ask Margaret to help us move your things? Then we can skype and see Clara Rose.

"Will all my Beanie Babies fit into Rose's bedroom?"

"You'll be able to have them in bed with you! Rose has a double bed. Under those lovely moon and stars. It is so pretty. And you'll be able to do your homework at the white table."

"It's dark in Rose's room. I like the playroom."

"Miranda, you need privacy. The playroom is the way into the garden. You don't want people marching through your room."

"I don't mind. It's only Clare and Rose, and their friends."

"Well, we need the playroom now for something else."

"what for?"

Gloria got up from the table and began to add the breakfast plates to the dishwasher. She turned around to look at Miranda who stared up at her, her head slightly cocked. Gloria had an uncomfortable feeling that Miranda knew exactly what she was going to say.

"A guest room for people to stay in. Simeon is coming to stay, Miranda. Your daddy will be living with us for a while."

"I want Clare to live with us. I miss Clare."

Gloria swept over to Miranda and kneeled at her chair, giving her a big hug.

"We all miss Clare, darling. But she will be back soon. She's on holiday."

"Can we skype Clare too? This afternoon?"

"Yes, though she's ahead of us. So, if we skype about 2ish it will be early evening, so we might get her then. In the meantime, let's go shopping and get a new lamp and duvet cover for your new room and some bookshelves. Maybe Simeon will put them up for us."

"Do I have to go to school tomorrow?"

"Yes, but you'll have so much to tell them…all about Rose's wedding in Red Rock and your new room."

"I don't want to go to school"

"Why not?"

Miranda shrugged

"I don't like it."

Gloria hugged Miranda again

"Why don't you like it?"

Miranda shrugged.

"Who is your best friend?"

"Michael."

"Michael?"

"He has a pet mouse."

"Really? How exciting."

"He keeps it in his pocket."

"I don't think that is allowed, Miranda. You better tell him. So why don't you like school?"

"I just don't. I prefer to be here."

"Well, Miranda, everyone has to go to school. It's the way of the world. Right, let's get a move on. I want to get the playroom sorted for Simeon."

"Mummy?"

"Yes."

"Has Simeon sent Clare away?"

"Miranda, of course not. Why do you think that?"

"Because he made Clare sad."

"What a funny thing to say. Clare loves Simeon, Miranda. Don't you like him?"

Miranda nodded.

"Yes."

"Simeon is a good man, Miranda. He is kind and considerate. He would do anything for you. You are lucky to have him for a father. You will see."

"I do see, mummy. I just wish Clare was home. And Rose. Everything feels the wrong shape."

"Oh, sweetie, they will be home soon. Maybe Christmas we'll all be together. You, me, Simeon, Clare, Rose and Clara Rose. In the meantime, you'll just have to put up with me."

Miranda got down from her chair.

"Can I go and see Margaret?"

"Yes, but don't bother her."

Miranda ran off and opened the front door. Gloria looked after her. What did she mean, Simeon made Clare sad?"

Chapter 40

As Simeon was packing up his flat his phone went. He had given the zookeeper his mobile number but was still surprised to see 'zoo keeper' come up as caller ID.

"Is that Miranda's father?"

Simeon was taken aback by the title,

"Yes, Simeon here."

"Sorry to disturb you but the zoo is having a Monkey Tea Party on Saturday. I thought of Miranda and wondered if she wanted to come along. She could bring a friend too. The tea parties are a lot of fun. The monkeys wear clothes and hats and are given a lovely dinner of bananas and nuts and presents to open and play with. It's a mad house for a couple of hours."

"That is very kind of you to think of Miranda, and call like this. She'll be thrilled."

Simeon decided to call around that afternoon to Gloria's to drop some stuff off and tell Miranda about the monkey party. She would be delighted.

Gloria let him in.

"We're skyping Clare. Come and say hello."

Simeon crouched down next to Miranda in front of the computer

"Clare! How are you? Wow, you look fabulous, you've got a great colour. How do you feel about being an aunt?"

Clare smiled. Now that her hair was away from her face, Simeon noticed how beautiful her bone structure was. He felt himself puff up with pride.

"Hello, Simeon. What are you doing there?"

"I've just come to tell Miranda that I'm taking her to a monkey's tea party at the zoo on Saturday. We've got a special invitation from the zoo keeper."

"A monkey party!" Miranda squealed, "What's a monkey tea party?"

"It's a tea party with monkeys. The monkeys wear hats, sit around a table, eat lots of bananas and nuts and have fun."

"Do I get to sit with the monkeys?"

"I think so. I'm not sure. We'll find out. And you can bring a friend."

Miranda's face fell just slightly.

"Wow, that's really exciting, Miranda," said Clare. "Ask that boy who keeps a mouse in his pocket, Michael, did you say his name was?"

Miranda beamed again.

"Oh yes." She jumped up and down on the couch. "When is the party?"

"Next Saturday!"

Simeon looked back at the screen. Clare stared straight at him. He wondered what she was thinking.

"How exciting, Miranda," Clare said. "Lucky you."

"So, Clare, how are you?" he said. "All going well? Have you seen Clara Rose?"

"Yes, on skype. She's beautiful. How are you?"

Clare's voice was level, but her usual warm timbre was absent.

"Fine, fine."

There was a moment's awkward silence. He wondered if Gloria had told her he was staying there.

"I hear Miranda has moved into Rose's room," said Clare. "All very exciting."

"Simeon is moving into the playroom," said Miranda.

The silence told Simeon Clare had not known.

"Just staying until I can get a place, which won't be very long," said Simeon.

"That's nice," said Clare. "I'm sure Gloria is delighted. Well, I'm glad everything is going well." She turned around to face a door behind her, and called, 'coming'. She turned back, "Sorry, guys, I can hear Angie call me. Miranda, I love you lots and lots, enjoy those monkeys."

"Hey, I haven't had a chance to talk to you," said Gloria. "I was just making Simeon a coffee. Don't go, I want to know if you can you come back for Christmas? Please. Rose is thinking of bringing Clara Rose. We could all be together. Think about it? Then maybe you could go to India in the New Year."

"India! Why would I go to India? If Rose is coming back with Clara Rose, it could be a little cramped for Christmas, particularly if she brings Finn. Anyway, I've only been here a couple of weeks."

"By Christmas, it will be nearly two months. You'll be ready to come home," said Gloria.

"Clare, you can sleep with me," said Miranda, "and you can tell me stories like you used to."

Clare put her hand to the screen, as if to touch Miranda.

"That would be lovely, Miranda. Now, I've really got to go. Angie's going mad. Love you, bye."

They saw Clare lean forward, press something and disappear. Miranda started crying. Simeon and Gloria looked at each other. Simeon picked her up.

"Come on, Miranda. Why the tears? We're going to a monkey tea party!"

"I wish Clare could come to the tea party."

"Clare does seem upset," said Gloria. "Something is not right. Do you have any idea, Simeon, what is upsetting her?"

"I'm not sure," said Simeon, thoughtfully. "Anyway, Monkey Miranda, are you going to show me your new room? Is it tidy? I want to see it at its best."

"I've got a new lamp, new bookshelves and a special hammock for all my Beanie Babies. We went shopping this morning." Miranda danced out of the room. "I'll get it all ready for you to see. Wait 'til I call."

"Ok, but don't be long."

Simeon turned to Gloria.

"Gloria, you must heed Miranda more. She understands more than you think."

"Oh, she's used to how we are. I'm more worried about Clare. She has not been herself for longer than I remember. Do you have any idea what might be wrong?"

"I don't know, but it could be possible that she is in love."

Gloria took a step back and laughed.

"In love? She'd have told me. Who could she possibly be in love with?"

"Possibly with me."

"With you? What do you mean? Why would you say that?"

"I'm not sure. Maybe I'm wrong. It's just that... it got strange between us. I tried to be affectionate and interested and well, I was affectionate and interested. Maybe she got the wrong idea. Both of us got a lot of pleasure being together. I loved looking at her, feeling her on my arm and maybe she took it the wrong way. In fact, I began to feel confused myself. It was why I withdrew for a bit, to get my head around it."

"You flirted with your own daughter?"

"Gloria, of course not. I didn't see it as that. Try to understand. I didn't know how to behave with her. Miranda was suspicious of me and I felt inadequate. However, I could relate to Clare, her being older. Yes, I think Clare and I fell in love. I don't mean romantically. We responded to something in each other. I think Miranda may have sensed it because when I'm with you and Miranda, our relationship feels easier, natural almost. You provide me with cues. Clare responded to me in a more grown up way I understood. I felt I was building a proper relationship. It was meaningful."

"What do you mean, 'grown up'?"

"Just that. Clare and I enjoyed being together. It was exciting. We talked, explored ideas. I suppose, it did feel a bit like a love affair. There was that frisson, almost. Actually, it was you saying that you fell in love with me when I told you about being described as a 'monkey god' by my mum that got me thinking."

Gloria felt her face blanche. A surge of anger rose from her belly.

"For God's sake, Simeon!"

Gloria wanted to punch him and also felt a shoot of jealousy. Jesus, she how could she feel jealous of her daughter? Miranda called up,

"I'm ready. Come and see my new room"

"Coming now," shouted Simeon.

"All this is completely absurd. Are you the reason Clare ran away to Thailand so suddenly? Are you what's making her so unhappy! I don't believe it. Jesus, what about me and how I feel? What a ridiculous situation. Shit. It's disgusting. Simeon, you better go! Get out."

Gloria steamed out of the room. Simeon heard her bedroom door slam. He closed his eyes, thought for a moment and went downstairs. Miranda was standing on the bottom step looking up. She looks such an angel, he thought, an angel amongst the madness.

"Where's mummy?" Miranda asked. "Has something happened?"

"She's got a headache and gone to lie down. Now, sweetie pie, show me your room. I saw a beautiful monkey mobile in Covent Garden. Maybe I could get it for you for Christmas."

Chapter 41

Simeon found a B&B in Victoria. From the window, he watched the London traffic on Vauxhall Road. What a mess!

Dear Clare,

I am so sorry. It seems I did not know how to be a father, so suddenly. I knew only how to relate to a beautiful young woman. On our walks and trips, I loved our discussions and exploring ideas. I realised when you and I had dinner that night in the Camden Brasserie that something irregular was happening and I didn't know what to do. Suddenly, I felt an emotion that was a little overwhelming. That is why I didn't contact you. I needed to think. I needed to work out what was going on. It didn't occur to me how it would upset you, Clare, please forgive me, I am truly sorry.

I am not moving into the house. I explained to Gloria why I think you are upset. She is furious, obviously. Clare. You have not done anything wron,. I promise. Clare, we will work everything out as it should be, as father and daughter. I am hoping you will come home to London for Christmas and we can talk. I think Rose is bringing Clara Rose over. It would be wonderful for her too to have you here. Clare, always. Simeon.

Ps please forgive me. Please take my calls. I do want to talk to you.

Clare wept as she read Simeon's email. There was something between them. She hadn't been wrong.

It was dark, always dark when she skyped Rose. On the wooden veranda that was beginning to become home, Clare was surrounded by mountains, seas, bush, and darkness but it smelt fetid. It was strange, she thought, how in contrast, Rose was always in a bright modern light in Red Rock, in the sunshine, against the white of the walls, shiny counters. Rose vibrated light.

"Come to London for Christmas, Clare. I am so desperate for you to meet Clara Rose. There is so much going on. I need to talk to you."

"What is going on?"

"It's like living on a film set here. I feel that I am in the middle of some show. It reminds me of that film with whatshisname, you know the one, where his life is in fact a televised series."

"The Truman Show."

"Yes. Anyway, I'm arriving in London on the 15th December. Please come."

"Is Finn going?"

"No, he has to work."

"Isn't he upset at you not being there for Christmas?"

"No, we discussed it. He's sad he won't be with Clara Rose, but he understands I have to come home, and she won't remember!"

"Well, Angie, Julie and I have booked into a moon party celebration on the 15th of December…

"Really? What actually happens at those?"

"The beach is lit up with lovely lanterns, and people party. I don't know, I haven't been to one yet."

"Well, fly back straight after so you can be there for Christmas."

"Gloria's begging for me to come back too. I never thought I'd see the day when Rose Van Standen thought we could have one big, happy family Christmas. Has Gloria invited Simeon?"

"Yes, Simeon is coming for lunch. And Clive, and Miranda will be so happy to see you. She misses you so much."

"I miss Miranda. But, I don't know if I can face it, Rose."

"Face what? Clare, I just want you to meet Clara Rose, my baby, your niece. Are you not interested at all?"

"Of course, I am. Let me think about it. I'll look into flights. But if I go home, I'll have to think about what I will do for the rest of my gap year. I can't come back."

"You can work in The Favourite. Get more money. Go to India. Hasn't Simeon got a new job? Gloria was telling me. He can fork out. Have you spoken to Simeon?"

"No. I don't know what to say."

"What do you mean you don't know what to say? 'Hello dad, can you lend me some money, I want to go travelling'. Having got a dad, you might as well milk him!"

"Rose, you don't understand."

"Don't understand what? Did something happen?"

"What do you mean, something?"

"I don't know, you were as happy as Larry in the summer, I was jealous, and then suddenly you wouldn't talk about him anymore and ran away to Thailand. At the wedding you were...I don't know. Something was wrong. What happened between you?"

"I just realised I needed to think about this father business. It all got a bit too much for me."

"What do you mean?"

"Rose, I know this sounds odd, but Simeon and I, I think we fell in love. It's why I left."

"In love? What do you mean?"

"In love. We fell in love. I thought it was just me, but I got an email from him saying he felt the same."

"How can you be in love, Clare, he's your father for God's sake."

"I know."

"Clare, of course, you're not in love and I'm sure he's not in love with you. It's ridiculous!"

"Rose!"

"What do you even mean, in love?"

"I don't know. I got so confused. He's one of the reasons I came here, particularly when he was with Gloria. I couldn't cope."

"With Gloria? What do you mean with Gloria? He's not with Gloria, is he? What's going on? You haven't had sex with him, have you? Oh Jesus. If you've had sex, it's child abuse."

"Rose. Of course, we haven't had sex, but I love him, for God's sake. He loves me. We are going to have to talk it out. He said so. It's not, like, gross. You don't understand."

"Clare, he's your father. Listen, just book flights and we can sort this out. You should go to the police."

"Police! Typical over reaction, Rose, and don't tell Gloria. You know how she feels about Simeon. It would really blow up then, her precious Simeon loving me."

"Just book tickets home, Clare."

"You promise you won't say anything to Gloria?"

"Okay! Just book tickets. I just want to see you and I want you to meet Clara Rose."

"I'll sort it out, I will. I promise. I'm just so happy it wasn't just me imagining it. He really does like me Rose!"

Chapter 42

On the plane, Rose's heart was like a wildebeest. Jesus, she thought, going away is almost worth the buzz of coming home. She walked out of the baggage hall with Clara Rose snuggled up against her breast, pushing the trolley, feeling ten foot tall. She didn't even have to look around. She heard Gloria scream before she saw her rush up. Gloria looked…,the word dashing came to Rose's mind.

"Rose, Rose, welcome home. Let me help. Look Miranda, its Rose and Clara Rose. Oh, you both look beautiful. Let me see. Can I hold her? How was your trip?"

Rose laughed. She saw Miranda standing back a little. "Miranda!"

Rose had never dreamed of being pleased to see Gloria, but she found she couldn't stop smiling. She lifted Clara Rose out of her baby carrier, kissed her head, and handed her to Gloria, giving her mother a kiss on her cheek. She bent down to Miranda and picked up Miranda, hugging her.

"Miranda! Hello. How's are you? Wow, you're so big after Clara Rose. So grown up!"

Miranda beamed. She is beautiful, Rose thought, so like Clare. In turn, Miranda thought Rose looked like the sun. Fiery, and warm. Gloria showed Clara Rose to Miranda who gave her a kiss on the nose.

"She's all soft like a Beanie Baby, except bigger, like a Beanie Buddy! Can I hold her."

"When you're at home and sitting down. She's heavy."

"Come on, let's go," said Gloria. "I cooked a stew, so we can eat when we feel like it. The Christmas tree is up. Miranda, Simeon and Clive decorated it. Clare is due back the day after tomorrow. It's so exciting."

Gloria took the Westway in from the airport. Rose noted the familiar landmarks along the Marylebone Road. She liked the dirty high-rise buildings, the art deco, the zebra crossings, the streams of traffic. Miranda and Clara Rose were tied into their car seats, side by side, at the back and Miranda was tickling Clara Rose's feet.

"Can I help you feed her, Rose?"

"Yes, and change her diaper!"

"What's a diaper?"

"Sorry, I mean, nappy. So, Gloria, you mentioned Simeon. How is he?"

Rose tried to keep the question general. She had kept her promise to Clare and not discussed it with Gloria, though it had taken huge will power. She had told Finn though what Clare had said. He had been quite sympathetic to Simeon.

"Jesus, imagine being told you have two daughters out of the blue. I don't know what I'd do. It must be so confusing, especially when one is a teenage beauty."

"But telling her he's 'in love' with her! That's not right."

"Did he, though? I'm sure he didn't say, 'I'm in love with you. They were probably enjoying the trips, the getting to know each other and it got a bit confused. I can understand why Clare fell for him. Here is this older man, bright, charming, handsome paying her attention. I guess it is easy to get confused about your emotions."

"So maybe I was lucky my dad was a revolting dead racist who raped women. No chance of my falling in love with him, then."

"Hah, Rose, you say the most ridiculous things. You might have to keep your tongue a little more tied now we have a beautiful daughter."

Rose bridled in response. How dare he say that? But, at the same time, Rose realised Finn was right. She did need to curb her tongue, or at least think before she spoke.

"Simeon is researching this project he's doing about new Indian immigrants to Britain," continued Gloria.

"And, he's helping me do a project on monkeys," piped up Miranda. "Rose, I'm going to work in a zoo when I'm grown up."

"That's a great idea, Miranda." Rose twisted around to give her a smile.

"So, all is peaceful on the home front?"

Gloria looked briefly across at her daughter.

"Fine, Clive and I are back giving it a go."

"Again? Well, good luck with that. And have you spoken to Clare recently? Is she alright? Is she looking forward to coming home?"

Rose looked at the profile of her mother driving closely. For the first time, she saw the similarity between them. Gloria was right, she was a chip off the old block. She had begun to feel like an alien in Red Rock. Her accent, her looks, her attitude made her stand out. It was nice to feel a part of a clan. Gloria stayed looking at the traffic in front.

"Have you not spoken to her?" Gloria asked with an ease she didn't feel.

"Not recently," replied Rose. "She messaged me saying she would be coming home for Christmas but, no skyping. I don't know, she hasn't been her normal self."

"No, I am worried about her."

"Clare said she couldn't wait to see me, and I can't wait to see her. I said she could sleep with me in your room, Rose. Mummy has given you and Clara Rose the playroom. It looks lovely, it's like a mini home."

Rose turned to her mother, "Oh, thank you, Gloria."

"I bought a few bits that you and Clara Rose will need: cradle, an arm chair, big bed for you. I put in a baby belling in so you can heat jars, make simple things. It gives you your own space. Clare can sleep in her own room, as well as with you, Miranda."

Rose sighed comfortably and leaned back in the seat.

"It will be so nice to be home." She turned around to Miranda.

"Shall we read Babar to Clara Rose later? Miranda, you can show her the pictures and tell her the stories. She'll love it."

"And she can watch The Magic School Bus with us. But I like The Simpsons now, too."

"Aren't you too young for the Simpsons?"

Rose wondered what Gloria truly thought. They could talk after Miranda was in bed. Everything felt a bit unreal. Rose sighed again. There was the bridge, and the pigeons sitting in the rafters. Nearly home. She was grateful to be here. It must have been hard for Gloria raising three children in a strange place. Rose felt a little ashamed. One day, she would have to apologise.

Chapter 43

Rose sat in the living room in the white leather armchair to feed Clara Rose her eleven o'clock night feed. Sasha was spread across the couch. The Christmas tree looked lovely. It was tall with the golden star on the top. There were new silver baubles in the shape of tiny gifts which tinkled. It was a blaze of shiny colour. Gloria loved to crowd the tree with everything she could find. Clare liked to see the green branches. Rose liked the tinsel best. At supper, Miranda had told her how she, Clive and Simeon decorated it. Mum had told them what to do. Gloria said she advised.

Now, feeding Clara Rose, Rose felt tired, and jet lagged. It had been a long day. She closed her eyes

"I'm tired. I love feeding Clara Rose but when she suckles, my head begins to feel drained."

"Do you want a glass of water. Or would you like a glass of wine?"

"I'll have water. I'm not really drinking because I'm breast feeding."

"Very sound. I didn't over worry about that when I was breast feeding."

Typical, Rose thought. Gloria plonked herself on the couch, swivelled around and put her feet up, facing Rose.

"Actually, smoothies are my favourite drink at the moment. I love them. I got a great juicer. Do you want one?"

"No thanks, not now. May be for breakfast. Gloria, I was thinking, I realised, living in the States, that it must have been hard for you raising me and Clare in a strange place. Was it?"

"Not really. It was an exciting time in London. I was busy with the ANC and had lots of help – as you so like to point out. I immersed myself in politics and protests. I think it sounds a little different in Red Rock. Funnily enough, maybe more like South Africa, a kind of veiled violence."

"Gloria, do you know why Clare went to Thailand instead of India?"

"Did she not tell you about Simeon?"

"Not much."

"Simeon thinks Clare might be a little confused about how she feels about him. He says they became very close while getting to know each other and neither of them knew how to handle their emotions. Did she say nothing to you?"

"She told me that she and Simeon were in love."

"Oh, God. What did you say?"

"I called it abuse on his part. Well, it is, isn't it? It's abuse."

"I suppose, but I don't think he intended it to happen. I couldn't believe it when he told me. I threw him out, but the worst part was that I was also jealous. Can you believe that? I was raging. I wouldn't let him near Miranda for a month. But Clive talked me around. Simeon is very upset. He says this mess is all his fault. He didn't realise what was happening. "

"Well Clare seems to be under the illusion that they love each other. He needs to tell her he doesn't love her, like that, I mean."

"I think she probably knows. I think it's why she left. She needed space. Don't worry, I think we can get over this.

"So, it's definitely over between you and Simeon?"

Gloria watched Rose feeding her grand-daughter for a moment.

"I did have strong feelings for Simeon but the idea of him and Clare being in love made me feel sick. Suddenly, I realised I didn't love him at all. I was furious. I could see him for what he is: a middle class, boring academic fool. I mean, he is clever, but so emotionally retarded. I think he'll be a good father but did I ever love him? Probably, back in the day, but maybe because he had rejected me. I had to prove that I could get him back. Crazy. Talking of relationships, how are you and Finn getting on?"

"Well. I do love him to bits. But Red Rock, it's not for me."

"I wondered. It's a strange place. Beautiful, but a little bit scary. So, what are you going to do?"

"Don't know yet. Finn is looking for a job here next year. We've discussed it. He agrees that London may be a better place to raise Clara Rose. Despite its wide-open spaces and its mountains, there is something claustrophobic about Red Rock."

"Well, it would be lovely if you stayed in London. I do miss you, Rose."

"Hah, I never thought I'd hear you say that."

"I don't know why we find it so hard to be nice to one another."

Gloria's mobile began to vibrate on the table. Gloria stretched out and picked it up to look at the caller ID.

"It's Angie. Clare must be out of juice. She must be confirming her arrival times. What time is it there? Hello. Angie? Clare?

"Gloria, its Angie."

The voice was very far away.

"You're very faint, Angie. I can barely hear you.

"Gloria, its Clare."

"Clare? Clare! Rose is here with Clara Rose. We can't wait to see you"

There was no answer

"Clare, I can't hear you. Can you hear me?"

"Yes, it's Angie, Gloria. It's about Clare."

Gloria sat up on the side of the couch. She looked at Rose.

"Angie, I can barely hear you. Speak clearly. Is Clare okay?"

She could hear the girl weeping.

"Angie? What has happened?"

"Clare. It's Clare. She drowned."

Gloria didn't understand. She couldn't understand the words. She waved Rose over.

"What do you mean? She can swim."

The girl's voice was flooded with tears.

"I am so, so sorry."

"I don't understand, Angie. What's going on? I don't understand what you are saying. What do you mean, drowned? That can't be right? She can swim. Angie what are you saying? I can't hear you."

Rose took Clara Rose off the breast and lay her on the chair. She had fallen asleep.

"Gloria?"

"Angie says Clare has drowned. But she can swim so it must be a mistake."

A man's voice came on the phone.

"Gloria Van Standen? Clare Van Standen's mother?"

"Yes, what's going on? Who are you?"

"I'm Doctor Praeawa Mitragul from the Koh Phangan hospital. I'm afraid there has been a terrible tragedy. Your daughter, Clare, drowned at the Beach Moon party. Her body was discovered four hours ago. I am terribly sorry."

Gloria leapt up, opened her mouth but only silence emerged. She dropped the phone and fell back in the chair. Rose bent down and picked up the phone.

"Hello,"

She listened. Her face lost colour. She nodded and sat down. She put down the phone.

"Mum?"

"Call Clive and Simeon."

Chapter 44

At six o'clock the next morning, finally the house was quiet. Margaret had come down with sleeping pills for Gloria which Clive had finally convinced her to take. They had phoned the doctor back but got no more information. Rose had gone up to Margaret's with Clara Rose at about 2am and Simeon had tried to rest in Clare's room but spent hours tossing and turning staring at the cracks on her ceiling, going over and over the events of the last few months. At six am, he got up, booked two tickets for Thailand, for Clive and Gloria as they had agreed last night. Then Simeon phoned the telephone number that Rose had scrawled for the Thai doctor and rang. The doctor explained that the autopsy showed Clare van Standen had drowned but that an autopsy showed she also had a high quantity of drugs in her blood stream. He had reported the death to the British Embassy who were now with her friends Angie Walters and Julie Shipley who said they had all been at a moon party at the beach. They seemed to have no idea of what had happened. Apparently, they had fallen asleep while Miss Van Standen went for a walk.

Simeon was making tea when he heard Rose come in through the front door. She looked exhausted. She stood at the kitchen door, holding on to the door frame. She was trembling, her eyes were as red as her hair. Her face was white, and her chin was still quivering from the tears.

"Rose. I've booked tickets for Thailand for Clive and Gloria. They leave at 2pm this afternoon. I'll take them to the airport. We need to tell Miranda. Who would be best to tell her?"

Rose shook her head.

"Where's Clara Rose?"

"Margaret's looking after her. She's asleep."

Gloria appeared at her bedroom door. She looked a mess, a loose bag of bones.

"What do you think happened?"

"Gloria, we don't know anything."

"Why didn't she talk to me? To us? To anyone? Rose, she didn't say anything to you about how she was feeling?"

Rose shook her head. "She seemed happy last time I spoke to her."

Rose looked at Simeon.

"This is your fault."

"Rose, Rose. Stop. Please," said Gloria

"It is no-one's fault," said Clive, appearing at the bedroom door. "We can't spend the rest of our lives blaming each other. Simeon, did I hear you book flights?

"Yes, 2pm departure. I'll take you to the airport.

"Mum, we have to tell Miranda."

"Oh my God. What do we tell her?"

Gloria crossed over to Rose and hugged her. They both stood there crying.

"What's happened? Why are you crying?"

Miranda was standing at the kitchen door in her pyjamas holding Bongo and her Babar book. Simeon went and picked her up.

"Sweetheart, Clare has had a terrible accident. She won't be coming home."

"But what about Christmas? Won't she be here for Christmas?"

It was Christmas Eve. Two days before, Gloria and Clive had returned home, bringing Clare's ashes. Gloria and Rose had decided to go ahead with Christmas and organise a memorial event in the New Year. How strange it had felt to be discussing such things. Nothing felt real. It was hard to believe Clare had gone. Gloria had the strange sensation of playing acting. Never had she felt this adult before, not even when she discovered she was pregnant with Rose.

Gloria was setting the table for Christmas Eve Dinner. She got the white Christmas tablecloth and shook it out over the table. Miranda was standing on a chair at the cooker with Rose, stirring the tomato soup. There was a melee of different cooking smells wafting around the house.

"That wine stain from last year didn't come out," said Gloria, "we can't use this."

"Just cover it with a table mat," suggested Rose.

"But it's on the corner."

"Well, we'll put the bread and cheese on the mat."

"But I wanted it to be perfect."

"For God's sake, Gloria, that is one thing this Christmas is not going to be."

Gloria shook her head. She laid out the golden place mats, the serviettes, knives and forks, glasses. She placed two silver candlesticks in the middle, then laid out five side plates, and a big wooden bowl of salad. Clare would have made it perfect. The doorbell went and Gloria went to open it. It was Simeon carrying two big shopping bags. She could see wrapped presents with ribbon and tags assembled in one.

"Simeon, come in."

"I brought samosas, spring rolls and a dahl as starter dishes," he said, lifting the others. "Can I put them in the oven to heat up?"

"Of course. Happy Christmas."

He looked at Gloria. Tears were pouring down her face.

"Happy Christmas, Gloria."

Simeon walked towards the kitchen. Gloria was following him when she heard the key turn in the lock. She turned back and watched Clive come in, looking rather smart, dressed in a suit, also carrying two shopping bags.

"I come bearing gifts,"

"Do you want to put them under the tree? And you, Simeon, put your presents under the tree. Then come into the kitchen for an aperitif. Supper is nearly ready. And I have something to say."

Rose shuddered but managed to keep quiet.

"Miranda, come and help me put the presents under the tree," said Simeon after he had put his dishes in the oven.

"I'm making the soup."

"You can let it simmer for a while," said Rose, lifting her down from the chair.

"Let's all have our drinks in the sitting room by the tree," suggested Gloria.

They assembled in the sitting room, having turfed the Sasha from the couch. Clive poured drinks. Miranda sat on the floor next to Clara Rose who was staring up at the tree from her baby seat and gurgling.

"I'll feed Clara Rose now, before we eat, if people don't mind." Rose bent down, picked Clara Rose up and sat down with her in the armchair. She lifted her shirt and Clara Rose clamped on to Rose's breast. Rose looked up at the crew looking down at her.

"You know, Clare would have said the Christmas tree is over decorated," she said, Gloria smiled.

"I want to say something. Rose and I were talking about how to cope with Christmas without Clare." She glanced up at the brown wooden urn up on the mantelpiece where they had placed the ashes.

"Obviously it's difficult, to say the least," Gloria choked, but swallowed it and continued. "But Christmas is Christmas. It's hard to cancel. So, as you know, we decided to go ahead. After all, Clare is with us, very much still with us in spirit, at least."

Gloria faltered again. Her eyes filled with tears and she turned away.

"So, what we thought," Rose continued, "is that instead of trying not say things about Clare, or silence our thoughts, that if we want to say something, we do. It's allowed. If we find tears on our faces that is fine. We allow each other the time and don't fuss."

Tears were pouring down Rose's face. Miranda got up and went and sat at her feet. Clive took Gloria's hand. Simeon got up and went to the urn, picked it up and examined it.

"Like now," Rose said, ruffling Miranda's hair with her free hand. "Let's just give ourselves a minute and we will get through it."

They were all silent. After a few minutes, Gloria said

"There are Christmas presents for Clare and from Clare under the tree. Clare bought them herself before leaving for Thailand and gave them to me. And all of us had brought her presents before she died, Clive and myself when we were in South Africa, Rose, in America, and I believe you have something, Simeon.

"I haven't got a Christmas present for Clare," cried Miranda.

"But you have, sweetheart. Remember that thing we saw that you said you thought Clare would love, when we went shopping to buy things for your room. Well, I bought it for you to give to Clare. So, as present giving is more about giving then getting, we thought we would give our presents to Clare and receive hers."

Simeon turned to face Gloria.

"Thank you, Gloria, thank you, Rose. I feel honoured to be here and humbled."

His voice broke and his smooth face crumpled. Rose thought how old he looked. Gloria got up and put a hand on his shoulder.

"Well, finally, rather ironically, I feel like I have a proper family. I used to dream about a happy family."

"Hollywood has a lot to answer for," Rose interrupted, sharply, "I don't know any happy families. And I wouldn't call us happy. We've just lost one of the most important people in our lives. Yet look, Christmas tree, beautifully laid table, a mountain of presents."

Gloria smiled.

"Life must go on, Rose. But I agree with you, what is a happy family? Over the years you and I have raged, argued, and said all sorts of terrible things to each other. My parents said terrible things to me. Maybe that is what family is about. We have learned. I feel hugely responsible for what happened I should have been more attentive, less self absorbed. And, the worse thing, is it was me who put the idea about drowning in her head with that stupid story about Rose's father."

Clive bent over and kissed her.

"Don't Gloria."

Gloria put her hands over her face and sobbed.

"Blaming ourselves will help no-one," said Rose looking directly at Simeon. "I'm sure that we all have our inner thoughts, and accusations, but we need to focus on how to help each other. After all, we are the people now through whom Clare will live. I suppose what I am trying to say, is that I will try to hold my tongue and not lash out. And maybe we should all try that, particularly over Christmas. Try not to blame ourselves nor each other but remember Clare and maybe behave in a more gentile manner, like she would."

Clara Rose started mithering. Rose stood up and walked around the room, trying to wind her. Tears were flowing down her cheeks

"To be succinct, shit happens." She took a deep breath and smiled. "We have to deal with it in the best way we can. No doubt, at some point all our feelings will all come out, in dribs and drabs." Rose again looked at Simeon, "Simeon, for example, I have mixed feelings about you. But the next few days are not the time. Now, let's get this show on the road. Gloria, we used to have a tradition of us children being allowed to open one present each on Christmas Eve. I am intrigued by Clare's present from Miranda. Can we open that one? Miranda is that okay?"

Miranda nodded. Rose passed Clara Rose to Simeon.

"Can you wind her?"

Simeon looked directly into Rose's face. He could see tracks of her eye liner in the lines around her eyes, flooded with tears.

"how?"

"Just pat her gently on the back and jiggle her up and down a little."

Rose knelt and scrabbled amongst the pile of presents, looking at name tags.

"Here it is. I'll open it."

She knelt back on her heels with a square flat box. The paper was gold with merry Christmas on it. She tore at the wrapping and revealed a beautiful hard back notebook with a golden ribbon page marker.

"This is beautiful, Miranda."

"Do you think she'd like it? Clare told me she wanted to be a writer, that she would write me stories."

"Miranda, it is beautiful. She'd love it, I think you should keep it and write stories for Clare or Clara Rose."

"That is a wonderful idea, sweetheart." Gloria kneeled on the floor next to Miranda.

"Now which present would you like to open, Miranda?"

"Can I open that one? I think it is for Clare too." Miranda pointed to a tiny square box wrapped up in red tissue paper. Rose picked it up and looked at the tag.

"No, it's not for Clare. It says 'from Simeon to Miranda. With much love.'"

Rose looked up at Simeon. He nodded and smiled.

"I think Miranda knows what it is. I showed her one day what I had got Clare for Christmas. I want her to have it."

Rose passed it over to Miranda. They all watched the little girl carefully unwrap a small jewellery box. Inside was a perfect silver monkey on fours looking as if its next action might be very wicked. Its eyes were two green jewels.

"It's beautiful," she smiled. "I love it." She hugged it to her heart.

"Show me," said Gloria. Miranda gave her the box.

"It's Hanuman, the monkey king?"

Simeon nodded.. Clara Rose burped and was sick on Simeon's shirt. Clive laughed. Clara Rose gave a gummy smile. Miranda giggled. Simeon said

"Hanuman, at work!"

"Whoops, sorry," said Rose, taking a tissue and rubbing Simeon's shirt. "Maybe it's time to eat."

"Won't Clare mind me having presents you bought for her?" asked Miranda.

"Of course not." Simeon looked at the wooden urn once again. He sighed at how ridiculous it all seemed. Him taking comfort from an urn full of ashes. His daughter! How could this be?

"Actually, could we open just one more present?" Clive asked. "Gloria, this is for you."

He handed her another small box, wrapped in silver paper.. Gloria looked down at it, and then up at him. Please, she thought, please don't let this be a ring.

"Oh God, Clive, you know I don't like surprises like this," said Gloria. "Surely we can open other presents tomorrow. The rule is only children."

"Please, now."

"The food is going to be overcooked."

"Gloria, open the present."

Gloria undid the wrapping carefully and there was a small box. She looked up at Rose, pleading for help. Everybody watched carefully as slowly she lifted the lid. A tiny enamel face on a spring leapt out at her. 'Happy Christmas' it said in a tinny cackle. Everybody heaved a huge sigh of relief and burst into laughter.

Chapter 45

It was Little Christmas, the 6th January. There was a sun, but it was weak, it came and faded in the distance against a pale white sky. Gloria knocked on the playroom door and stuck her head in. Rose was sitting on the armchair by the French windows looking out at the winter garden, feeding Clara Rose. She was smiling.

"Oh Gloria, come in. I've just been skyping with Finn. He has been offered Social Media Assistant Editor with the Camden Journal!"

"Oh, Rose, that is brilliant. When does it start?"

"5th February. He'll come over in three weeks."

Gloria looked down at Clara Rose who had fallen asleep.

"She'll be a proper little Londoner."

"Do you think she looks like anyone in particular?"

"Actually, don't you think she has the imprint of Finn? Kind of lanky, brown eyes, but, lucky her, she has your hair. I think she is going to be a startling little thing."

"Not a look of Pieter about her then?"

"No. He was blonde with blue eyes, and stocky. No, she looks nothing like him. So, will you stay here? This could be your kitchen/living room and you could use Clare's room as your bedroom. You have the bathroom. Of course, Miranda would keep her room. But you could be more or less, self-contained. I mean, you don't have live with me, sorry, us, me and Clive, share meals etc."

"As a start, yes, thank you. I'm sure we will find our own place after a while, but, to start with, yes.. Finn's job is such good news. I can't quite believe it after … You know, I feel guilty though about feeling happy."

"Don't. Clare would hate that. Can I make tea?"

"Work away."

Gloria put the kettle on and tea bags in a tea pot.

"Where is Miranda?" asked Rose.

"She's gone with Clive to the airport to meet Margaret who is back from Ireland today. That's why I popped down, actually, I wanted to see if you'd help me take down the Christmas tree. It's the 6th January. If we put away the decorations, Clive can take it to the recycle station when he gets back."

"Ok. We can do it now. Clara Rose has fallen asleep. I'll put her down."

"Don't you want to wind her?"

"It's ok, she just burped in her sleep. I'll be glad to see the Christmas tree come down. Christmas was okay. We did well. But I'd like to just get back to normal, though what that is now, I'm not sure.

"You were amazing over Christmas, Rose."

"I just had to keep my mouth shut. You didn't say much either. Relief all round for everyone, I guess. Mind you, I don't think silence is necessarily a good thing."

"Is there something in particular that you want to say?"

"I don't know yet, exactly."

"Well, when you do know, practice it in front of the mirror first!"

They climbed the stairs. At the top, the bannister rail had re-grown its coat pile. Gloria could smell its damp, furry must.

"Last year the tree stayed up until, God knows when, around the 20th January," said Gloria. "Clare decorated it with McDonalds cartons."

"I don't think it was decoration. I think it was a form of protest. It was that cleaning weekend that everything kicked off, wasn't it?"

Gloria nodded.

"I'm sorry, Rose. I am truly sorry for everything."

Rose started to take tinsel off the tree and put it in the cardboard box Gloria had left out.

"Clare did this last year," Gloria said. "I found all the decorations neatly assembled in the box. She'd organised them well. She'd wrapped the lights around strips of newspaper so that they didn't get tangled."

She held up the coiled newspaper.

"We'll do it again."

Gloria began to take the tinsel from the tree.

"Tinsel first, then baubles, and finally the lights. You start on that side."

They were silent for a while. They stripped the tree aside from the lights and folded the decorations into the box.

"This feels very final," said Rose. "I feel like I'm packing Clare away. A burial of sorts."

"Yes, I know what you mean." Gloria clambered up on the arm of the white leather armchair to reach for the star at the top of the tree.

"One of my new year's resolutions is to try to think before I speak. It's amazingly hard. You don't need to be silent, Rose, just think before you speak."

Rose turned to look at Gloria who stumbled and righted herself against the wall.

"Be careful," said Rose. "You know, Gloria, you've put on weight over Christmas! You're getting fat."

"What was I just saying about think before you speak?" Rose laughed.

"Well, you needed to fill out. Who wants a skinny mum with no curves to cuddle?"

Gloria laughed.

"Cuddle? Rose! Not really our thing, is it, cuddling! But there's a reason."

Gloria got down off the armchair and laid the star into the decoration box and turned to unwind the string of lights.

"Rose…" Gloria took a breath. "I'm going to have a baby."

Rose froze as the words sunk in. She fumbled to get the last bauble off the tree. She refused to look at her mother.

"Don't tell me this is some pathetic attempt to replace Clare?"

"Rose! I was pregnant before Clare died."

Rose looked across at Gloria. Her stomach churned. Jesus, whose was it? She prayed not Simeon's.

"Tell me its Clive's?"

Gloria nodded. Rose turned back to the tree.

"I suppose you think this is good news."

"I don't know. I did and then I didn't, and then I did. It won't be the same, Rose. It's not the same. Everything has changed."

"Yeah, Clare is dead. And you think you're fit to be a mother?"

"Rose, please. I wasn't trying to get pregnant. But it happened. Clive and I have thought about this. We truly want the baby."

"Is Clive happy?"

Gloria nodded and smiled.

"Delighted but like you said earlier, we both feel a little guilty feeling happy."

"Amazing how life moves on," Rose mused, "I used to think I had more control of it."

Clara Rose started to mither. Rose picked her up and walked to the mirror. She looked at the reflection of herself, her baby and Gloria in the background. She held Clara Rose up and examined her little face. She couldn't see anyone in there.

"To new life and another year," Rose looked back at Gloria's reflection. "Congratulations, Gloria. I hope you'll be very happy."

"Thank you, Rose."

Rose continued

"You know, I've not practiced saying this in front of the mirror, but I'm trying to say it as nicely as I can: I don't think I can stay here. It's too much for me. Miranda will be fine. She has Simeon, Margaret. But I have to go. I'll pack up today and book into a hotel

Gloria started to speak. Rose held up her hand to silence her and sat down, heavily.

Gloria nodded,

"Ja."

Chapter 46
October 2022

Miranda closed the notebook she had bought for Clare, tears running down her cheeks. She didn't know if she was crying for Clare or if it was because, having written the book, Clare was now finally laid to rest. She heard Josie gallumphing down the stairs, shouting

"Miranda, it's mum. Come quick."

She met Josie at her bedroom door.

"It's mum! I think she's dying." Josie was hysterical.

"Josie, calm down. I'm sure she is not. You know Gloria."

Her little sister was already galloping back up the stairs.

"She is so!"

Miranda hurried up the stairs after her. She could smell the coats hanging over the rail and for the millionth time promised herself she'd clear them. As Miranda ran into the kitchen, the lino stuck to the bottom of her slipper making a slapping noise under her feet. She stopped at the door into Gloria's bedroom and looked around at the bed. Gloria was wearing a blue silk scarf with peacocks strutting across it tied around her head.

"Mum?"

Gloria looked up at her and smiled weakly.

"Better warn the clan. Get them here."

"Why?"

"I want to say my goodbyes."

Gloria started coughing, her body convulsing. Josie sat on her bed, put her hand on her mother's humped body.

"Gloria, you're not dying," Miranda said.

Gloria glared at her

"Miranda, that is a comment I would expect from Rose, not from you."

"Rose said this would happen. Mum, she can't drop everything. Simeon is in Mumbai. Josie can phone Clive. Josie, go ring your dad and tell him Gloria wants him to come over. And don't worry, Josie, mum isn't going to die. Mum, you're upsetting Josie."

"My phone's in my room. I'll go get it." The girl ran off.

"Miranda, truly. I'm scared."

Miranda looked at her

"Mum, I know you're sick but you're not going to die today, or tomorrow, come to that. Anyway, I need you to do something for me before you do. I've been writing. About us, about our family, about the year Clare died. Writing it down has helped. I've made it my story, and finally I have what Clive might call, some perspective.

"Perspective? Good Lord. But you were only five. How can you know anything?

"Mum, it's what happened as I see it. I want you to read it and then I'll be ready to move on."

Gloria squeezed her daughter's hand.

"Miranda, is that what you've been up to, holed up in your room, writing" She smiled. "You were so young, how can you know what happened?"

"Mum, I was there. It happened to me too."

Gloria frowned and took Miranda's hand.

"Okay, darling, bring me your story. Cancel the family reunion, I can wait until Christmas. Oh, and Miranda, could you make Josie some supper and I'll have a glass of wine!"

．

Printed in Great Britain
by Amazon